Trial by Fire

GOING DOWN IN FLAMES

Chris Cannon

D1040367

Entangled Publishing, LLC
2614 South Timberline Road
Suite 109
Fort Collins, CO 80525
Visit our website at www.entangledpublishing.com.

Ember is an imprint of Entangled Publishing, LLC.

Edited by Erin Molta
Cover design by Louisa Maggio
Cover art from Deposit Photos, iStock, and Shutterstock

Manufactured in the United States of America

First Edition April 2016

This book is dedicated to my family for all their encouragement and support. Especially to my husband who moved band practice to someone else's house so I could have quiet time to write.

Chapter One

She must've been insane when she'd planned this. Sure it had seemed like a good idea at the time. Let's throw a Welcome Back to School party so students injured in the attacks on campus would receive a formal invitation to return to school. This was meant to circumvent the Directorate's policy of suggesting injured students stay at home with a private tutor. The Directorate's sucky rationale? Something about culling the weak from the herd, which was total crap since the Directorate had failed to protect the students in the first place. So, this may have been her plan, but it was her grandmother and Jaxon's mother Lillith's idea that she host with him. She didn't know what his problem was, but he was being more obnoxious than usual.

"Jaxon, I swear to God, if you don't stop bitching, I will set your hair on fire." Bryn spoke through clenched teeth as she smiled and nodded at the students streaming past her into the Welcome Back to School Gala. "Aren't you supposed to have this fake socialite crap down to a science?"

"It's not the greeting people I mind." He nodded at

a group of students who entered the dining hall. "It's your proximity."

That was it. She didn't care what her grandmother and Lillith wanted. If she had to listen to Jaxon make one more rude comment, she was going to lose it and roast him like a marshmallow.

"Bryn." Garret walked toward her, his dark complexion a bit pale for a Green dragon, his brown eyes appeared wary, and his injured left arm hung limp in a sling.

And now she remembered why she was doing this. "I'm so glad you came." Only half of all the students injured during the attacks at the Institute for Excellence, aka shape-shifting dragon school, had been willing to return. The other less-than-perfect dragons had allowed the Directorate, the governing body of Dragon society, to bully them into private tutors.

A ghost of a smile crossed Garret's face. "I told the Directorate my left arm may not work and I may not be able to fly, but my mind was still functional, and they owed me for failing to provide adequate protection. You should've seen the looks on their faces."

"Good for you."

Garret headed toward the tables where the Green dragons sat. The color-coding still threw Bryn sometimes. All the Greens had the same dark hair, eyes, and skin as Garret. All the upper-class Blues, like Jaxon, had golden-tan skin, blond hair, and blue eyes. The artsy Black dragons always looked a bit Goth with their ivory skin, black hair, and dark eyes. The middle class Reds seemed Irish with their red hair, green eyes, and freckled skin. The two lone Orange dragons with their bronze hair, skin, and eyes, looked Hawaiian. Since her mom had been a Blue and her dad a Red, Bryn didn't fit in with any group of dragons. She wasn't as thickly muscled as the Reds and not as graceful and lithe as the Blues. She'd changed her blond, red, and black striped hair to blond, to make peace with her grandfather, but she still didn't blend in with the Blues. Far from it.

She envied the greeting Garret received from his Clan and loved that they acted like nothing was wrong. Then again, they were the smartest dragons, so it made sense they'd figured things out. Now, if only the rest of the Clans would catch up and realize the injured students didn't reflect badly on them, life would be good.

"You think this is a positive development," Jaxon said, "but you're wrong."

"That's it." Fire crawled up the back of Bryn's throat. Smoke drifted from her lips as she spoke. "Get the hell away from me."

"Gladly." Jaxon stalked off to join his Clan-mates.

Bryn's best friend, a Black dragon named Ivy, bounded over with her boyfriend Clint in tow. "I won," Ivy announced.

"You won what?" Bryn asked.

"She bet you'd try to roast Jaxon within the hour." Clint ran his fingers through his Mohawk. "I bet within the first thirty minutes."

"You made it forty minutes." Ivy grabbed Bryn's hand. "I declare your door greeting duties officially over."

Once they were seated at their usual table, Bryn sighed. "Finally, I can relax."

Ivy's eyebrows went up. "Maybe not."

Bryn heard the click of high heels on the marble tile. She cringed. That had to be her grandmother, Marie Sinclair.

"Bryn, why aren't you greeting people at the door?"

Turning to face her grandmother, Bryn gave a tight smile. "Most of the guests are here, my feet hurt, and I was five seconds from setting Jaxon's hair on fire." The woman could choose whichever reason she liked.

Her grandmother frowned. "It's inappropriate to leave the entrance unless you find someone else to greet your guests."

"This isn't my party. It's a school party."

"That's not what we discussed," her grandmother said.

"I didn't realize you meant I had to stand at the door all night."

Marie Sinclair appeared unswayed.

Bryn pushed to her feet. "If I find someone to greet people, will that make you happy?"

"No." Her grandmother said in her cold, upper-class Blue dragon tone. "But it will do."

"Fine." Bryn scanned the room. Who did she want to dump door duty on? Better yet, who could she convince to do it?

Rhianna stood on the outskirts of the Blue Clan, clutching a glass of punch. Coming back to school after her injury was one thing. Playing hostess was another. Still, it didn't hurt to ask.

Bryn approached Rhianna and spoke in a quiet voice. "I have a favor to ask. My grandmother won't let me sit down unless someone else takes over greeting guests. Do you think you're up for it?"

"I'm not sure." She nodded at her classmates. "My reception hasn't been what I hoped for."

"Idiots." Bryn frowned. *Where was Jaxon?* And then it came to her. "You could ask Jaxon to go with you. He'd be far happier standing up there with you than he was with me."

"Maybe." Rhianna caught Jaxon's gaze and waved.

He said something to the group of males he stood with and came over to hold Rhianna's hand. "What's wrong?"

"Bryn needs someone to take over greeting at the door. Would you do it with me?"

"Of course. We should have done it that way in the first place."

Okay, he was being nice to Rhianna, but did he have to

be such a jerk to her? Not wanting to deal with him, Bryn clamped her lips shut and rejoined her friends at their table.

Clint pointed to her hair. "I see you decided to go native."

She rolled her eyes. "My grandfather interpreted my red, blond, and black-streaked hair as lack of pride in my Blue Clan heritage. So I went blond to appease him." She reached up to touch the inch-wide red streak by her temple. "He still hates this nod to my father's Clan, but I refuse to change it."

"I miss the black stripes." Ivy said.

"Me, too. But my grandparents took me in, so I'm trying to keep the peace." With her parents gone, it's not like she had anywhere else to go. If she alienated her grandfather, she'd be homeless. "Let's talk about something happier."

"I got my driver's license," Clint said.

"That's great." And it gave her an idea. "Maybe you could teach me how to drive."

Ivy shook her head. "Not a good plan. He drives like a maniac."

"I do not." Clint puffed out his chest. "I'm a fabulous driver."

"You took out the bushes at the end of my driveway, on both sides." Ivy laughed. "I don't know who gave him his driver's test, but they must've been caffeine deprived."

"If I could have your attention." Mr. Stanton, the Elemental Science teacher and head of the Green Clan stood near the punch bowl holding a microphone. "I'd like to welcome all of you back after the Christmas Holidays. I'm sure the new year will be an exciting time for all of us. The Directorate has taken security measures to protect the campus from any more disturbances."

Disturbances seemed like an understatement given the severity of the attacks that had occurred on campus before Christmas.

"Please enjoy your friends' company but remember,

classes start bright and early tomorrow. Make sure you rest up this evening."

"Please." Clint threw his arm around Ivy's shoulders. "I'll be a zombie no matter what tomorrow. We might as well stay up tonight and have fun."

A growl echoed through the room. Bryn whipped around to see Jaxon facing off with a male from his Clan. "Rhianna does not reflect poorly on our kind."

The other male narrowed his eyes. "Really? Then why did your father void your marriage contract?"

Uh-oh. Jaxon wouldn't speak against his father or the Directorate, which left only one option. This was about to get ugly.

The air around Jaxon shimmered as he shifted to dragon form. The other male shifted, but backed up a step. Big mistake. Ceding ground showed weakness. Jaxon lunged, blasting frozen flames and striking out with his talons. The coppery scent of blood filled the air.

Jaxon backed the boy up to the wall and pinned him there with his talons digging into the boy's neck.

"That's enough." An all too familiar voice boomed through the room. Her grandfather, Ephram Sinclair, was here. Great.

Jaxon released the boy's neck, but didn't retreat.

"Shift back," her grandfather ordered. "Now."

Even though he shifted back to human form, Jaxon never took his gaze from his opponent.

"Jaxon Westgate, what do you have to say for yourself?" her grandfather asked in a voice that rang throughout the room.

"What I have to say, sir, is that the members of my Clan will treat Rhianna with respect."

"Not just me." Rhianna stepped forward. "My injury wasn't my fault. Neither was Garret's or any of the other students who were injured in the attacks. We have every right to be here. Don't you agree, Mr. Sinclair?"

Holy crap. Rhianna had just called her grandfather out in front of all these people. Bryn wasn't sure if she should cheer, or duck and cover.

"You raise an interesting point, young lady. It was brave of you and the other injured students to return to the Institute," her grandfather said. "I would like to think your classmates would recognize that bravery and treat you accordingly. Now, I believe it's time for everyone to retire to their dorms."

The injured Blue slunk away, blending in with the other members of his Clan. How many of them felt Rhianna didn't belong? Would they act on that feeling? Jaxon couldn't fight all of them. Then again, if he went all Westgate on them and proved he was the alpha male, he might not have to.

"Is it me," Clint said, "or did your grandfather wiggle out of answering that question?"

"He's a master of Directorate double-speak," Bryn whispered.

Chapter Two

Bryn headed toward the door with her friends. She'd had enough drama for the evening. If her grandmother thought she was going to play the polite hostess by hanging around at the entrance and thanking everyone for coming, she was about to be disappointed.

The noise of chairs scraping on the floor and students gathering their things was a familiar, comforting sound. Who knew she'd miss school?

"Incoming," Ivy said.

Now what? Bryn turned to greet her grandmother. "I don't suppose you're just coming over to give me a hug good-bye?"

Her grandmother appeared at a loss for words. "Well, that would be nice, but I thought I'd accompany you to your new room and say my good-byes there."

"New room?" Bryn hoped she'd misunderstood.

"Yes. Your grandfather and I discussed it. Since you've been legally recognized as a member of the Blue Clan, it's only right you stay in the Blue dorm."

Bryn sent a mute appeal to Clint and Ivy for help.

"We like having Bryn in our dorm," Ivy said.

"We'd be happy to move her things back," Clint offered.

"I appreciate the kindness you showed my granddaughter when she first came here. I see nothing wrong with you continuing to be friends, but her grandfather and I believe her place is with her Clan."

"Is this more him than you?" Bryn asked, knowing the answer already.

"I mentioned you might not want to be uprooted from your current location, but your grandfather felt strongly about the issue. There is a silver lining. Since Rhianna's roommate asked to be reassigned, you'll be able to move in with her."

"Oh, that part I like. I don't suppose Rhianna could move into the Black dragon's dorm with me?" That way they'd be farther away from the people who weren't so friendly toward both of them.

"No." Her grandmother's answer was succinct and gave no opportunity for argument.

Bryn groaned and turned to Clint and Ivy. "I'll call you with my new room number, and we'll figure out some way to mark my terrace, so you won't land on the wrong one and have to deal with anyone's attitude."

"I've always wondered if their rooms were fancier than ours," Clint said. "I guess now I'll find out."

"All right. That's settled," her grandmother said. "Let's join Rhianna and tell her the good news."

Rhianna stood outside the dining hall with Jaxon by her side. Crap. Rooming with Rhianna would mean more exposure to him.

"Hey, roommate," Bryn said with a grin.

"Oh, good. Your grandmother talked to you. I wasn't sure how to bring it up."

"You'd be better off on your own." Jaxon spoke like Bryn

wasn't standing right there in front of him.

What the hell? "You can turn back to your non-asshat self any time now."

"Why don't we go see your new room," her grandmother said, like she hadn't heard their comments. Odds were, she'd heard, and this was her way of telling both of them to suck it up and deal with it.

Bryn waved to Clint and Ivy and then followed her grandmother toward the one dorm on campus where she didn't want to live. The Green dragons' dorm had been nice, before she'd been poisoned, and she'd liked the Black dragons' dorm because she'd been closer to her friends.

Rhianna seemed to know what Bryn was thinking. "It will be all right. Most of the other girls will be so caught up in their own lives, they won't pay attention to us."

Would she be ignored or shunned? Did it matter? Not really. It's not like she was expecting to make friends, though it would be nice.

Entering the Blue dorm gave her a sense of deja vu. When she'd first come to school and entered the Green dragons' dorm, they had stared and whispered. The Blue dragons stared as she and Rhianna entered the lobby. Maybe they were too polite or too fearful of her grandmother to whisper. Still, the view before her was like a sea of golden tan skin and blond hair. Her light freckled coloring would never blend in, or truly be welcomed, here.

Despite the cold greeting, the dorm lobby seemed comfortable. There were several sets of couches and wingback chairs scattered about the room. The furniture made of leather and dark polished wood looked like expensive antiques. Rather than a standard cafe in the back of the room like the other dorms, there appeared to be a sit-down restaurant where waiters took your order. To say this was nicer than the Black and Green dragons' dorms was a severe understatement.

There was, of course, the same marble staircase, and no elevators. "Do you think the Directorate will ever modernize the dorms and put in elevators?" Bryn asked.

"No," her grandmother and Jaxon spoke in unison.

"That's a shame." Rhianna held the handrail and climbed the stairs with her uneven gait.

Jaxon's cheeks colored. Good. He should feel embarrassed at the Directorate's closed-mindedness. None of the buildings on campus at the Institute for Excellence, aka Dragon School, were wheelchair accessible. When she'd asked about this, she'd been told medics were able to heal almost all injuries by manipulating Quintessence, or the essence of life. Bryn was actually quite skilled in this area and hoped to become a medic one day. However, the recent attacks on campus had left multiple students with injuries that the medics had been unable to treat or repair. The students with limited mobility might need ramps or elevators, but it didn't seem like the Directorate planned on updating the buildings any time in the near future.

"What floor is our room on?" Bryn asked.

"The second," Rhianna said. "I used to live on the third floor, so this is an improvement."

They reached the second floor landing. Jaxon took both of Rhianna's hands in his and then leaned in and kissed her on the cheek. "Call if you need anything." Then he continued up the steps.

Rhianna blushed, which was cute, because most of the time Blues didn't show emotions in public like the other Clans. The three of them walked down the hall and stopped at the third room on the right where Bryn's grandmother presented her with a set of keys.

Inside the doorway, Bryn came to a dead halt. "You've got to be kidding me."

"What?" her grandmother asked. "Don't you like it?"

"It's twice the size of the rooms in the Green and Black dorms." Though the front room held the two obligatory roll-top desks with their hideously uncomfortable chairs, the floors were hardwood, rather than carpeted. An antique couch, wingback chairs, and a coffee table took up half the space. The other half had floor to ceiling bookshelves and a library table.

Bryn walked over to one of the shelves to check out the sculptures, which ranged from intricate glass figurines to carved wooden boxes. "What's all this?"

"Art," her grandmother said.

Sure. Everyone needed art in their living room. She resisted the urge to roll her eyes.

"Come pick which bedroom you want," Rhianna said.

There was more than one bedroom? That was new, too. In the other dorms, the roommates each had their own beds in one big room. Not so here. She walked down the short hallway that ended in the window, which opened onto the terrace. A door on the right led to a bedroom with a four-poster bed covered in a silk sky blue comforter. The fleur-de-lis wallpaper was a bit much. There was a dresser and a nightstand on either side of the bed, like her other rooms. The door on the far wall opened to reveal a claw foot tub.

Bryn went back out into the hall and entered the other bedroom. The cream colored walls and the sleigh bed with the navy comforter barely registered. She saw the door on the far wall. Suspicion confirmed. "We each have our own bathroom?"

"Of course," Rhianna said.

"Roommates in the other dorms share a bathroom," Bryn said.

"The Blue Clan did fund most of the buildings on campus," her grandmother said. "And we are used to living a certain lifestyle."

"But you don't spread that information around," Bryn said.

"No one ever asked," her grandmother said. "Now, which room would you like?"

Bryn looked at Rhianna. "I like this one, if you don't mind."

"Good," Rhianna said. "I like the four-poster bed better."

"Go open your wardrobe," her grandmother said.

Bryn opened the mahogany armoire door to find her clothes already inside. "How'd you know I'd pick this room?"

"You seem to like simpler lines, so I thought you'd choose this one. Rhianna, I had your clothing placed in your wardrobe as well." She clasped her hands in front of her waist in the same manner she did when saying good-bye to guests at her home. "I should leave you girls to prepare for bed."

Rhianna ducked out the doorway and across the hall.

An odd sense of unease trickled down Bryn's spine, like cold rain dripping down the back of her shirt collar. She was happy to be back at school, but she'd miss her grandmother. Despite her outwardly proper appearance, she wasn't the iceberg Bryn had originally imagined. After moving in with her grandparents, she'd grown much closer to her grandmother, though her grandfather was still a bit scary. She hadn't quite found her footing with him.

Not sure if it was the right move or not, Bryn embraced her grandmother and was relieved when she hugged her back.

"I'll miss you." Bryn meant it.

"Let's plan to have lunch this Saturday," her grandmother said. "I'm sure something in Dragon's Bluff will be open."

"Sounds good." Bryn stepped back. "Someone better keep an eye on Lillith now that Jaxon is gone." God knows

Ferrin, Jaxon's father, wouldn't be much comfort.

"I'll check in on her." Her grandmother cleared her throat. "I should go. And I think I'll use the terrace exit."

. . .

Classes the next day were oddly normal. If you didn't count the guards posted at the front door of every building and the undercurrent of animosity toward the injured students who'd returned to school.

"Is it me," Clint said as they walked across campus to the dining hall for lunch, "or do the guards seem a little tense?"

"They're supposed to be on guard," Bryn said. "It's part of the job description."

"On guard is one thing," Clint said. "I sneezed when I walked out of the restroom, and the guard in the hall shifted and growled at me…because I *sneezed*." He emphasized that last part like she might not have gotten it the first time.

"The solution is simple," Ivy said. "Stop sneezing."

"I'll get right on that." Clint slowed as they reached the steps to the dining hall. "In my head, I thought, 'wouldn't a pizza from Fonzoli's be good right now.' Then I remembered about the attack on Dragon's Bluff. Every time, it's like a smack in the face."

"I know what you mean." The attack on Dragon's Bluff had come in the form of fire. Bryn and many other Blue dragons had tried to beat back the fire by combatting the flames with ice. Still, damage had been done. None of the attacks made sense. If the enemy wanted to overthrow the Directorate, then they should attack the Directorate, not everyone else. Bryn trudged up the steps and nodded at the Red guard who opened the door for her.

Ironically enough, the buffet was loaded with Italian food. Bryn inhaled. "Hey…that smells like Fonzoli's."

"It should, since a Fonzoli made it."

Bryn whirled around. Valmont Fonzoli, her knight—a human who'd been bound to her when a dormant spell in his blood had been activated by an act of chivalry—stood there smiling, wearing a pair of dark jeans and a white shirt with Fonzoli's Catering stitched across the pocket.

She dropped her book bag and threw her arms around him in a hug. He laughed, wrapped his arms around her waist, and picked her up off the floor.

There was that happy warmth again, which she associated with him. He set her down. "And here I thought you might not be happy to see me."

"What? I'm always happy to see you."

"As heartwarming as this is, you're blocking the line for food." Jaxon's voice came from the small crowd gathered behind them.

Reluctantly, Bryn released Valmont and grabbed her book bag. "Can you stay and eat lunch with us?"

"Planned on it." Valmont gave a small bow. "After you."

A part of her brain knew the joy she felt when she was with Valmont was a side effect of the Knight-Dragon bond but who cared? He made her happy. She made him happy. It was a win-win situation.

After filling their trays, they joined Clint and Ivy.

Ivy opened her mouth. Clint cut her off. "You have thirty seconds to tell Ivy what's going on between you two before she explodes with questions."

"Hey." Ivy whacked her boyfriend on the arm.

"Am I right?" he asked.

"Yes. But that's beside the point." Ivy rearranged the pepperoni on her pizza in a symmetrical pattern. "So what's new with you two?"

Valmont shrugged. "We spent time together over the holiday break, and now we're closer than ever."

"That's the boring version." Ivy pointed at Bryn. "Show him how it's done."

"Well..." How much should she say? "We did spend a lot of time together over break, and we fought together when Dragon's Bluff was attacked, so I think our bond is stronger now." She glanced out of the corner of her eye at Valmont. She couldn't read his expression. "But it's more than that. He makes me happy, and he's incredibly handsome."

Valmont puffed out his chest and nodded. "I am, you know. It's the caterer's uniform. Girls love a man in uniform."

Clint and Ivy laughed. Bryn relaxed and leaned her shoulder against Valmont while they ate because whenever he was near, she felt the urge to touch him.

"So how goes the recovery process in Dragon's Bluff?" Clint asked.

"Thanks to your Mr. Stanton and the Green Clan, we were able to restore power and communication. Now, we're working on finding homes for those who lost their houses." Valmont leaned back in his chair and frowned. "I don't understand..." He clamped his lips together and looked into the distance like he was trying to push down his anger and keep his emotions inside.

"There's nothing to understand," Bryn said. "Because whoever did this isn't logical." She grabbed Valmont's hand and laced her fingers through his.

"You're right." He shook his head like he was trying to shake off the negative emotions. "So what's new at school?"

"Bryn's grandma kidnapped her from our dorm and forced her to move in with the Blues," Ivy said.

Valmont cringed. "Sorry about that."

"The upside is I'm rooming with Rhianna. The downside is I'll probably see more of Jaxon."

"So he's continuing their relationship despite his mother and your grandmother's deranged plan that you two should have an arranged marriage?" Valmont said.

"Yes." And she respected the hell out of him for it. Females who the Directorate declared unfit to marry had only one option. It was a weird yet sanctioned game where an older male, normally a Blue, offered to be the female's benefactor, no matter what Clan she was from. Which meant he'd keep her as his mistress after she graduated. And that's what Jaxon had promised to do for Rhianna. In this world where the Directorate was all-powerful and could deny marriage petitions without giving a valid reason, Jaxon was trying to do right by the girl he'd been promised to marry.

Clint snorted. "Every time I think of you and Jaxon together, I imagine fireballs flying."

"You need to come up with a plan on how to deal with that nightmare of a situation," Ivy said.

"I have a plan." Bryn said. "It's called denial. I choose to believe the Directorate will not take me off the unfit-to-marry list."

"After you finish school, we could run away to Vegas," Valmont said. His tone was teasing, but she knew true emotions lay underneath it. She needed to tread lightly.

"That's a great plan, except my grandfather would personally hunt us down and make sure we were punished to the full extent of the law."

Her friends stared at her like she'd said something wrong. "I'm not joking. He is a scary, determined man who isn't above hurting people to get his message across."

Valmont stiffened. "Did he do something to you?"

"It's not a big deal. We were talking, and he grabbed my arm to make a point. He squeezed a little harder than necessary. That's all. It didn't even leave a bruise."

Valmont leaned in and touched her cheek. "He's family. He's supposed to protect you, not hurt you."

His gaze dropped to her mouth. And it was like someone

sucked all the oxygen out of the room. Oh, this could not be happening in the middle of the dining hall. She would not have her first kiss with Valmont in front of the entire student body.

"We can't do this here." She forced a laugh.

"We could." He grinned, and his single dimple made an appearance.

Straightening in her chair, Bryn picked up her soda and took a drink. It did nothing to cool her hormones.

After lunch, Valmont said his good-byes and left.

When he was out of hearing range, Ivy pounced. "Oh my God. What was that?"

Bryn groaned in frustration. "I don't know. This thing between us has been building, and I'm not sure what to do."

"He likes you, and you like him," Clint said. "What's the problem?"

Bryn relayed the short version of her terrible encounter with his evil grandmother. "She thinks, since I'm a dragon, I'll hurt him. I don't want her to be right."

"Allow me to use my brilliant deductive skills to tell your future." Clint put his hand to his forehead. "I see Jaxon and Rhianna having a life-long relationship. You might have to marry him, but she will be his true wife. Whenever your grandmother hints at grandchildren, Jaxon will whisk you away to a science lab where they'll do that turkey baster thing so the two of you don't have to get naked together. While all this lunacy is going on, you will carry on a torrid affair with your knight." He dropped his hand. "See, it all works out in the end."

Bryn put her hand to her own forehead. "If you ever mention my name and Jaxon's in the same sentence with the word turkey baster ever again, you'll be dodging fireballs."

Ivy cracked up and then kissed her boyfriend on the cheek. "You have to give him points for coming up with a decent solution."

"I guess," Bryn said. "We could buy one of those obscenely large houses where we'd each have our own wing. Jaxon and Rhianna could live in one wing, while Valmont and I shack up in the other." Not a bad plan, until you considered the whole living-a-lie thing. Best not to think about it. Who knew, maybe this uprising, or war, as her grandfather now referred to it, would end the Directorate's reign, and everyone could be with who they wanted. Better yet, maybe she could find a community of nice hybrids who weren't trying to kill everyone and she could live her life the way she wanted.

Chapter Three

After spending the evening hanging with her friends in Ivy's room, in the Black dorm where she'd still rather live, Bryn flew back to her new and far less friendly home. Rather than deal with all the frosty stares from her Blue dorm mates when she entered the building by the front door, she opted to fly up to her terrace.

Rhianna had come up with the plan of tying an aqua scarf to a chair on the terrace, to make finding the right one easier. With the cold welcome both of them received from the Blue Clan, neither of them wanted to mistakenly land outside someone else's room.

Bryn spotted the scarf, came in for a landing, and stumbled, knocking over the chair. Stupid landings…she always miscalculated. She shifted back to human form and righted the chair. When she tried to open the window to go inside, it wouldn't budge.

What the heck? She knocked and nothing… Where was Rhianna? She should be home, unless she was with Jaxon. Now what? Flying around to the front of the dorm, dealing with the other Blues, and then climbing the stairs would be a pain in the butt.

Solution? Knock louder and peer inside. A pile of clothes lay in the hallway. That was weird. The hair on the back of her neck stood up. Something was wrong. Shifting to dragon form, she knocked out the top pane of glass and then shifted back so she could reach inside and unlock the window. Sliding the window open, she listened carefully for anyone moving about inside, but it was dead quiet. Producing a fireball in her left hand in case she came across some non-friendly types, she climbed into the hallway.

Creeping forward, she listened again for anything that would tell her another person was in the room. The silence stretched out. *Now what?*

"Rhianna?"

No answer. Both the bedroom doors were closed, which was weird since she hadn't closed her bedroom door when she'd left for class that morning. Right hand on the doorknob, she raised her left hand holding the fireball higher so she could blast anyone who might be inside. A twist of the knob, and she shoved the door open. Nothing was out of place. Her room appeared untouched.

What did that mean? Back out in the hall, she kicked the clothes strewn about on the hall floor. Some of them still on their hangers. And now that she really looked, she realized they were all Rhianna's. Fireball in hand, she opened Rhianna's door and let out an involuntary cry. Clothes were tossed about the room, like someone had reached into Rhianna's closet and played a twisted version of fifty-two pick-up, scattering clothing far and wide. Red paint splattered the walls, floor, and bedding. *Oh God. Please let it be paint.* She sniffed a patch of red on the wall. It smelled of chemicals rather than the copper scent she associated with blood.

"Rhianna?" No answer. Where would she be? Bryn ran

to the phone in the front room and dialed Jaxon's number.

"Hello?"

"Is Rhianna with you?"

"Yes."

Bryn breathed a sigh of relief. "Both of you need to get over here, right now."

"We're almost done with our homework," Jaxon said. "She'll be there in half an hour."

Why did he have to be difficult? "Someone redecorated Rhianna's room, and it isn't an improvement."

"What are you talking about?"

She slammed the phone down, hanging up on him. That should get his uncooperative butt moving.

Five minutes later, Jaxon stalked into the living room with Rhianna trailing warily behind him. He headed straight for her room. As soon as he crossed the threshold, a low growl rumbled from his chest.

Rhianna stood in the doorway, surveyed the mess and then walked over to her four-poster bed and sat on an area of the comforter devoid of paint. Elbows on her knees, she leaned forward so her long blond hair covered her face like a curtain. "Someone is trying to send me a message, and they aren't bothering to be subtle."

The air around Jaxon shimmered, and sleet shot from his nostrils, which meant he was about to lose control.

"Did you lock the window to the terrace when you left today?" Bryn asked.

"What does that have to do with anything?" Jaxon snapped.

Fire banked in her gut. He was being protective of Rhianna. She'd focus on that, and not get mad at him. "The window was locked when I tried to come in."

"I didn't lock the window." Rhianna sat up straight. "How did you get in?"

"Once I saw the clothes in the hall, I was worried you might be hurt, so I broke the glass to reach the lock."

"Thanks for worrying." Rhianna stood and walked over to a splash of red paint on the wall and ran her finger through it. "This should clean up, right?"

"That's not the point." Jaxon waved his arms around at the mess that used to be her room. "This is unacceptable."

"This," Rhianna copied his flailing gesture, "is petty and stupid. In order to show the idiots who did this they can't run me off, I'm going to make a big deal about hiring decorators to come in and redo my room."

Jaxon looked at her like she'd lost her mind. "What in the hell will—"

"That's what my grandmother would do," Bryn cut him off. And then she had an idea. "Why don't we ask *her* to redesign your room?"

Rhianna stood and walked to the phone in the living room. "That's not a bad idea."

"We need to report this," Jaxon said. "Not cover it up."

"The individuals who did this are cowards." Rhianna picked up the phone. "I'd rather not give them the satisfaction."

"I'd rather rip them apart with my talons." Jaxon paced the room.

"If you knew who did it, you could." And then Bryn had another idea. "Give me the phone. Let's call Garret or Mr. Stanton. One of them might be able to figure it out."

Garret arrived fifteen minutes after Bryn called. He took a sample of paint from the walls and then walked around the room. "Did you touch anything?"

"I sat on the bed," Rhianna said.

"Jaxon shot sleet on the carpet," Bryn said, which caused Jaxon to glare at her. "What? I'm trying to be helpful."

Garret exited the bedroom and studied the window Bryn had broken. "They couldn't have left and then latched the window." He walked into the living room, and they followed along behind him. "They must have exited through the door, setting it to lock automatically, which means it was an inside job, and the perpetrators probably still have the paint cans in their rooms."

Jaxon grabbed the phone and dialed. "I'd like to report an act of vandalism in the Blue dorm. Someone painted anti-Directorate graffiti on my friend's wall." Loud voices could be heard through the phone. "No, you don't need to see the message. You need to find who in the Blue dorm has red paint in their room. They are the perpetrators."

Jaxon slammed the phone down.

Garret pointed at him. "You just lied to the Directorate."

"No, I didn't." Jaxon headed back into Rhianna's bedroom and grabbed a paint-splattered blouse off the floor. Holding it in his left hand, he smeared the paint on the walls to form the letters DIRECTORATE and then drew a line through them.

Garret nodded in appreciation. "Crude, yet effective."

Jaxon tossed the blouse on the floor and then went to wash his hands in the bathroom.

Garret approached Rhianna and touched her gently on the shoulder. "You're staying. Right?"

"Yes."

"Good." Garret blushed. "Those of us who were injured… we need to stick together."

Rhianna leaned toward him and spoke in a low voice. "Your Clan-mates, how are they treating you?"

"At first, it was awkward, but then we talked science and math, and it was all okay."

Jaxon emerged from the bathroom and caught sight of Garret touching Rhianna. "Thank you for coming over, Garret. I'd hate to keep you from whatever you were doing. Feel free to leave."

Garret laughed.

"What's funny?" Jaxon asked.

"The way you make it sound like you're letting me leave and kicking me out at the same time. It's amusing." Garret dropped his hand from Rhianna's shoulder. "Some of the walking wounded are meeting for coffee this Wednesday night in the dining hall, if you want to join us. It's kind of a support group."

"I'd like that."

Unable to help herself, Bryn spoke in a singsong voice, "Garret just made a date with your girlfriend."

Garret laughed again. "That's even funnier." Then he headed out the front door.

Rhianna blushed. She walked over to Jaxon and took his hand. "Are you jealous of Garret?"

"No," Jaxon said, and then he kissed her.

"Gross." Bryn covered her eyes and headed for her own room. She changed out of her school clothes into black yoga pants and a purple T-shirt. Then she sorted through her homework and laid out her clothes for the morning and waited for some sort of all clear sign so she wouldn't accidentally see more of Jaxon and Rhianna making out.

Tap. Tap.

"Come in."

Rhianna peeked inside. "Jaxon is gone."

"I can't believe he was jealous of Garret."

A sly smile blossomed on Rhianna's face. "Do you have any idea how often I've had to watch girls flirt with him?"

The concept of being attracted to Jaxon was beyond Bryn. "Serves him right."

"He's going to call when he has news of the investigation." Her smile dimmed. "I guess I should go see what I can salvage from my closet."

"Don't bother. You can borrow a pair of my pajamas and sleep in here."

"Thanks."

"Did you call my grandmother yet?"

Rhianna nodded. "Jaxon spoke to your grandfather, too."

"What did he have to say?"

"The words I heard coming through the phone aren't words I'd repeat." Rhianna frowned. "He was more worried about the anti-Directorate sentiment than the fact that I was targeted."

"Sounds like my grandfather."

• • •

The next morning, Bryn and Rhianna flew down to breakfast together. By unspoken agreement, they parted company at the buffet line, Bryn went to eat with her friends, and Rhianna went to eat with Jaxon.

Over French toast and coffee, Bryn filled in Clint and Ivy on what she'd found the night before.

"That's weird," Ivy said. "A Blue wouldn't normally do something so...normal."

"What do you mean?"

"You'd expect Blues to pull high class pranks. Like delivering expensive gifts with paint bombs inside of them or something," Clint said. "Regular graffiti seems so middle class."

True. "I don't think anyone but a Blue could walk into the dorm unnoticed." But a hybrid who could manipulate Quintessence to control their coloring probably could. She couldn't mention that to her friends without explaining she'd seen other hybrids in Dragon's Bluff the night it had been attacked, but sharing that information might endanger them. So she kept the idea to herself.

• • •

When she returned to her room after the last class of the day, Bryn found her grandmother sitting at the table in the living room pointing and giving orders. Rhianna sat next to her flipping through wallpaper swatches.

Two men had dismantled Rhianna's bed and were in the process of leaning it against the far wall by one of the roll top desks. "What's going on?" Bryn asked.

"There you are." Her grandmother pointed at the empty spot on the couch beside her. "Come pick out your new wallpaper."

"Not that I plan on arguing, but why am I picking out new paper when you're redoing Rhianna's room?"

"If I'm redecorating Rhianna's room, I might as well redo yours so the decor is cohesive."

Sure. That made sense. "Sounds like fun."

"I like this one." Rhianna pointed to a swatch of pale gray wallpaper that looked like silk.

"It's pretty," Bryn said. "But it looks more like a comforter than wallpaper."

"This is the bedding I'd recommend." Her grandmother flipped through another sample book. Swatches of material flashed by, until her grandmother stopped on a robin's egg blue silk with a silver gray floral pattern.

Rhianna sucked in a breath. "I love that."

Crap. Bryn was going to be stuck in a girly-girl room.

"I thought you might like this one." Her grandmother turned the page and pointed at a sky blue silk with a silver gray stripe.

"I do like that." Bryn had caught sight of another pattern a few pages back. She reached over and flipped pages until she came to the one she wanted. It was charcoal gray with silver and sky blue stripes. "I like this one, too."

"It's a bit masculine." Her grandmother flipped through a few more swatches and stopped on a silver gray comforter with the faintest navy pinstripe. "How about this?"

"I like that."

Men exited Rhianna's room carrying buckets of red rags. "Were they able to clean the walls?"

"They'll be good as new by the time we're done with them. Better, actually." Her grandmother marked the swatches they'd chosen and opened a shopping bag sitting next to her chair. "Now, let's pick out the accessories for your rooms."

Odd as it seemed, looking through pages of shower curtains and wall hangings was fun.

Rhianna shoved a catalog under Bryn's nose. "Look at this."

The bathroom was done up in charcoal gray and silver, but there were flowers on the shower curtain. Damn it all if she didn't like it. "I can't believe I'm about to say this, but I like the flowers."

After another half hour of playing pick-a-pattern, Bryn's stomach protested the lack of food by making a loud gurgling sound.

"Sorry about that. I need food."

"First let me speak with the staff, and then we'll figure out where to eat."

Did the workers mind being called staff? It seemed weird. *Whatever.*

Her grandmother returned a moment later. "Why don't we eat in the cafe downstairs?"

Rhianna froze. "I'm not sure that's a good idea."

"Why not?"

"Our dorm mates aren't...." What was the word Bryn was looking for..."overly friendly."

Her grandmother slammed a book shut. "That is ridiculous." She stood. "Follow me, and pay attention."

They took the stairs down to the dining hall. Every time they encountered another Blue, her grandmother stopped to ask questions.

"How is your grandmother?" she asked a girl Bryn didn't know.

"She's fine, Mrs. Sinclair. Thank you for asking."

"Do tell her I'd like to meet for coffee soon."

The girl brightened. "She'd love to meet for coffee. I'll have her call you."

It took them three times as long as it should have to make it down the stairs to the small cafe in back. Once they were seated and the waiter had delivered menus and iced tea, Bryn pointed back the way they came. "What was all that about?"

"That," her grandmother said with an arched brow, "was networking. Something you must learn how to do. Whenever those women call to make plans, I'll insist they bring their granddaughters along so you and Rhianna can network, too."

"Isn't that social blackmail?" Bryn asked.

"It's a game, Bryn. One you need to learn how to play."

After dinner, they returned to their dorm room. There wasn't a sign in the living room that a major project was taking place in the bedrooms. Rhianna stepped foot into her bedroom and smiled. "Oh, it's lovely."

What could the workmen have done in the amount of time they'd been gone? Bryn peered around the doorframe. "Wow." A soft silver glow covered the walls, like they were lit from within. "How did they do this while we ate dinner?"

"All you need is the right amount of workers, and you can complete any job in a short span of time," her grandmother said. "The bedding and the bathroom accessories will be delivered tomorrow."

In her own bedroom, Bryn found a surprise; her walls were also covered by the silver gray silk. "I love this wallpaper.

It's so—"

"Happy?" Rhianna said.

"Yes." Bryn hugged her grandmother. "Thank you. This place feels more like mine now."

"I'm glad you like it. I'll come back tomorrow night and we'll finish up."

. . .

"Dang." Ivy spun in a circle taking in Bryn's newly redecorated room. "This is unbelievable."

Clint stood in the doorway frowning. "I can't believe they have separate bedrooms."

"Sorry," Bryn said. "If you want to bleach your hair and get a tan, I'll try to sneak you in."

"No thanks." Clint's eyes narrowed. "Wait a minute. Is that a bathroom over there?"

"I'm going to start on my tan tomorrow," Ivy said. "I can't believe you have your own bathroom."

This was awkward. What could she say? *Sorry, the Blues have all the money so they built themselves better dorms.* "You could lodge a complaint with someone. Maybe they'd build you your own bathroom."

"Excuse me," Rhianna said from behind Clint. He stepped aside to let her come in. "Fair warning, Jaxon is coming over."

Bryn nodded at her friends. "Do you guys want to stay here and study in the living room or head back to your place?"

"Let's stay here," Clint said. "If for no other reason than to annoy Jaxon."

"We'll study at the table and you guys can have the couch, if that's all right," Rhianna said.

"One question," Ivy said. "Does your swanky cafe downstairs deliver pizza?"

Rhianna shook her head. "No."

Clint grinned. "Bryn, I will do your homework for a week if you call Jaxon and ask him to pick up a pizza on his way over."

"He won't do it if I ask." Bryn batted her eyes at Rhianna. "Can you ask your foul-tempered boyfriend to pick up pizzas for us?"

Rhianna struck a snotty posture. "Westgates order food. They don't deliver it."

Bryn laughed and then headed for the phone in the living room. "I'll call in a pizza, and we'll go pick it up."

"I volunteer." Clint brushed his fingers through his Mohawk, twisting it and making it stand up taller.

"Going for shock effect?" Rhianna asked.

"Of course."

"It won't work." She spoke in a sad tone. "They'll act like they can't see you."

Clint cracked his knuckles. "You underestimate my ability to piss people off. It's an art form."

Knock. Knock.

"That must be Jaxon." Rhianna rushed to answer the door.

"She's got it bad, doesn't she?" Ivy said.

"I so don't understand it, but yeah, she does." Bryn picked up the phone and dialed the restaurant downstairs.

Jaxon had barely stepped foot into the room, when he spotted Clint and Ivy. The scowl he directed at Bryn was hard to interpret.

"What? You're annoyed by me, or you don't like my friends?"

"Being annoyed by you is a given. While I don't dislike your friends, I don't like them being here."

Clint flopped onto the couch and stretched out, taking up as much room as possible. "I claim this couch as my new home." He winked at Bryn. "You don't mind if I sleep here tonight, do you?"

Jaxon glared at Clint and then stalked over to the table on the opposite side of the room and removed a notebook from his book bag.

Bryn remembered something. "Rhianna, isn't this the night you're supposed to meet Garret for coffee?"

"Yes, but it's not until later."

"I wish you'd reconsider." Jaxon flipped pages in his notebook. "Gathering together with the other injured students is like painting a target on your back."

"Then come with me," Rhianna said.

Jaxon's hand froze for a second, and then he resumed turning pages. "I would be happy to take you for coffee someplace else."

"It's not about the coffee and you know it." Rhianna smacked her textbook closed.

"I'm not sure if my presence at that meeting would help or hurt you," Jaxon said. "I don't think my father would approve."

"We already know he doesn't approve of me," Rhianna stated.

Jaxon shot Bryn a look. "Would you excuse us?"

It took her a minute to realize what he wanted. "You want me to leave so you can talk in private?"

"Yes."

"Fine. We'll go wait for our pizzas."

Bryn, Clint, and Ivy headed out the door.

"That was interesting," Ivy said.

"Jaxon is trying to do the right thing, but he's trapped between his father and the way he grew up and what he thinks is the right thing to do. One of these days he's going to snap, and I don't want to be there when it happens."

"You're defending Jaxon," Clint said. "That's new."

How could she explain? "Even though I want to shoot a giant fireball at him most of the time, he's doing right by Rhianna. He's standing up for her, and I respect that."

By the time they made it back to the room with the pizza, Rhianna and Jaxon were nowhere to be seen. Their books still lay on the table like they might be coming back to study. Bryn settled on the couch and put the pizza boxes on the coffee table. Clint stretched out on the floor, and Ivy sat in one of the wingback chairs.

"I hope they don't expect any pizza." Clint grabbed a slice of sausage pizza and shoved half of it into his mouth, grinning as he chewed.

"Impressive." Bryn took a normal bite.

Ivy laughed. "Don't encourage him. At my tenth birthday party, he shoved an entire piece of cake in his mouth."

"I was trying to impress you." Clint snagged another piece of pizza.

"When we have kids, let me tell the boys how to impress girls," Ivy said. "Or they're going to be lonely."

"What are you talking about? We're together, aren't we?"

"In spite of the cake," Ivy said. "Not because of it."

Bryn finished off her first piece of pizza and grabbed another. One of the major perks of being a dragon was a fast metabolism. She could eat whatever she wanted and not gain weight.

The sound of running water came from Rhianna's room. Then the door to her bedroom opened, and Jaxon came out followed by Rhianna.

"I told you I smelled pizza." Rhianna grabbed a piece of pizza, placed it on a paper plate, and then headed over to the table where her books were laid out.

Jaxon did the same.

Clint raised his eyebrows, glanced toward the blond couple and then to the bedroom they'd exited.

"Not a word," Ivy said.

"You're thinking the same thing I am," Clint said.

"No way," Bryn whispered. When she'd been paired with

Rhianna, she knew Jaxon would visit, but she hadn't thought through what he and Rhianna might be doing while they were there.

"I could ask," Clint said.

Ivy smacked him on the shoulder. "Behave."

"Where's the fun in that?" Clint polished off another piece of pizza, and then smiled at Ivy like he was up to something. "Bryn, are you going to the dining hall for coffee with Garret and the others later?"

"I wasn't invited," Bryn said.

"You could go with me," Rhianna spoke up from across the room.

Wanting to be supportive, she turned and smiled. "Sure, I'll go with you."

"No," Jaxon stated. "You won't."

He did not just pull that lord and master crap on me again. "You can't tell me what to do."

Jaxon reached up and rubbed the bridge of his nose. "We've had this conversation before."

"Which is why you should know better than to speak to me like that."

"Before you start in on another rant, perhaps you'd like to hear why I don't want you to go with Rhianna."

Whatever his reason was, it wouldn't be good enough. "Fine. Talk."

"Strategically speaking, if you go with Rhianna, it makes her look weak, like she can't stand on her own two feet."

"I hadn't thought of that," Rhianna said.

"That must be some weird Blue Clan logic," Clint said. "In my Clan, friends go places together to support each other."

"Yes. And you also do strange things to your hair and mar your skin with tattoos."

Lightning crackled in Clint's palm. "I bet I could make your hair stand on end."

Chapter Four

They so didn't need this right now, so Bryn tried to calm her friend. "Clint, being offended by Jaxon's snobbiness is a waste of time. It's ingrained."

Rhianna cleared her throat. "We just had our rooms redone. I'd appreciate it if you two didn't mess them up."

Clint closed his palm and the lightning dissipated. "Fine, but he needs to understand one thing. Your Clan may be different than mine, but it's not superior."

Jaxon opened his mouth to reply.

"Don't even think about it," Rhianna said. "For me. Please let it go."

Lips clamped together, Jaxon nodded and went back to his book.

Maybe having her friends over here wasn't such a good idea. She needed a way to get them out of the room without making it look like she wanted them to relocate. "After we eat, do you guys want to go flying?"

"Yes," Clint said. "Being trapped in a classroom all day makes me claustrophobic."

After dinner, Bryn, Clint, and Ivy departed by the terrace window, fixed courtesy of her grandmother's staff. The brisk night air was invigorating. She dove and performed a barrel roll. Ivy copied the move. All three of them took turns performing aerial acrobatics, then playing follow the leader.

Below them, Bryn spotted Rhianna walking by herself toward the dining hall. Consciously or not, she edged toward the dining hall with every maneuver.

"Are we spying on her?" Clint asked.

"No, just making sure she's safe," Bryn said.

"I guess that's what the asshat is doing, too," Clint said.

Bryn glanced around. Sure enough, Jaxon was flying laps near the dining hall. "See, that's why I can't hate him. He truly is trying to take care of her."

"That's all right," Clint said. "I can hate him enough for both of us."

Later that night, Rhianna returned to the room with a smile on her face.

"Have fun?" Bryn asked.

Rhianna joined her on the couch. "It's the strangest thing. I never would've associated with half those students before my injury, but I liked them a lot. They all have a positive attitude. And Garret is funny. I didn't know Greens could be so funny."

"Uh-oh. You better not say that in front of Jaxon. He'll be jealous."

Rhianna pulled her knees up to her chest. "Garret is cute, and he blushes whenever he talks to me."

"If you run away with Garret and leave me to deal with Jaxon, I will *never* forgive you." Bryn was only half joking.

"Please, I would never leave Jaxon, but it is kind of nice to have someone else pay attention to me."

• • •

As the week went on, Bryn watched for any sign one of her classmates might be a hybrid but never noticed anything. The other students on campus adjusted to their injured friends' presence. Everyone except, of course, the Blue Clan. Saturday afternoon, Bryn asked Rhianna to accompany her to Dragon's Bluff where she planned to meet her grandmother for lunch.

"No, thank you. I'm tired of dealing with everyone. I want to hide out here for a while."

"I know what it's like to have everyone staring at you and making you crazy, but are you sure you want to be alone? Fonzoli's reopened. Valmont saved us a table."

Rhianna shook her head. "You go ahead. Have fun."

She thought about flying to Dragon's Bluff, but her grandmother had already planned to pick her up. When the car arrived, her grandmother wasn't in it. "Am I having lunch by myself?" Bryn asked the driver.

"Your grandmother left for Dragon's Bluff early this morning to oversee some of the details on the rebuilding. She'll meet you at the restaurant."

"Oh, okay." If her grandmother was in charge of the recovery efforts in Dragon's Bluff, the place would be back to normal in no time.

On the drive through campus toward the back gate, Bryn people-watched, or rather dragon-watched. *Ugh.* Would she ever stop thinking of herself as a human? Probably not.

Students congregated at the new picnic shelters that had been installed around campus since so many of the trees had been demolished during the attacks last semester. Granite tables and benches sat underneath the shelters, which had decorative copper roofs. The official story claimed they were meant to provide shade. Of course, they would also provide protection from most aerial attacks. Not that the Directorate mentioned that part. Did they think the students wouldn't figure it out, or were they supposed to be polite or obedient enough not to say anything? Too bad for them she was short on both counts.

When they reached the back gate leading off campus, there was another change. The guard post where students had to sign in and out had transformed into what looked like a military bunker, complete with a dozen guards, camera surveillance, and an observation deck with something that looked suspiciously like a gun turret on top. Rather than a gun, there was something that resembled a cannon with a javelin sticking out of the barrel.

"What's that thing on top there?" Bryn asked as the car stopped at the gate and a guard approached the vehicle.

The driver ignored her question in favor of rolling down the window.

"State your business," the guard said.

"I'm transporting Bryn McKenna to Dragon's Bluff to meet her grandmother for lunch."

The guard checked an electronic tablet he held in his hand. "I don't see your authorization permit."

"Last minute change of plans," the driver said.

"I'll need to see your ID."

The driver pulled a badge from his pocket and flashed it at the guard. "We shouldn't keep Mrs. Sinclair waiting."

Unmoved by this statement, the guard tapped away on the tablet. "Miss McKenna, I'll need to see your ID as well."

That was going to be a problem. "I didn't bring any ID with me." Since her grandmother was paying for lunch, she hadn't even grabbed her wallet.

The guard frowned. "Please step out of the vehicle. I can scan you and check it against the photo ID online."

That was new. Bryn tugged on the door handle, but it didn't open. "The child safety locks must be on. Can you let me out?"

"Sure." The driver leaned away from the window, where

the buttons to release the locks would be, and reached toward the passenger seat. An uneasy feeling grew in Bryn's stomach. Something about this wasn't right.

"Miss McKenna, exit the vehicle. Now." The guard drew a gun and aimed it at the driver.

Holy hell.

The driver turned, knife in hand, and lunged at Bryn. She sucked in a breath and blasted him with flames as she scrambled over the seat into the back of the SUV. The driver roared in pain but still managed to dive partway over the seat and grab her ankle. She kicked out, making contact with something that caused the driver to curse. What the hell was going on? The interior of the SUV was smoldering and smoking. She didn't want to risk any more fire. Focusing on cold, she blasted him with ice. He countered with flames, melting the ice and filling the car with a cloud of steam. Now what? If she shifted in this confined space, she'd probably break a wing, so she kicked again, and missed. The back window of the SUV shattered, a new guard grabbed Bryn's arms and pulled, but the driver still held her ankle.

"Let go." Bryn kicked again. Razor sharp pain sliced through her leg. She twisted and kicked.

Bam. Bam. Bam.

Gunshots reverberated through the car. The grip on her ankle fell away, and the guard holding her arms tugged her through the jagged edged window. Glass sliced through her clothes, biting into her skin.

"Down." The guard shoved her to the ground as the militia surrounded the vehicle.

She sucked in a breath. The cuts on her back and arms stung, but they weren't fatal. Her leg throbbed.

"Is it over?" she asked. The sound of water trickling under the car caught her attention. Then the fumes hit her. Not water. Gas. And the inside of the car was still smoldering.

Not good.

"Shift!" Bryn shouted. She lunged away from the car, shifted and *Boom*. The SUV went up in a ball of flames. Fire engulfed her body, playing across her scales, doing little damage.

Screams came from behind her. The guard by the door was engulfed in flames. She blasted him and the burning remains of the SUV with sleet, dousing the blaze. Everyone around her screamed. Dragon wings beat through the air. She eyed the sky. Friend or foe? How was she supposed to tell?

Half a dozen Reds descended and stood guard around her. She turned in a circle checking the sky. Everything seemed okay. She sat down, oddly exhausted and unable to catch her breath, like someone had knocked the wind out of her. What was going on? The cut on her leg hadn't been that bad. She checked the gash on the back of her right calf. If she were human, she'd need a few stitches. Since she was a dragon studying to be a medic, she'd healed minor wounds before, so she focused on the angry red line. Reaching inside, she gathered her life force like a small sun in her chest. Then she tried to direct the Quintessence, which she could normally do without breaking a sweat. While channeling her energy, a strange smell like rotten meat hit her. She gagged. Damn it. The blade must've been poisoned.

More wing beats filled the air. A green dragon landed and shifted.

"Bryn? What's wrong?" Medic Williams shifted to human form. "Shift for me."

She tried, she really did, but the world was going all swimmy. Whenever she tried to focus her energy, it slid through her fingers like water through a sieve. She opened her mouth to speak, but no words came out.

Someone shouted. Medic Williams laid her hands on Bryn. Heat surged through her body. A weird vibrating sensation started in her wings. It swept through her core. She felt stretched tight like a rubber band and then snapped back to her human form. Limp, she lay on the ground, unable to blink or speak, or move in any manner. The only thing she felt was the rising tide of panic clawing at her chest.

The medic lifted Bryn's leg, which was puffed up like a tick full of blood. That wasn't right.

"You've been poisoned. I'm going to burn it out." Quintessence shot through her veins, and her body convulsed. It felt like she was watching someone else. The heat from the procedure...she should be able to feel it, but she couldn't, and that was wrong. She willed the sensation of heat or burning or even pain, but there was nothing. Closing her eyes, she reached inside, trying to focus on the rancid smell, but her own Quintessence now felt like tar, unable to flow or move.

There were more voices, and then she felt another pair of hands on her legs and another on her shoulders. A faint warmth, like sunshine through a window, enveloped her body. That was nice. The sensation grew warmer, and warmer.

"This is going to hurt," someone said next to her ear.

Of course it is.

Warmth flowed and turned into heat, the heat turned into a low burn, the low burn turned into a blowtorch searing her from the inside out, and she couldn't even scream.

• • •

Why couldn't she open her eyes? Bryn inhaled and smelled disinfectant. They must have moved her to the medical clinic. *Come on eyelids. Move.*

A slit of light came into view. Maybe talking would be easier. She forced her lips apart, and a groaning sound came out.

"Bryn?" She knew that voice.

"Grandmother?" At least that's what she tried to say. It came out as a muffled mess.

Fingers pried her eyelids open. A beam of light aimed at her pupil sliced through her head. She tried to turn away, managing to move a little.

"She's coming around. It will take a while."

Back at school less than a week, and someone had tried to kill her—again. Damn it. So much for a safer school. Then again, if all those guards hadn't been there, the driver, whoever he was, could have driven off into the woods, killed her, and dumped her body.

That was a freaking cheery thought.

She wanted to blast someone to cinders. At the very least, she wanted answers. Just lying here and not being able to move or talk pissed her off. So, time to concentrate.

She'd start with her eyelids. They'd moved a little before. Lifting them was like trying to lift a boulder. Focus. The slit was bigger this time. Now she could see light again.

"Bryn." Her grandmother stood over her, studying her. "You can hear me, can't you?"

"Yes." It came out like "essss" but at least she was talking.

"Thank God." Her grandmother sat down next to her on the bed and grabbed her hand. "I'm beginning to think scaring the life out of me is your new hobby."

Bryn laughed. It was a dry, raspy sound.

Her grandmother's lips set in a thin line. "I can't tell you how furious I am that something like this happened again."

She didn't love it herself.

"Excuse me." Medic Williams came to stand on the other side of her bed. "You're awake enough now. I'm going to channel energy into your body to support you, and I want you to burn out whatever remains of the drug in your bloodstream."

Why couldn't Medic Williams do it by herself?

"And yes, I could do it myself, but since you were unable to shift back to human form after the poisoning, we need to jumpstart your system and make sure everything is working properly again."

Would her Quintessence respond this time? The idea of losing the ability to manipulate her Quintessence and giving up her dream of being a medic made her afraid to try. But that was stupid. Of course she'd be able to do this. She hoped.

Medic Williams placed her hand on Bryn's shoulder. "Any time you're ready."

Bryn focused on gathering her Quintessence. Rather than tar, it was thick like oatmeal, but she could move it. Slowly, she reached into her blood and detected a milk-gone-bad sour odor and little flakes, like ash, floating in her blood. That must be the problem. She focused and torched the flakes wherever she found them, drawing Quintessence from Medic Williams.

As the ashy flakes disappeared, energy returned to her body and transformed into that strange pins and needles feeling she got when she'd slept on her arm wrong, except it was her entire body tingling. Not the best sensation she'd ever had, but it was more annoying than anything.

Twenty minutes later, she couldn't find any more. "I think it's all gone."

The medic channeled a little more energy into Bryn. "We'll check again tonight."

Bryn opened her eyes and smiled at her grandmother. "I guess we'll have to wait on lunch."

Her grandmother didn't say anything. She pulled her into a hug and kissed the top of her head. Bryn hugged her back hard.

When her grandmother released her, she sat in a chair by the bed. "Tell me what happened."

Bryn relayed the events leading up to the attack. "I guess the moral of the story is never get in a car with a driver unless you're sure he works for your grandparents."

"That's just it. He did work for us. He's worked for us for more than a dozen years."

"What the hell?"

"Exactly. I can't imagine what someone could've promised him or threatened him with that he would try to harm you. None of this makes sense."

One thing she did know, her grandfather was going to be furious. "Has the Directorate heard about this yet?"

Her grandmother's eyebrows came together. "An SUV exploded on campus. Of course they've heard. And your grandfather is incensed. He's interrogating our staff and the other guards here at school."

Interrogating, not questioning. Interrogating. By the time he was done he'd probably have more enemies than before he started.

"I've made a decision." Her grandmother sat up straighter. "There is only one person I trust to guard you."

"If you say, Jaxon, I will run screaming from this room."

"He would've been my first choice, but he's busy taking care of Rhianna. So I'm going with option number two."

"You're dragging this out to torment me."

"Think of it as payback for scaring me senseless." Her grandmother grinned. "Don't worry, I think you'll approve."

The door flew open, and Valmont stormed in. "What's going on. Are you all right?"

"I'm recovering."

He sat on the side of the bed opposite her grandmother and grabbed Bryn's hand. "Someone will pay for this."

"Yes they will, young man. In the meantime, you are responsible for my granddaughter's wellbeing. Are you up to the task?"

"Yes."

It was like the dark of night had turned into a bright,

sunny day. "Valmont is my personal guard?"

Her grandmother nodded. "Your grandfather will have a fit, but I think Valmont is the right choice."

"He's a fabulous choice." Bryn squeezed his hand.

"Of course, there will be a few wrinkles to iron out," her grandmother said. "For now, he will accompany you to classes and anywhere else you go on campus. The housing situation is a concern." She shot Valmont a look. "If I allow you to share Bryn's room and sleep on her couch, you will behave with the utmost propriety."

"Yes, Ma'am."

Holy crap. Valmont was going to be living with her. Laughter was an odd response, but it's all she had. "I can't wait to see the look on Jaxon's face when he learns about this."

• • •

"Absolutely not." Jaxon stomped his foot like a toddler throwing a tantrum.

Valmont sat on the couch in the living area of Bryn's dorm, seemingly unaffected by Jaxon's hissy fit. "If you'd like to take this up with Bryn's grandmother, feel free to do so."

It was even funnier than Bryn imagined. "Calm down, Jaxon. Look at the positives. Rhianna will benefit from the added security."

"No. She won't. Not only is her roommate suspect, the entire school will hear about this ridiculous living arrangement."

"I'm sure he'll be a perfect gentleman," Rhianna said.

"There is not a chance in the world your grandfather knows about this." Jaxon paced the room. "Have you thought about what people will say?"

"I'm sure they'll all want a handsome knight of their own, by the week's end," Valmont said.

She tried not to laugh, but Rhianna giggled, and Bryn's dam of self-control broke.

"You think this is funny?" Jaxon turned on Rhianna. "Do you have any idea how hard I've worked to make sure our Clan treats you with respect? And this is how you repay me?"

A weird sense of deja vu hit Bryn. Hadn't her former boyfriend Zavien said the same words to her not long ago when he didn't want Valmont spending the night to guard her after she'd been poisoned the first time? Sadness tugged at her insides. No. She wouldn't think about her ex. What they'd had…any trace of a relationship or friendship…it was done. Over.

The smirking knight on her couch cared for her…and she cared for him. More than that, she trusted he would never hurt her. He would never choose someone else over her.

"You know how much I appreciate everything you've done," Rhianna told Jaxon. "You know how much you mean to me. This isn't about me, or about what anyone else thinks, it's about keeping Bryn safe."

Valmont sat forward. "This isn't open to debate. Until Bryn, or her grandmother, tells me otherwise, I'm camping out on the couch."

"Then Rhianna is moving." Jaxon pointed at his girlfriend. "Don't even think about arguing. I don't care if you spend time here during the day, but you will officially reside in a different dorm room. Up until this point, my father has tolerated our relationship. If he hears of this, he will order me to sever ties." Jaxon's voice softened. "After everything we've been through—"

"I'll do it." Rhianna stepped closer to Jaxon. "If you think it's important, I'll move."

His posture relaxed. "Good." He grabbed her hand. "Let's go take care of this right now."

Rhianna shot a nervous glance at Bryn.

"It's okay," Bryn said. "I don't like it, but if Jaxon thinks his dad will go psycho, it isn't worth it. But you have to promise you'll still hang out here."

"I promise."

Jaxon tugged Rhianna out the door.

Bryn flopped onto the couch next to Valmont. "Well, this sucks."

"Sorry." Valmont put his arm around her shoulders. "I expected Jaxon to freak out and then calm down. I didn't expect him to kidnap Rhianna."

"He knows how the rest of his Clan thinks." She snuggled into Valmont's side. "Not that I approve."

"They are an uppity bunch," Valmont said.

Bryn laughed. "It's strange. Just when I think I understand how my grandparents think, or what the Clan will take in stride, something comes up to blow my whole outlook. You've been around them longer than I have. Do you have any insights?"

"No." He pulled her closer so she laid her head on his shoulder. "But there is a time honored tradition in the Fonzoli household. Every Sunday afternoon a sacred ritual takes place. We call it a nap."

"That is a tradition I'm happy to continue."

"Good." He put his feet up on the coffee table and closed his eyes. "After the nap comes food."

"Works for me." She closed her eyes and drifted off to sleep using his chest as a pillow.

. . .

That night, Bryn helped Rhianna organize her new room down the hall, while Valmont stood guard in the hallway outside the door.

"I hate this," Rhianna said, hanging clothes in the armoire.

"Then why did you agree to move?"

After placing the last dress on the rod, she closed the armoire door. "Jaxon felt it was important, and he's been wonderful to me. And I'm not sure he's wrong. People will assume certain things since Valmont is sharing your room."

Bryn plopped down on the bed. "That's ridiculous. Half the people on campus spend the majority of their time in someone else's room."

"Yes, and everyone talks about them."

"They do?"

"Yes." Rhianna laughed. "Of course, I'm out of the loop now because most of my Clan doesn't talk to me anymore."

"Idiots."

"At least Jaxon keeps them from being rude to my face." Rhianna frowned. "I miss my other room already."

What could she say to make this better? "Think of it as having two rooms. One you sleep in and one you live in."

"That is a more positive spin." She nudged Bryn and spoke in a quiet voice. "You and Valmont can have some time alone together now. How do you feel about that?"

"Excited and terrified." Bryn glanced toward the door. "I'm afraid I'll hurt him."

"That's his evil grandmother in your head. You care about him, and he cares about you."

"Which he's willing to admit, in public." Not that she was bitter.

The sound of raised voices came from the hallway. Bryn jumped off the bed and went to investigate.

Valmont stood leaning against the wall wiping down his broad sword like he didn't have a care in the world while a Blue male ranted at him.

Valmont grinned at Bryn. "Ready to go?"

The Blue whirled around. "I should've known this would be your fault."

Bryn took a deep breath and gave the polite smile her grandmother used when someone was being a jerk. "I'm sorry if my knight's presence bothers you, but my grandmother, Marie Sinclair, ordered him to stay by my side. If you have a problem, I suggest you ask your mother to take it up with her."

The Blue cursed and stormed off down the hall.

"You're getting good at that," Rhianna said. "Your grandmother would be proud."

"It's kind of fun."

"You wield your grandmother like your knight wields his sword." Jaxon came toward them with a less than friendly look on his face. "I moved Rhianna to keep her away from you. Why are you here?"

"First. Bite me," Bryn said. "Second, I helped her unpack."

"Go away." Jaxon made shooing motions with his hands. "She can come to your room. You're not allowed in hers."

Valmont cleared his throat and held out his sword as if he was admiring the way the light reflected off the blade. "You could say that in a nicer manner."

"I hate to tell you, but that was him being nice," Bryn laughed and grabbed Valmont's hand. "Let's go before he tries to tell me what else I can't do."

Chapter Five

Bryn sat at the table in her living room and double-checked her homework assignments, which were due tomorrow, while Valmont talked to his dad on the phone. All her assignments were good to go. Not perfect, but good enough. There was only so much time she could devote to homework when someone was trying to kill her.

She zipped up her book bag. Now what? She needed to say something. There was no reason to be nervous. This was Valmont. It's not like he was going to kiss her or anything, not that she'd have a problem with that scenario, but still, she was being stupid.

After Valmont ended the call, she said, "I guess you'll follow me to class tomorrow?"

"According to your grandmother, I'm supposed to be your shadow. She didn't give specific details."

Her grandmother expected Valmont to drop everything to protect Bryn, and he'd agreed—no questions asked, and with no thoughts to his living arrangements. The suitcase he'd brought with him leaned against the far end of the couch.

"Since Rhianna moved out, why don't you move into her room? You can unpack and make yourself comfortable."

"Are you sure? If I'm on the couch, I'm between you and the front door."

True. "Though someone could come in from the terrace entrance, too. If you're in her room, with the door open, you'd be in the middle of the two entrances."

"I hadn't thought of it that way." He stood and grabbed his bag. "I guess I'll unpack."

It was on the tip of her tongue to offer to help him unpack, but he couldn't have much in the one bag, and he might want some time to think. A few minutes later, she heard the sound of furniture moving.

What could he be doing? She poked her head in his new room where she witnessed him moving the four-poster bed toward the door.

He must have his reasons. She waited for him to finish.

"There." He adjusted the bed so it was two feet inside the room. Now, I can jump out of bed and be out the door as soon as possible."

"Good idea." She yawned. "Speaking of bed, I think I'm going to turn in."

"Okay." He closed the distance between them and pulled her into a hug. His arms around her made her feel safe. It would be great to fall asleep with him on the couch. A nap was one thing, sleeping in his arms all night long might not be a good idea. Actually, it sounded like a fabulous idea, but her grandmother most certainly would not approve.

• • •

The next morning, Bryn checked the mirror and frowned. Pale skin and tired eyes stared back at her. Using Quintessence she darkened her lip color, gave her cheeks a healthy glow, and darkened her eyelashes. That was better. She might not be a morning person but that didn't mean she had to look like she was still asleep.

Valmont walked her to breakfast. Clint and Ivy acted like it was normal for Valmont to join them. Everyone else, not so much.

"Should I stand up and introduce myself to everyone in the dining hall?" Valmont asked.

Clint shook his head. "Believe me, everyone knows who you are."

Valmont gave a movie-star grin, and his single dimple appeared. "Looks like I'm famous. Do you think they'll want me to sign autographs?"

Bryn chuckled. Good thing her knight didn't mind scrutiny.

"Hey, look at that." Ivy pointed toward a table where Rhianna and Jaxon sat with several others of their Clan. The girls were talking among themselves, and they were including Rhianna.

"Yeah, I guess moving out of my room bumped her back up the social ladder."

"Hello?" Ivy waved her hands in front of Bryn's face. "Did we forget to share with the class?"

"Sorry. Everyone staring at Valmont distracted me." She told them about Jaxon insisting Rhianna move out.

"It sucks that he might've been right," Ivy said.

"It sucks that my grandmother made me move to the Blue dorm in the first place."

"I wonder how long it would take her to hear about it if we moved you back to our dorm?" Clint said.

"Unfortunately, that would constitute an act of war, as far as my grandfather is concerned." Bryn stirred a packet of sugar into her coffee. "Though when I lived in your dorm, I felt like I belonged. The Blue dorm is not so friendly."

"They're a bunch of pompous asses." Valmont spoke in a voice quiet enough for only their table to hear. "Too bad they control all the money and have all the power."

"They don't," Clint said. "I mean, they have most of the money, but they wouldn't survive a week without the rest of us. Who creates the art they love to buy? Who heals them when they're sick? Who runs all the businesses they love to spend their money at?"

She'd never thought about it that way. "I guess all the Clans need each other to play their roles."

"And the Blues are like the prima donnas of the company," Clint said. "We put up with their snotty behavior, while we secretly fantasize about knee-capping them."

. . .

In Elemental Science, Mr. Stanton approached Valmont and had a quick whispered conversation before class started.

"What was that about?" Bryn asked.

"You'll see." Valmont grinned like a kid who'd been offered a trip to Disneyland.

Mr. Stanton stood behind his desk and waited for everyone to settle down and face him. "As you can see we have a visitor today, and he has generously agreed to help with today's lesson."

This could be really great or really awful.

"I'm sure you've all heard that Valmont is Bryn's knight. I've asked him to explain how this came to be."

Oh crap. She grabbed Valmont's hand as he stood. "You don't have to do this."

"Afraid I'll name names?" he asked.

Did she care about that? "Maybe."

He laughed. "Fine. I'll just use an unflattering description."

And everyone would know who he was talking about, anyway. She wanted to crawl under her desk.

Valmont strode to the front of the room exuding

confidence and way too much sex appeal. He leaned his left hip against Mr. Stanton's desk and grinned at her.

"Once upon a time—"

Several students laughed.

"What? It really does start like that." He cleared his throat. "Once upon a time, Bryn and several of her friends came to Fonzoli's for lunch. We met, and I could tell there was something special about her."

Bryn felt her face color.

"A few days later, she returned to the restaurant, asking for a gallon of lemon ice and a spoon. Given my experience with females, I knew this meant something wasn't right in her world. We talked, and then the source of her irritation, who we shall refer to as the spiky-haired moron, showed up and tried to push past me to continue his confrontation."

Oh, God. Zavien would hear about this. She was sure of it.

"As any good descendant of a knight would do, I blocked his path to protect Bryn from more verbal abuse." Valmont zeroed in on Bryn. "And in that moment, she became my world, the only thing worth living for, and I knew I would lay down my life or take another's to protect her."

A tingling sensation started on Bryn's scalp and traveled through her core all the way down to her toes. It was like magic pulsed in the air between them. Female students from all Clans whispered among themselves, while the male students muttered under their breath. Not that she could blame the girls for being impressed and the boys for being jealous. Her knight was awesome and hot, and why did these I-must-kiss-him feelings always seem to hit her when they were in a crowd? It was damn inconvenient.

"Thank you for that illuminating explanation, Valmont." Mr. Stanton shuffled papers on his desk. "You may return to your seat."

Seeming larger than life, Valmont strode back toward her.

More than half the girls tracked his progress across the room, which earned more scowls from the boys. Did Valmont mind? Of course not. Maybe that was the reaction he'd been going for. He did love to stir up trouble, but in her heart she knew he meant every word he'd said.

When he reached her, he moved the chair so he sat beside her, took her hand, and laced his fingers through hers. It was only by sheer willpower that she didn't crawl onto his lap.

He leaned in and whispered, "I know what you're thinking."

Her face grew hot. "No. You don't."

"You're blushing." He sat back in his seat and gave a self-satisfied grin.

She tried narrowing her eyes at him but ended up laughing instead. "Knock it off."

"Class, as you just witnessed, the bond between a dragon and a knight is strong. There hasn't been a knight in our society for more than a hundred years. Normally, dragons and the descendants of knights don't interact in a way that makes stepping in to protect someone a common occurrence. However, now that there is an outside threat, you need to be aware that every grown human in Dragon's Bluff has the ability to take on the mantle of a knight. Take care when you're there, not to bring about the transformation by accident."

"Could a dragon saving a human bring about the transformation?" Garret asked.

Mr. Stanton frowned. "The history texts are vague on that account. In ancient times, dragons used to adopt entire towns. The people kept their dragon's identity a secret and the dragon protected people from any invaders. The dragons shared their magic with the humans, imbuing them with extra strength and turning them into knights."

"This brings about so many interesting theoretical questions." Garret tapped his desktop with his good hand. "What if a human had a transfusion from a dragon? Would that activate the spell since the magic is literally from the dragon's blood and the latent spell is in the human's blood?"

"That is an interesting hypothesis. One you would not be allowed to test." Mr. Stanton spoke sternly.

"It's not like I'd kidnap someone," Garret said, "but maybe someone could volunteer."

"Can the process be reversed?" Jaxon asked.

An involuntary growl poured from Bryn's throat.

Jaxon rolled his eyes. "Calm down. I'm not talking about your knight in particular. It's a theoretical question. If Garret found a volunteer, and he managed to bring out the latent powers of a knight, could he change the person back?"

"Once a bond is forged, it can only be broken by the dragon. Not that I am giving approval of any sort for this experiment, but if Garret was able to change someone, that person could be released. They would go back to their normal life. On the battlefield, if a dragon is mortally wounded, she can release the knight in order to give him peace. If either the dragon or knight dies while still bonded...well, you've seen the dragon atop the hill for which the town was named."

Bryn swallowed hard. "That isn't a statue?"

"No," Mr. Stanton said. "Her knight was gravely injured in battle. She could have released him, but instead she chose to stay by his side until he died. He was buried on the bluffs. She sat by his grave every day. Eventually, the magic of the bond turned her to stone so she could watch over him forever."

Tears filled Bryn's eyes. She'd thought that story had sucked when she believed it was only a myth. Now that she knew it was true, it was heartbreaking.

Valmont put his arm around her shoulders and pulled her close. "I will never put you in that position. If worse came to worse, I'd ask you to break the bond."

That didn't make her feel any better, but she nodded like she was okay with it, because what else could she do?

Chapter Six

As they walked across campus, Valmont said, "I can't believe you're allowed to work in the library by yourself for an hour while your friends go to history class."

She gave him a brief overview of her confrontation with the history teacher who had banned her from class for disagreeing with her. "So, I still have to do the work, but I turn it into Mr. Stanton instead."

At the front desk, Miss Enid surprised Valmont with his very own library card. "You're the first knight entered into the computerized library system."

He examined the card. "Thank you. I should have plenty of time to read in the evening while Bryn is doing homework."

Valmont had put his entire life on hold to spend twenty-four hours a day with her. His family, not to mention his evil grandmother, probably weren't thrilled with the situation. Guilt made her feel twitchy.

As they ascended the stairs to the third floor where she normally studied, Bryn tried to put her concerns into words. "Your family, are they okay with this?"

"With what?"

Seriously? "With you walking away from your everyday life, the restaurant, and time with your family, to take care of me."

He opened the door to the third floor. "I can talk to them on the phone whenever I want. I'm sure they miss me, but they understand."

Her grandparents wouldn't understand if she took off to live with someone twenty-four hours a day. "I'm not sure if I'm allowed to leave campus, but if I am, we should go have dinner with your family."

"I appreciate the thought." They reached the table where she normally studied. He pulled out her chair and then sat next to her. "But your grandmother already informed me that you aren't to leave campus."

If she thought about that too long, she'd become claustrophobic. "I'm sure there's some way we can set up a visit."

Valmont placed his hand under Bryn's chin and tilted her head up to look into his eyes. "Stop worrying about me. It's my job to worry about you."

"I can't help—"

"Stop it." He grinned at her. "I might miss my family, but there is no place in this world I'd rather be than by your side."

He spoke with such conviction. The world narrowed down to his bright blue eyes. Her scalp started tingling again and the sensation flowed through her body. Was it just her? Was it the bond, or something more?

"Can you feel that?" she asked.

"Yes. I've felt that since the first day I became your knight."

Oh, God. He'd felt this way all along, and he'd had to watch her moon over Zavien. "I'm sorry… That must have been hard for you."

He dropped his hand and looked away. "You've no idea

how much I hated Zavien for hurting you." He turned back and met her gaze. "And the guilt I felt because I was thrilled he turned out to be such an idiot."

"If it's any consolation, I feel guilty for wasting my time on him."

"Why don't we stow away all this guilt and move on with our lives." Valmont's gaze dropped to her lips. "And I know how we should start."

Time seemed to slow down as he leaned down toward her. The tingling sensation she'd felt before intensified. This was right. This was magical. This was…due to the bond? No, she refused to believe that. She'd thought Valmont was hot the first time she'd met him, pre-bond. Even Ivy had commented on how attractive he was. Closing her eyes, she leaned in.

A door banged closed, shattering the moment.

Valmont stood and moved around to the front of the table placing himself between Bryn and anyone who might come toward them.

"It's not unusual for people to come up here," Bryn said.

"Until I know it's *not* a threat, it's a threat."

Students Bryn didn't know came into view and turned down a different aisle.

Now what? Would he try to kiss her again?

He rejoined her at the table and leaned back in his seat. "This probably isn't the best place to finish what we started."

Too bad. "Maybe you can help me with something else. Do you remember how I told you the dragons who attacked Dragon's Bluff were different?" She didn't want to go shouting the word "hybrid" in case anyone was nearby.

He nodded.

"I think there have to be some peaceful dragons like that, hiding out here on campus, keeping their real identity a secret. And if there are, I need to find them to show everyone that not all of them are dangerous."

He tapped his fingers on the table. "What if the ones on campus sympathize with the arsonists? Wouldn't you be putting yourself in danger?"

Crap. She hadn't thought of that. "There has to be proof somewhere in this giant building that *different* dragons exist. If I could find something: a map, a relic, maybe I could use that to figure some of this out." She pulled on her necklace and showed Valmont the small golden key pendant with red and blue stones decorating both sides. "Onyx gave me this protection charm. He could have placed the charm on any piece of jewelry. I think he gave me this for a reason. I think it's supposed to lead me to something."

"Did you ask him about it?"

"He claims it was something he had lying around, and it reminded him of me. I took it to Talia at All that Sparkles. She said it was old and real gold, but that didn't mean it was anything but a piece of jewelry."

"Did she tell you the story of Wraith Knightshade?"

Bryn nodded. "Some of it. What did she tell you?"

"She didn't tell me the story. I read it in a book."

This was news to her. "There are books with that story? Where? I searched all over this library and couldn't find them."

He frowned. "There are several books of fairy tales which include stories of the time before the Directorate took control, but they're told from the knight's perspective, which might be why they aren't included here. Talia's grandmother used to read to us at the library in Dragon's Bluff when we were kids."

"There's a library in Dragon's Bluff?"

"Of course. It's attached to the school." Valmont stood. "I think we should go see if Miss Enid can arrange for an interlibrary loan."

They found Miss Enid still sitting at the front desk, checking out books for students. When she was free, Bryn filled her in on their request.

"Do you remember the name of the set?" Miss Enid asked as she typed away on her keyboard.

"*Days of Knights*," Valmont said with a grin.

"Are puns part of the knightly code?" Bryn asked.

"Maybe." Valmont grinned. "Although that isn't exactly a pun."

"Close enough." Miss Enid clicked through several screens. "I think I can arrange an unofficial interlibrary loan with the Dragon's Bluff School librarian. You shouldn't go around talking about this. The Directorate must have a reason for not housing those books in the campus library."

"Mums the word." Bryn grabbed Valmont's hand. "Come on. We don't want to be late for my favorite class." Basic Movement was like gym class, but far cooler. "You're going to love it."

Chapter Seven

For some reason, Basic Movement was a bit awkward. While Bryn had seen Valmont in a shirt and jeans before, she'd never seen him in a too-tight Directorate-issued T-shirt and track pants. And she might have felt the muscles beneath his shirt, but now she could see the outline of pecs and biceps. Where Jaxon and the Blues were lean and muscled like runners or swimmers, Valmont was built thicker through the shoulders and chest. Not nearly as muscular as the Reds who were built like pro-wrestlers, but somewhere in between. He walked toward her with an evil grin on his face, and her temperature spiked.

"Funny that his body type is somewhere between the Red and the Blues," Ivy said. "Sort of symbolic, don't you think?"

When Valmont reached them, he jerked his thumb over his shoulder toward the jousting platforms. "Any chance I can face off with Jaxon?"

Clint laughed. "I'd pay to see that."

"That's probably not a good idea." In fact, Bryn knew it was a terrible idea. "Jaxon has been working his butt off to prove he's the alpha of the Blues, so people will leave Rhianna alone."

"You're right," Valmont said. "When I beat him, it would cause problems for Rhianna, and I like her."

"I am secure in my masculinity and therefore have nothing to prove." Clint put his arm around Ivy's shoulders. "But I think a lot of the other males are wondering how strong your knight is. You better pick an activity he and you can do alone, before someone challenges him."

Valmont winked at her. "We could finish what we started in the library."

"And what did you start it the library?" Ivy asked in far too cheery a tone.

Bryn whacked Valmont on the arm. "Knock it off."

Mrs. Anderson waved at Bryn from across the room and pointed at Valmont, then gestured they should come see her.

"Maybe she has something planned for you two," Ivy said.

Valmont grabbed Bryn's hand, and they walked over to investigate the situation.

"I heard you two fought together in Dragon's Bluff," Mrs. Anderson said.

Valmont's grip on her hand tightened. "We did."

"Flying with a knight on your back had to feel different than flying by yourself. I think you two should practice aerial maneuvers."

And Mrs. Anderson was her new favorite teacher. There was only one problem. "We'd need a saddle and a place to practice."

"Follow me."

They wandered to the lockers on the far wall where different sports equipment was stored. Mrs. Anderson unlocked one of the larger lockers and stepped back. Saddles and lances rested inside, encased in what looked like giant Ziplock bags.

Valmont opened one of the bags and pulled out a saddle. The saddle at her grandparents' house had been made of highly polished tooled leather. This scuffed leather saddle was purely utilitarian.

Next he grabbed a lance, testing its balance in his hand. "Too bad there isn't someone to joust with."

"With the way things are going, I fear that won't be a problem for long," Mrs. Anderson said. "Leave the lance, and follow me."

They exited the large gymnasium and headed back toward the door, which lead to the new ice rink addition, which was under construction. The memory of Zavien taking her back there for a tour of the place, which had turned out to be an excuse to kiss her where no one would see them together, pestered Bryn like an annoying mosquito. A few weeks ago, the memory would have flattened her. Now it was more irritating than anything. That must mean she was moving on with her life. Which was good. Or sad, depending on how you looked at it.

Two stories high, the ice rink would be impressive when it was completed, but now it was just an open room with a high ceiling. "This is under construction, but it gives you a place to maneuver away from curious eyes."

Nervous excitement shot through Bryn's body. "Cool." She shifted and crouched down.

Valmont threw the saddle onto her back, settling it between her wings.

"Move your tail around for him to use as a step," Mrs. Anderson said.

So that's how this was supposed to work. Bryn moved her tail around, and Valmont climbed onto her back. As soon as he was in place, a sense of power filled Bryn.

Mrs. Anderson sucked in a breath. "You're glowing. The legends are true."

"What legend?" Valmont asked.

"When a knight and dragon fly, their powers flare up and combine, which is what the glowing signifies."

Bryn itched to take flight. "Ready, Valmont?"

"Always."

Bryn pushed off and flapped her wings, flying in a tight circle. Flying outside with the wind and the sunshine would have been better. Still, flying anywhere was awesome, especially with Valmont along for the ride.

"Try a few dives," Valmont shouted. His voice rang loudly in her ears.

"Talk in a normal voice," Bryn said.

"How would you hear me?"

"I don't know, but I just did." It had to be due to the bond. "Hang on." She spiraled up toward the ceiling and then dove into a low glide. "You okay up there?"

"That," Valmont's breathing came faster, "was amazing."

"So no dizziness or fear you won't stay seated? Because I worried about that."

"No problems."

They flew until Mrs. Anderson blew her whistle.

"Hold on," Bryn said. "You know landings aren't my strong suit." Concentrating, she dove to the floor and landed in a crouch. She stutter-stepped a bit but managed to stay upright in a semi-dignified fashion.

"Not bad." Valmont dismounted and removed the saddle.

A sense of loss swamped Bryn. She shifted and threw her arms around him in a hug. He hugged her back, kissing the top of her head.

"Sorry to intrude on this personal moment," Mrs. Anderson said, "but you two need to be careful about how far you let the bond take you."

Valmont cleared his throat. "What are you saying?"

Bryn turned around to face Mrs. Anderson. Valmont kept

his arms around her, and she leaned back against him.

"I can see the bond has created a connection between you two. From everything I've read on the subject, that's part of what makes it work, but be aware of the magic's influence and don't do anything that would endanger your future relationships."

Oh my God. Was Mrs. Anderson telling her not to hook up with Valmont? Not that she was thinking about that. Much. They hadn't even kissed. It's not like she was in the habit of jumping into bed with some guy on a moment's notice.

"I have the utmost respect for Bryn, and I would never do anything to hurt her," Valmont said. There was an edge of anger to his voice.

Chapter Eight

At lunch, Valmont was oddly quiet.

"What's wrong?" Bryn whispered.

His eyes showed he was waging some sort of internal battle.

On impulse, she leaned over and kissed him on the cheek. "Don't let what Mrs. Anderson said distort what we have. I thought you were hot before you became my knight."

He brightened at this news. "Really?"

"Hello?" Bryn waved her hands toward his face and then down to his feet and back up again. "Have you seen you?"

"I am rather handsome, aren't I?" His trademark single dimple appeared.

Now he looked like her knight again. "Yes. You are."

Clint's eyebrows went up. "We may have a problem."

"What?" Bryn turned around and caught sight of Jaxon stalking toward their table. "Great."

Jaxon didn't bother to sit down. Instead, he slammed his palms down on the table and leaned into Bryn's personal space. "We need to talk."

Valmont leaned back, draping one arm over Bryn's shoulder. "Good afternoon, Jaxon. What's got your knickers in a twist?"

Clint choked on his pizza.

Bryn bit the inside of her cheeks to keep from laughing.

The temperature around them seemed to drop as Jaxon turned his ice-cold glare on Valmont. "I wasn't speaking to you."

"You weren't speaking to Bryn, either. You were barking orders." Valmont leaned forward. "You might want to try a more polite approach."

Oh, hell. She did not need Jaxon and Valmont facing off in the dining hall.

"For Rhianna's sake, why don't you two dial back the testosterone?" Bryn spoke in a calm tone, even though she wanted to smack Jaxon.

"I'm not the one with the problem," Jaxon bit out. "Meet me in Rhianna's room after Proper Decorum. And leave your knight in the hall. He's not invited inside." With that parting shot, Jaxon stalked back to his table.

"He moves pretty fast for someone with a giant stick up his ass," Clint observed.

Valmont laughed, and Bryn joined in.

"I don't know why he has to be such a jerk," Clint said.

"Maybe he's jealous," Ivy said.

The laughter stopped. "What?" Bryn and Valmont said at the same time.

"Officially, he might have to marry you," Ivy said. "Maybe he doesn't like watching you two together."

"Or watching the whole campus watch you two together," Clint said.

"Watching us do what?" It was ridiculous. So they held hands, and she'd kissed him on the cheek when he was sad. It wasn't like they were doing the wild thing on the dining hall table.

"In Elemental Science this morning, the looks going back and forth between you two were pretty intense," Ivy said.

"Half the campus thinks you're an item," Clint added.

"We could finish what we started in the library and confirm their suspicions." Bryn leaned toward him.

Valmont looked down at his plate. "That's probably not a good idea."

Wham. His lack of interest punched her right in the gut. She sucked in a breath and turned away. This could not be happening *again*. Her face burned from embarrassment. He'd wanted to kiss her earlier when no one was around. Was she doomed to date guys who were ashamed to be seen with her?

"Bryn." Valmont touched her arm. "It's not what you—"

"Don't." She jerked away from him.

"Bryn, please. I promised your grandmother I'd be honorable. Doing what I want rather than what's right isn't honorable."

Smoke shot from her nostrils. "And what do you want?"

"I gave up my entire life to come watch over you. I want to tuck you away somewhere safe, where no one can come after you. I want to be the first thing you see in the morning and the last thing you see at night before you fall asleep in my arms. I want us to be together in every sense of the word, and above all, I never want to hurt you... Ever."

At his touching words, Bryn's anger and the fire in her gut receded.

"Are we okay?" Valmont asked.

"I'm 90 percent sure I no longer want to shoot a fireball at your head."

Chairs scraping across the floor and students talking signaled it was time to go to class.

"You're in for a treat," Ivy said. "Our next class is Algebra, and then it's off to Proper Decorum."

"Proper what?" Valmont asked.

"De-cor-um." Bryn enunciated each syllable. "It's the class where they teach us all the pointless social crap my grandmother believes so strongly in."

"Like don't chew with your mouth open?" Valmont asked.

"Wait and see," Clint said. "We spent weeks memorizing different kinds of utensils. I never knew there were so many different kinds of forks."

As they walked across campus, Valmont reached for Bryn's hand and laced his fingers through hers. The warmth of his touch reassured her. She squeezed his hand and glanced over at him. "You still want to kiss me, right?"

"Yes. It's the venue I objected to." He checked his watch. "In exactly two hours, I will prove I'm telling the truth."

"In two hours, I have my mandatory meeting with Jaxon."

"He'll have to wait."

All through Algebra and Proper Decorum, Bryn fantasized about kissing Valmont. It was what she wanted. She was sure of it. But how much of it was due to the bond? Damn Mrs. Anderson for putting that thought into her head.

When class ended, a nervous frisson of excitement grew in her stomach.

"Call me later," Ivy said. "I want to know what has Jaxon in such a fabulous mood."

"Sure."

Ivy and Clint headed for their dorm. She and Valmont headed up to her room.

Jaxon standing in the hall outside her door put a crimp in her romantic plans.

"Come on," Jaxon said. "Let's get this over with."

"I'd like to drop my book bag off first." *Asshat*, she

mentally added.

"Give it to your knight," Jaxon bit out the last word. "Isn't that part of his job, to carry heavy things?"

"One of my jobs." Valmont took the bag and gestured down the hall toward Rhianna's room. "As he said, let's get this over with. We have more important things to do."

Valmont waited outside in the hall, while Bryn followed Jaxon into Rhianna's room. Once the door shut, Jaxon paced the living room. Rhianna emerged from the bedroom with a frown on her face.

"What's wrong?" Bryn asked.

"It's your grandfather," Jaxon said. "He's managed to have you taken off the unfit to marry list."

"Holy Hell."

Jaxon snorted. "Wait. It gets worse. He also completed the lineage check to see if you and I would be compatible for a marriage contract."

"And it came back negative, right?"

Jaxon didn't respond.

"It came back positive? What kind of bullshit is that? We're like oil and water. How could our lineage be compatible?"

Rhianna sniffled. Jaxon walked over and wrapped his arms around her, pulling her close and tucking her head under his chin. "It means nothing."

There was a strange itchiness under Bryn's skin, like it had become too tight. The results had to be a mistake. Was the Directorate on drugs? What did this mean, anyway? "Jaxon, what happens now?"

"Run off with your knight, and nothing happens."

Dare to dream. "I can't do that to my grandmother."

"If you stay, your grandfather will file a petition for approval of marriage between our families which my father, being far more sane, will fight."

She never thought she'd utter these words. "Please tell

me your dad outranks my grandfather and can make this go
away."

Jaxon stepped away from Rhianna and rammed his hand
back through his hair. "They are fairly evenly matched. I'm
not sure how the vote will go when it hits the Directorate. I'm
sure it would amuse some of my father's enemies to handicap
his son with an unsuitable wife."

Unsuitable? That should piss her off, but he could call
her whatever he wanted if it would stop this nightmare from
becoming reality. Bryn shot across the room toward Jaxon.
"This can't happen. You need to talk to your father, have him
bribe, threaten, or murder whoever he has to, in order to stop
this insanity."

"Are you calling my father a murderer?" Frost shot from
Jaxon's nose.

"Oh, grow the hell up. If my grandfather has had people
killed, your father probably has, too. That's not the point. The
point is, I don't care how your father does it. This," she pointed
back and forth between Jaxon and herself, "cannot happen."

"On that we agree." Jaxon slumped onto the couch and
held his hand out to Rhianna. She joined him, curving against
him like a comma, resting her head on his chest.

The sight of them like that, gave Bryn another idea.
"Don't get mad at what I'm about to suggest." Bryn took a
deep breath and blew it out. "You and Rhianna seem to have,"
good God, how do I say this, "an intimate relationship. What
if after we graduate, and before we get married, Rhianna
became pregnant. You'd have to marry her. Right?"

Jaxon went very still and then closed his eyes. "Sometimes
I forget how absolutely ignorant you are. Pregnancy outside
of marriage is an unforgivable betrayal in our Clan."

She looked at Rhianna. "Do you agree with what he
said?"

Rhianna gave a curt nod. "I would never bring such

shame upon my Clan."

They were both insane. "You're worried about shaming the Clan. If the Clan has its way, I'll have to marry Jaxon." She laughed. "Clint's turkey baster idea is sounding better and better."

"What are you talking about?" Jaxon said.

She repeated Clint's idea of a marriage in name only, which would allow Jaxon and Rhianna to be together while she and Valmont were together and how a child would be created through absolutely no bodily contact.

Jaxon sat up. "That's not a bad idea. Except for the part about you carrying on with Valmont. I wouldn't allow that."

Fire roared through Bryn's body. Sparks shot from her lips when she spoke. "What makes you think you're allowed to tell me what I can and cannot do? And why would I agree to you carrying on with Rhianna while I had no one?"

"That's the way it works," Jaxon said.

She wanted to bludgeon him with a chair. "You are not going to dictate how I live my life in some sham of a marriage."

"She's right," Rhianna said. "If you and I continue our relationship, she deserves to have someone, too."

"Are you insane?" Jaxon snapped.

The door to Rhianna's room sprung open and smacked back against the wall. Valmont strode into the room, grabbed Bryn's arm, and spun her around.

Off balance, Bryn clutched at him. He solved the problem by wrapping his arms around her and pressing his mouth against hers. And just like that, the rest of the world vanished. His mouth moved against hers. Magic and heat flowed through their bond, setting off various nerve endings in her body. She growled deep in her chest.

Valmont pulled back. "Did you just growl at me?"

She nodded. "But in a good way."

He grinned and rubbed his nose against hers. "You're

mine. I'm not giving you up no matter what the Directorate says."

She melted against him. "Agreed."

Rhianna giggled.

Right, they had an audience. Bryn turned toward the couch.

Rhianna wore a huge grin. Jaxon looked like he wanted to eviscerate someone.

"I'm not going anywhere," Valmont said. "Deal with it."

Frost shot from Jaxon's nostrils. "If Bryn and I are forced to marry, no one can know about your relationship. It would make me appear weak."

"Why are appearances so important to you?" Bryn didn't get it. And then something occurred to her. "If you're so concerned about how things look, then you shouldn't carry on in public with Rhianna, either."

"Double standard." Jaxon smirked. "No one cares what I do."

The urge to shoot a fireball at his head consumed her. She took a deep breath and counted to ten. Didn't help. She still wanted to fry him.

"If," Rhianna said, "worse comes to worse, then all four of us will carry on discreetly. Agreed?"

"Agreed," Valmont answered. "How long do we have until we start playing our parts?"

"What do you mean?" Rhianna asked.

"If you're approved for marriage," Valmont cringed as he spoke the words, "do you two pretend to break things off while I pretend to be nothing more than friends with Bryn?"

"Not necessarily," Jaxon said. "We could agree to see other people until we graduate. That's not uncommon."

That was a relief.

On the way back to her room, Bryn prayed to any higher power that might be listening. *Please don't let the Directorate approve our marriage contract.* Because no matter how good the plan sounded in theory, in real life it would suck. Sure, behind closed doors, she and Jaxon might live apart, but they'd have to go to all the stupid balls and charity events as a couple. She'd have to put up with his stellar personality, and sooner or later, she might snap and kill him.

"What are you thinking about?" Valmont held the door to her dorm room open so she could enter. He dropped her book bag on the floor and turned so he was staring into her eyes. "Bryn, you're not having second thoughts about us, are you?"

"No." She threw her arms around him and pressed her face against his chest, breathing in his warm sunshine and soap smell. "You're the only thing that makes sense in my life right now."

He took a deep breath, his chest rising and falling beneath her cheek. "Thank God. I worried that I might have scared you."

She squeezed him tighter. "Nope. You're stuck with me."

"Till death do us part?"

Chill bumps raced down her spine. "You aren't allowed to die."

"Hey," he smoothed his hand up and down her spine, "it was a joke. That's the last line of a wedding ceremony."

"I know." God, what was wrong with her? Her emotions were all over the place lately. "The thought of losing you and being stuck with Jaxon would make any girl a little clingy."

He laughed and kissed the top of her head. "True. Don't worry, I'm not going anywhere."

• • •

Tuesday morning, Bryn shared the news of her possible marriage with Clint and Ivy.

"So, my turkey baster idea wasn't so bad, after all," Clint said.

"Can we please refer to it as 'the sham marriage idea?'" Bryn said. "The whole idea of a turkey baster makes me queasy."

"Better than the idea of naked-time with Jaxon," Clint said.

Valmont focused his entire attention on Clint. "Do not utter those words again."

"Do they make you queasy?" Clint said.

"No," Valmont said. "They piss me off."

"Told you." Clint grinned at Ivy. "It's my special skill set."

"I'm so proud." Ivy rolled her eyes. "Now let's change the subject. Did you hear about the students who were arrested for being out after curfew?"

What the hell? "No. How do you know about it?"

"You're not plugged into the Black Clan's grape vine." Ivy leaned in and spoke in a quiet voice. "The Directorate had the students arrested, for real. They said anyone out after curfew will be considered a criminal."

"So they'll be suspended?"

"No." Clint glanced around like he was worried someone might overhear. "Rumor has it they're reverting to old laws."

That sounded bad. "They're kids. What can the Directorate do to them?"

"Incarcerate them without food or water for twenty-four hours, for starters. There's talk of worse."

"Worse?" What did that mean? "Are they going to put students in stockades in the middle of campus or something?" Clint didn't laugh like she thought he would. "Are you kidding me?"

Ivy shook her head. "It could get bad. The best plan is to stick to the curfew and not push the Directorate. I bet they're dying to make an example of someone to keep the rest of us in line."

Great. Ferrin drunk with power… That's all she needed.

. . .

That night in her room, Bryn sat on the couch reading her Proper Decorum assignment until her eyes glazed over.

"Is it that boring?" Valmont asked.

Bryn's head snapped up. "Boring enough to render me unconscious." She yawned and stretched. Was Valmont staring at her? "What, did I drool on myself?"

"No." He plucked the book from her hands, scooted close and wrapped his arm around her back so she leaned against his shoulder. "There we go. That's better." He propped his feet up on the coffee table, leaned his head back against the top of the couch, and closed his eyes.

His body heat warmed her, which would have relaxed her except for the fact that he was a hot guy. He would kiss her, right? She waited. The only sound she heard was Valmont breathing. Seriously? They hadn't discussed the kiss they'd shared last night. She assumed it would be the first of many. Maybe not.

She wiggled against him, trying to get comfortable.

Valmont's left eye opened. "That's distracting."

He seemed amused.

"Sorry, just trying to get comfortable." Her nearness didn't appear to have the same effect on him that his had on her. Damn it.

She sighed and cuddled against him. A nap. That's what she needed. Not.

"You have two choices," Valmont said. "Lie still and we'll take a nap, or keep wiggling around and we'll do something else."

"Like what?" She wanted him to say he wanted to kiss

her.

"I don't know. Play cards. Memorize china patterns." He opened his eyes. "Or I could kiss you senseless."

"I vote for option C."

"Are you sure? Because I was thinking about brushing up on my poker skills."

She smacked him on the chest. He laughed, catching her hand and pulling her close.

Her heart sped up as his lips touched hers. Magic flared through the bond, increasing their connection. His mouth moved against hers and suddenly, it felt like she was flying.

Valmont jerked away from her. "What was that?"

It took a minute for her brain to adjust to the no longer flying/kissing sensation. "What was what?"

"You didn't feel that?"

"Are you talking about the cold vacuum of air that rushed in when you stopped kissing me? Because that's what I'm feeling right now."

"No. It felt like we were flying."

"That's not a bad thing." Why was he freaking out about this? She leaned toward him.

He scooted backward, putting distance between them. "That's not normal."

"Maybe it's normal for us." Why did he care, and why didn't he want to kiss her anymore?

A shadow of sadness passed over his face. "What if you don't really feel the way you think you feel?"

To sum up... The guy she wanted was looking for explanations she didn't have. "Valmont, you have two choices. Kiss me and be happy about having the added feeling of flying, or don't kiss me and ask a bunch of stupid questions." Wow...that came out bitchier than she intended.

Valmont cupped her face in his hands. "I would rather kiss you, but I want to know what's happening between us is real and not some side effect of the bond."

"Why does it matter? Can't you think of it as a bonus?"

He dropped his hands. "I'm not sure."

"I told you. I liked you before the bond."

"Not enough to dump Zavien."

"Hey. It's not like I have a lot of experience with these situations. I needed to figure out what was going on with Zavien before I moved on. And why are you picking a fight with me?"

He blinked. "I am, aren't I?" He shook his head like he was trying to clear his thoughts. "I think the bond magnifies things between us—our emotions, my lingering resentment about Zavien, and your insecurities about being abandoned."

Could he be right?

"I don't claim to be an expert on healthy relationships, but even if the bond amplifies our emotions, they're still our emotions, right? The bond can't *create* feelings between us."

"Are you sure about that?" he asked.

She stared at him for a moment, fighting to keep her temper under control. "Before you became my knight, we met. What did you think of me? Did you think I was hideous?"

"No. Of course not."

"Did you think I was cute or pretty or the type of girl you might want to ask on a date?"

"Yes."

"Okay. We've established you were interested pre-bond. Now, the magic of the bond might be amping up our emotions, but it isn't brainwashing us. Can't you think of the bond like sprinkles on ice cream?"

He cracked a grin, and his single dimple appeared. "Sprinkles?"

"Yes. Normal ice cream is great, but when you add sprinkles, it's extra good." She needed him to be okay with this. Being pushed aside for a stupid reason was unacceptable.

She wasn't above playing dirty. Moving closer, she played with the black curls at the nape of his neck. "Sprinkles are good."

His eyes narrowed. "You're trying to distract me from logic."

"Logic sucks." She grinned. "You should kiss me."

He didn't move toward her. He didn't make a witty comeback. He didn't do much of anything but sigh. And then he said, "I'm not sure what's going on between us is appropriate."

Chapter Nine

What the hell? "Last night *you* kissed *me*. You started this. You said we'd be together till death do us part. Where'd that guy go? Because I liked him."

Valmont's cheeks turned a mottled shade of red. Was he mad, or embarrassed? Time ticked by at a glacial pace as the awkwardness between them grew.

"Is that it?" Bryn asked. "Don't you have anything else to say?" The next words out of his mouth better be an apology, or she was going to lose it and roast him.

"The way the bond works, I'm not sure I can trust your feelings for me."

Smoke shot from her nostrils. "What does that mean? Where does that leave us?"

He reached up to rub his forehead. "I don't know."

Seriously? Whatever. "Let me know when you've figured out what you want." She willed her body to stand up and walk away, but hope rooted her to the spot. If she sat there, maybe he'd say what she needed to hear.

"Bryn, I'm sorry."

Thank God. Relief washed over her. She leaned toward him.

"I can't do this."

"Can't do what, exactly?"

He stood and paced the length of the coffee table. Back and forth he went as she waited for him to speak. "What's going on between us...the bond...us being romantically involved...I'm not sure it's a good idea."

She shot to her feet. "What?"

He held a hand out to signal she should stop talking. "I need time to think. It would be best if we went our separate ways for a bit. I'm going to bed." And with that, he headed into his bedroom and slammed the door.

Shocked, Bryn stared after him. This could not be happening. He was supposed to be her rock. He was her knight. And she still had no idea what the hell he meant. Should she go pound on his door until he answered her questions? When he said they should go their separate ways, he'd meant he needed time to think alone. Or did he mean he didn't want to be romantically involved anymore? That would suck, but even if he never wanted to kiss her again, he still wanted to be her knight, no matter what, right?

What if he meant he didn't want to be her knight anymore? That idea had her stomach twisting into knots. Did he want to be released from their bond? Is that what he meant? If she released him and they kissed and they were still attracted to each other, would that set his mind at ease?

And if she ended the bond, and he didn't want to be her knight anymore, then what would she do?

Damn it. What was wrong with her? She was not some emotional female, some weak girl who had to have a man in her life. She would not stress over another guy who couldn't figure out what the hell he wanted. She was better than that, stronger than that. It had to be the bond making her feel all clingy and screwing with her head.

Maybe by morning, Valmont would have *his* head on straight. Moron. And if he came up with a really good apology *maybe* she'd forgive him. Right now she couldn't decide if she wanted to kiss him or kick his ass. She headed into bed, changed into comfy yoga pants and a tank top, brushed her teeth, and gave herself a pep talk in the mirror. "It will all be okay. No matter what happens. It will be okay."

She collapsed on the bed and closed her eyes, but sleep didn't come. She tried to focus on other things. A history paper was due soon. What did she want to write about? Her brain refused to play along. All she could think about was Valmont. What if he didn't want to be her knight anymore? What if he wanted his normal life back? Could she fault him for that? Not really. So… If he didn't want to be her knight anymore, she'd deal with it. She might need some therapy and some mood-altering drugs, but it would be okay.

She stared at the ceiling. Sleep eluded her, but a slow burning sensation built inside her gut. The fire in her body felt like it was closer to the surface of her skin, or like she had a fever. *Great.* Now she felt sweaty and itchy. Maybe a shower would help, but that seemed like too much effort. If she could just *freaking* fall asleep.

After an hour of tossing and scratching, she dragged herself into the bathroom and took a shower. All her muscles ached. Was she coming down with some sort of flu? And why did her skin itch so badly? Was she having some sort of allergic reaction? Did her bad luck know no bounds?

She slathered on lotion, dressed in a different tank top and yoga pants, and crawled back into bed. Now she was freezing. Chilled and shivering, she pulled the covers up around her neck and prayed for sleep.

• • •

Her alarm was going off, and she didn't care. Her heart hammered in her chest as the piano music became louder and more discordant, performing its function of increasing her stress level by encouraging her to rise and shine. She didn't care about classes or going to breakfast or shutting off the annoying alarm. The rest of the world and all its occupants could move along without her for one day. She planned on staying right where she was, curled up under the covers until she felt like her normal self. Attending classes when she felt like crap was not on her agenda.

Her door flew open. Valmont stalked across the room and smacked the top of the alarm. "I hate those things. Why didn't you turn yours off?" His eyes met hers, and he paled. "Bryn, what's wrong?"

She didn't have it in her to talk about their bizarre relationship and the you-don't-really-care-about-me-it's-just-the-bond issue right now. "Go away." All she wanted to do was sleep until she was over this stupid flu.

He rushed to her side. "Bryn, do you feel all right?"

Rolling away from him, she closed her eyes. "No. I'm sick. Leave me alone."

He touched her forehead. "You're burning up. I'm calling a medic."

That was probably a good idea. She clutched the covers tighter as a wave of cold passed through her bones and then she drifted back to sleep.

Sometime later, a knock sounded on the door, and she heard voices and footsteps.

"Bryn, it's Medic Williams. What's wrong?"

"I have a stupid cold or something." She rolled over and pushed herself up.

Medic William's eyes widened. "When did this start?"

Geez, how bad did she look? "Last night after I went to bed."

"Are you in pain?" the medic asked.

"No." Another chill made her teeth chatter. "I must have some type of flu. I'm hot, and then I'm cold. The worst part is, everything itches." She reached up to scratch her head and something coarse came away in her hand. "What the hell?" How had she gotten straw into her hair? This didn't make any sense. She studied the blond stick-like strands in her hand. Wait a minute. "Is that my hair? Oh my God. What's going on?"

"Don't panic," Medic Williams said. "Tell me what you did last night before bed. Maybe this is some sort of poison. Did you eat or drink anything different?"

"No." Smoke crawled up the back of Bryn's throat, making her cough. Sparks shot out onto the bed sheets and smoldered.

Valmont patted down the ashes. "That's not good."

"Focus on cold," Medic Williams ordered. "Before you burn the dorm down."

She concentrated until she sprayed sleet when she coughed. Not that she wanted to cough much more. "Can you give me some medicine? My throat feels raw."

"I'm going to scan you." She placed her hand on Bryn's forehead. The warmth of Quintessence flowed over her skin. "I can't detect any foreign substances. This makes no sense. Dragons rarely catch colds, unless they are ancient. Tell me exactly what happened yesterday."

Bryn described her day, skipping over the fight with Valmont. That was too embarrassing and personal.

"That's it. You're not leaving anything out?"

Valmont cleared his throat and touched Bryn's shoulder. "Tell her everything, or I will."

She rolled her eyes, which made her kind of dizzy. "Fine. Valmont and I argued."

"I need details."

"Fine. Valmont," — his name tasted sour on her tongue — "decided he wasn't into this whole knight thing. It doesn't make sense to him, so he doesn't want to play anymore."

"Bryn, that's not fair." Valmont sat on the bed next to her.

"Fair?" Sleet shot from her nostrils as her anger grew. "I'll tell you what's not fair. Trusting someone and then having them freak out and walk off when things become confusing… That's not fair."

"You need to calm down and listen to me," Valmont's placating tone upped her irritation.

"No. You need to suck it up and make a choice."

"A choice about what?"

"About whether you want to be my knight or not."

"Bryn, I—"

"Did you reject her?" Medic Williams asked.

"No," Valmont said.

"Liar. Liar. Pants on fire." She knew she was being childish, but she didn't care. "You walked away from me. You left me standing there in the living room like an idiot." Bryn growled, but it turned into a coughing fit that took her breath away. She forgot to focus on cold, but rather than sparks, ash shot from her mouth. That was weird.

"You did this." Medic Williams pointed at Valmont. "Through the bond, you did this to her. You are sworn to protect her, to lay down your life to defend her, and instead you rejected her."

Valmont's eyes widened with panic. "No, I didn't. It's just that I don't understand what's happening between us."

"The bond is strong. It binds your spirits together with magic. If you don't want to be bound to her anymore, then ask to be released, but you can't make her feel abandoned, because her spirit will wither and fade along with her body."

"Like hell it will." Bryn gasped and coughed.

"It's not your conscious choice, Bryn. This is ancient

magic we're dealing with. The bond is bound with your Quintessence, your life-force." She pointed at Valmont. "You need to decide. Now. Either you want to be Bryn's knight or you don't. If you don't, then she needs to release you."

Even though she was pissed at him for being an indecisive wuss, she realized he'd never made the choice to become her knight. The ancient magic in his blood had chosen for him when he'd stepped forward to help her that day. Just like she wasn't asking to be sick right now. The magic kind of did what it wanted. He deserved to make the choice on his own, not be forced into it.

Sitting up tall, she spoke in as calm a tone as she could manage. "Valmont, becoming my knight wasn't something you decided to do. It happened through the magic in your blood. You deserve to have a say in your life. And I understand if you want your old life back. So it's up to you. Do you want to continue being my knight?"

"Of course I do."

"Keep talking to her," Medic Williams said, "I'm going to call for more medics."

Bryn reached to touch Valmont's face and froze. That couldn't be her hand. It looked dry and weathered like she'd been washing her hands with bleach. "Holy shit. What's wrong with me?"

"Nothing the medics can't fix," Valmont said. "Right now, you need to understand I will never leave you, ever. I will never ask you to break the bond."

"Are you sure? You're not just saying that because you feel guilty."

"Yes. I'm sure."

"What about the sprinkles?" she asked, hoping he'd understand she was referring to their kiss, which she didn't want to mention since Medic Williams was nearby.

"I will never question the sprinkles again. No matter how

strange they might be. I promise."

His words were like a soothing balm. She leaned into him, and he wrapped his arms around her. Her thoughts came clearer and with the clarity came embarrassment. "Getting sick like this…I didn't do it on purpose."

"I know." He ran his hand up and down her back.

"I'm not the type of girl who freaks out and tries to off herself over a guy."

He laughed. "I know. Listen to me. This wasn't your fault. It was mine."

"It was the magic of the bond." Bryn took a deep breath. She knew what she had to do. "Seriously, I don't want to force you to be with me. I could release you."

"Shut up. You're stuck with me. End of discussion."

"Thank God." She enjoyed the warmth from his body, and from the bond. They sat like that until voices came from the living room.

Bryn sat up and nodded at the two medics who followed Medic Williams into the room. Both stared wide-eyed, before sliding their professional masks back into place.

"I look that bad?"

"We'll have you fixed up within the hour, I'm sure." Medic Williams accepted a camera from one of the other doctors. "We need to take a few pictures for medical purposes."

Great. She was a freaking science experiment.

Once the pictures were over, the medics placed their hands on Bryn's neck, back, and shoulders. Warmth flowed over her 'til it felt like she was floating in a pool of warm honey. Nothing hurt, but her scalp itched. She reached to scratch, and Valmont caught her hand.

"You probably shouldn't do that," he said.

"It itches." And not just a little bit. It felt like ants were swarming on her skull.

"You can scratch in a minute," Medic Williams said.

"Repairing hair takes less time than regrowing it from scratch."

Oh hell. "I have bald spots?"

"Just one," Valmont said, "and I'm sure they'll fix it."

Warmth continued to flow through Bryn's body. Her eyes drifted shut. "Can I sleep while you do this?"

"No," one of the medics snapped.

Okay, then. Her skin prickled like she had a case of goose bumps. The prickly feeling changed into an odd stretching sensation. "That feels weird."

"Why don't I distract you with a story," Valmont said. "Once upon a time, there was an unbelievably handsome waiter who worked in an Italian restaurant in Dragon's Bluff."

Bryn grinned. "This sounds oddly familiar."

"It should. This waiter was happy, but he always felt like something was missing from his life. One day, a girl with striped hair came into the restaurant and ate an entire pizza by herself, which he found very alluring."

"Right."

"One day the girl had a fight with a stupid boy, and the waiter stepped in to offer his help, and once he did, he was transformed. He felt whole, like he'd found his true purpose in life. The girl was a bit slow. It took her awhile to realize the handsome knight was the one for her. Once she came around, they discovered true love and lived happily ever after, except for a minor bump where the knight did something stupid and made the girl sick. After that one time, he promised he would never do anything to hurt her ever again, and they lived happily ever after. The end."

"I like that story." Bryn yawned. "I'm sleepy."

"I'm not surprised." Medic Williams removed her hand from Bryn's forehead. "You're stable. I want you to rest. I'll be back in a few hours with food. Then we'll see what more needs to be done." She pointed at Valmont. "With the exception of using the bathroom, you are not to leave her side. Do you understand?"

"Yes."

After all the medics were gone, Valmont kissed Bryn on the forehead. "I swear to you, no matter what happens between us personally or romantically, because there are bound to be some bumps as we figure all this stuff out, I will never ask you to break the bond."

Her body sagged with relief. "Thank you."

He lifted up the covers and climbed in next to her, so she could lay her head on his chest. Wrapped in his arms, she fell asleep.

. . .

"What in the hell do you think you're doing?" A male voice shouted.

Bryn swam through the fog of sleep, and was greeted with the image of Jaxon standing next to her bed scowling. Clint and Ivy stood by his side.

"I believe it's called spooning," Clint said.

Bryn realized she and Valmont had shifted positions while they slept. Her back was pressed against Valmont's chest, and his arm was wrapped around her waist.

"Medic's orders," Valmont said. Bryn could hear the smirk in his voice. She pushed upright to a seated position.

"What's going on?" Bryn asked.

Ivy pointed at her. "That's my line. You weren't at breakfast, and Mr. Stanton refused to tell us why you weren't in class, so we shanghaied Jaxon and made him bring us into your room."

How much should she tell them? What happened was too personal to share with Jaxon. "Thanks for letting them in, Jaxon. You can go back to whatever it was you were doing."

"Right. They dragged me here. I'm not leaving without an explanation."

"She woke up sick," Valmont said. "Medic Williams ordered me to stay by her side and take care of her, which is what I'm doing."

"I doubt this is what she had in mind," Jaxon said.

"What made you sick?" Clint asked.

So much for getting out of this situation without an explanation. "Valmont and I had a misunderstanding, and the bond made me sick," Bryn said. "But now that we understand how this works, we won't let it happen again, so it's not a big deal."

Ivy moved in and hugged her. "I'm glad you're okay. We'll do girl talk later."

Clint and Ivy moved toward the door.

"Wait," Jaxon said. "We need to have our stories straight. People are going to ask questions."

Okay. What should they say?

"Tell them I brought up going back to work at Fonzoli's," Valmont said, "Due to the bond, Bryn became sick because she thought I meant I didn't want to be her knight anymore."

"How close to the truth is that?" Clint asked.

"Close enough," Valmont said. "There's your story. Feel free to pass it along through the rumor mill. Now, go to class so we can sleep."

Sometime later, Bryn felt the mattress shift, and then cold air hit her back. She opened her eyes. "Valmont?"

"I'll be right back. Someone knocked on the door."

It was probably Medic Williams coming back to check on her. Hoping for the best, Bryn ran her fingers over her scalp. While her hair no longer had the texture of hay, it didn't feel normal.

Medic Williams entered the room carrying a bag of something, which smelled like French fries. Bryn smacked her hand over her nose as her stomach rolled. "That smells awful."

"Now I'm worried," Medic Williams said. "How can you not want French fries?"

"I don't know." Bryn inhaled and her insides squirmed. "Please get that out of here before I throw up."

Valmont took the bag and exited the room.

"You have to eat," Medic Williams said. "Does anything sound good?"

Bryn ran through all her favorite foods in her mind. Nothing sounded good, which was so not her. Then she remembered eating the deer after the fire in Dragon's Bluff, and saliva filled her mouth. "Gross. I want a deer."

"A deer, as in venison?" the medic asked.

"No. As in a fur-covered animal. God, that's disgusting. Bring the French fries back in. I'll eat those."

"I think it's your dragon nature that was most injured by this, so it makes some sense that you wish to eat as a dragon."

Valmont came back into the room. "What's up?"

"I want a deer," Bryn said. "And it's freaking me out."

Valmont didn't look concerned about her feelings, but he did look perplexed. "Who can we call to have a deer delivered? It's not like ordering pizza."

Pizza. She should just eat pizza. Her stomach rolled again. *Deer*, she thought and her stomach growled. "Crap."

"Let me make a few calls." Medic Williams left the room.

Valmont wore a neutral expression on his face, which wasn't normal.

"You think I'm disgusting. Don't you?"

"No." He sat and put his arm around her shoulders. "It's kind of funny."

After several phone calls, Bryn was led to the terrace patio where the carcass of a deer had been left. This was so wrong. She drooled and shifted to dragon form. Sick and wrong. She grabbed the carcass in her teeth and bit down trying not to think about it. In two bites, it was gone. And she wanted more.

After she'd eaten the deer, Medic Williams treated her with Quintessence again. "That should do it. I'll be by tomorrow morning to check on you. Don't even think about leaving your room."

"Can I take a shower?" Between the deer and her illness, she felt disgusting.

"Shower, but be careful not to run the water too hot. Your hair and skin are still recovering. You don't want to dry them out."

A lukewarm shower. Fabulous.

Valmont escorted the medic from the room and then came back to sit by Bryn on the bed. "You have no idea the self-control I'm exerting not to make a joke about helping you in the shower."

"I appreciate that." She patted him on the arm and headed for the bathroom. Twenty minutes later, she felt refreshed, but not exactly revived. All she wanted to do was crawl back in bed. And not just because Valmont lay there reading a book.

He smiled as she came toward him with wet hair and no makeup. That right there was a true test of love. "My hair still feels a little stiff."

"You probably need more rest." He patted the bed beside him.

"Aren't you hungry?"

"I'm good. I ate the burger and fries while you ate the deer."

"I'm praying that was a one-time craving. I know it's natural, and I tell myself that, but I grew up watching *Bambi*, so the guilt is built-in."

"The next time you feel hungry, we can call Clint or Ivy to bring whatever you want. That way they can visit and you can eat."

She crawled into bed and cuddled against him. "Thank you."

"For what?"

"For staying with me, letting me use you as a pillow, and for wanting to be my knight."

...

When the alarm went off the next morning, Bryn startled awake and tried to climb out of bed. "I've got it," Valmont said. He smacked the button on top of the alarm, went to his room across the hall to do the same, and then climbed back in bed with her. "Until Medic Williams gives you the all clear, I think we should sleep in."

Great idea, but she didn't think it would happen. "Sorry, I feel twitchy."

"What does that mean?"

She scratched her head. Her hair felt like she'd forgotten to use conditioner for a month. That was better than the straw hair yesterday. "I feel like I've been cooped up, and I need to fly."

"That is not happening without medical consent." Valmont grabbed both her hands. "You have to take it easy."

The idea of heading out to the terrace, shifting, and taking flight consumed her. "I can't just sit here. I need to do something."

Valmont walked over to the dresser and picked up a legal-size envelope. "This is a copy of the photo Medic Williams took of you. She dropped if off last night while we slept." He held the envelope out so she could read the writing on the front.

Bryn read it aloud. "If Bryn tries to do anything stupid, show her this." That was a bit harsh.

Valmont opened the envelope and upended it so the

picture slid out into his palm, and then he handed it to Bryn. Her heart jumped around in her chest. That couldn't be her. Straw-like hair stuck out from her head, her skin was scaly and pale, and veins showed beneath the surface. Bryn backed up to the bed and sat down. "I was that bad?"

"Yes." Valmont took the picture and set it on the nightstand. "You scared the hell out of all of us."

"I would like to point out, again, that I did not get sick on purpose."

Valmont scratched the back of his neck. "It's not like the bond came with directions. Maybe we should try to find some information in the library so we don't mess up again."

Bryn's stomach growled loud enough for Valmont to hear, breaking the tension between them.

"That's a sure sign you're feeling better. Should I call out for another deer?"

Bacon, she thought, and her stomach growled. *Good. I am back on people food.* "This morning, I'll take whatever the cafe downstairs is serving."

"There's one problem with this scenario. Your snooty cafe doesn't deliver. I can't leave your side, and you aren't allowed out of bed." He squinted his eyes and stared off into space, and then he laughed. "What's Jaxon's number?"

"Are you serious?" He'd never bring her food. "You realize that's like poking a bear with a stick."

"That's what makes it fun. Besides, he'll do it to keep me from hanging out with you at Rhianna's room every day for a week."

"Blackmail…that might work."

Valmont called Jaxon. Bryn could tell from his end of the conversation it wasn't going well. When he hung up, his eyes narrowed. "That didn't work how I expected."

"What happened?"

"He outmaneuvered me, said he'd bring Rhianna here to

your room and hang out every evening for a month. I wanted to call his bluff, but if he didn't back down that would have meant putting up with him for an entire month."

"And that would end in bloodshed." Bryn's stomach growled. "I'll call Ivy. I bet she'd fly over some carryout from the dining hall before she goes to class."

Ivy showed up half an hour later on the terrace with two Styrofoam cartons and passed them to Bryn. "Sorry, I can't stay to talk."

Ivy took off. The longing to fly increased as she watched her friend glide through the air.

"Don't even think about it." Valmont grabbed her hand and pulled her back inside.

Chapter Ten

Medic Williams came by at noon and examined Bryn head to toe. "Besides being a bit dehydrated and fatigued, you're doing well."

"She wants to fly," Valmont said.

Bryn stuck her tongue out at him for ratting her out.

"Sorry, but I know you," he said. "Once something is in your head, you don't give up."

"Flying has to wait until tomorrow. Today you need to eat and sleep." Medic Williams pointed at Valmont. "While I'm here with Bryn, why don't you go down to the cafe and pick up some food. Make that a lot of food. The more calories, the better."

"All right. Any special requests?"

"Dessert." Bryn's mouth watered at the thought of chocolate.

"What kind?"

"Anything but cake." It might be stupid that she refused to eat cake, but once a food is a vehicle for poison, it loses its appeal.

Valmont took off, and Medic Williams's demeanor changed. "Bryn, we need to talk." She headed for the couch and sat.

Oh, crap. She was using that I'm-going-to-say-something-which-will-tick-you-off voice. Bryn sat on the couch and waited to see what new tragedy was about to befall her life.

"What's happening between you and Valmont is dangerous. You need to control your emotions. Getting as sick as you did, as quickly as you did, well, it's unprecedented."

Wait a minute. "I didn't do it on purpose. What do you have to compare it to, old medical records? How do you know it wasn't normal?"

"Whether it's normal or not isn't the point. I've never seen a case like this, and when we treated you, we were guessing. You can't let this happen again."

How had this turned into a game of blame the victim? "I didn't do it on purpose. And there won't be a next time."

"I hope that's true. Valmont cares about you, but he's human and human behavior can be erratic."

Where was this coming from?

"I appreciate your concern, but it's unnecessary. I care about Valmont, and he cares about me. Everything will be okay."

"I hope you're right."

They sat in uncomfortable silence waiting for Valmont to return. When he did, the tower of takeout boxes he carried was stacked higher than his head.

"What did you buy?" Bryn asked.

"A little of everything."

Medic Williams stood. "I'll let you eat. Bryn, I'm glad you're feeling better. Let's keep it that way." And with that, she left.

Valmont set the stack of containers on the library table and popped the nearest lid. The savory scent of steak drifted across the room. "What's the verdict? Do we need to send out for another deer?"

"No." She inhaled, and her stomach growled. Bryn worked her way through a steak, two potatoes, a hamburger and half a pizza.

"Are you even chewing?" Valmont asked.

"Yes." Mostly. "Now I'm ready for dessert." She reached for the chocolate pie and then stopped. "If you want a piece, call dibs now, or I'm eating the whole thing."

"I planned ahead." He opened a small Styrofoam container to reveal a single piece of chocolate pie.

He'd bought her a whole pie. "You are the best knight ever."

She polished off every last crumb and then leaned back in her seat and yawned.

"Why don't you lie down while I clean this up?" Valmont stacked the empty boxes.

"I can help."

"No need." Once the containers were in the trash, Valmont led her to the couch. "Nap time."

He stretched out on the couch. She joined him. Medic Williams's words kept spinning through her head. Bryn pushed them aside. So she and Valmont had a hiccup in their relationship. Not a big deal.

A knock sounded from the terrace window startling her. That was odd.

They both sat up. Grabbing his sword, Valmont headed down the hall. While she doubted attackers would be polite enough to knock, she didn't bother to point that out.

Miss Enid waved at Bryn from the terrace while Valmont unlocked the window, allowing the librarian to enter.

"Sorry to bother you, but I thought you might want some reading material while you recuperated."

Bryn took the small black nylon duffel bag Miss Enid

offered. "Thank you. Are these more legends books?"

"If anyone asks, that's the answer you should give," Miss Enid said in a conspiratorial tone.

The bag contained several faded black leather books with silver bindings and *Days of Knights* stamped on the cover along with volume numbers.

Valmont grabbed volume three. "This was my favorite. Talia's grandmother must have read these stories to me dozens of times." He flipped through the pages, which were covered in calligraphy.

"Are these hand written?" Bryn flipped open Volume One.

"The originals were." Miss Enid ran her fingers over a page reverently. "These are replicas made on a printing press, but they are still old and fragile, so treat them with care."

Bryn felt like she'd been entrusted with a secret treasure. "Thank you."

"You're welcome." Miss Enid checked her watch. "I believe I'll exit through your dorm rather than flying back."

"Why would you want to do that?" Valmont asked. "You'll have to deal with all the Blues staring at you."

"When I was a student, that might have bothered me, but as a member of the faculty, I enjoy throwing the Blues off-balance a bit."

"You sound like Mr. Stanton." Bryn suspected Miss Enid and Mr. Stanton were involved even though their marriage petition had been denied. After all, they'd both refused any other alternative. It was kind of romantic to think about them sneaking around having a love affair.

Miss Enid grinned. "After all this time, maybe he's a bad influence on me."

Was that a confirmation? Bryn couldn't tell. After showing Miss Enid out the front door, she joined Valmont on the couch. "What was your favorite story?"

He thumbed through the pages. "I'll read it to you."

Once upon a time, there was a young man named Gray Everscale who lived in a small fishing village. He dreamt of running away to seek adventure and glory. One day, while he sat fishing in his boat in the middle of the lake, he noticed something bright in the water. Curious, he dove in, barely making a splash. No matter how far he swam, the sparkling lights seemed just out of reach. When he finally stopped to look at his surroundings, he could no longer see his boat floating above him. His air was running low, so he swam toward the underground caverns the villagers hid in whenever the village was under attack.

As soon as he surfaced, he saw a beautiful maiden swathed in an iridescent white robe. Parts of the robe darkened, turning reddish brown.

"Have you come to steal more of my treasure?" the young woman spoke in a calm voice, pulling a dagger from her robe.

"I have no use for treasure." As he spoke, the stains on her robe grew larger. "Are you injured?" He moved toward her but didn't presume to touch.

She tossed a few sparkling stones at his feet. "Go. Leave me in peace."

He kicked the jewels aside. "You're bleeding." Pulling off his shirt, he said. "Let me bandage your wounds. Then I'll bring back a healer."

She laughed. "And why would you go to such trouble for me, human?"

Freezing for a second, he tilted his head and stared. "You're a dragon?"

In the small village, he'd met a few of the dragons who claimed the forest the villagers lived in as their territory, but they'd always been male.

"Aye." The woman drew herself up to her full height, even though doing so must have caused her pain. "Do you still wish

to help me?"

Common sense dictated he ask why she was here in another dragon's territory, but he couldn't bring himself to do that. Instead, he tore his shirt into strips. "I will bind your wounds. What happens after that is up to you—"

"Nyana," the girl responded. "My name is Nyana."

Gray bound the lacerations on her arms. Resentment boiled inside of him at the thought of someone hurting such a beautiful creature. "Tell me of your injuries."

"I was sent here to treatise with Wraith Nightshade, but he did not care to listen. I offered him jewels, which he readily took, but then he set his knights upon me. I escaped to this underwater dwelling where I planned to bide my time while I healed."

Gray sat next to her on the rocks. "Then I will wait with you."

While she didn't send him away, she didn't seem thrilled with his company. Over the next few hours, she made several demands. She required water, food, and a fire. Each of these tasks he performed without complaint. He'd no idea how many hours had passed when a man emerged from the water.

"There you are." The man moved toward her with his sword at the ready.

From his belt, Gray grabbed the knife that he used to gut fish. "Who are you?"

"I'm the one who will end your life." The man spat.

With the practice of a boy who'd grown up playing with his father's knives, Gray flung the blade, burying it up to the hilt in the man's right eye. He went down on the spot, sinking back into the water. While he should have felt bad at taking another's life, all Gray felt was peace, as a warmth of purpose filled his soul. He turned to Nyana and sank down on one knee. "You will never face battle alone again, my lady."

A day later, once she was able to travel, Nyana and Gray

emerged from the lake. She moved in with his family while he brokered a peace with the ruling dragons, and they lived happily ever after."

Valmont shut the book and looked at her expectantly.

"I get that the knight rescued the dragon, but the whole knife in the eye thing was a bit gruesome. Why is that story your favorite?"

Valmont chuckled. "Don't you get it? A nobody saved a dragon, and they lived happily ever after. And just so you know, I can hit an apple with a steak knife at sixteen feet."

"Okay...why do you know the exact measurement?"

Valmont grinned. "That's how wide the kitchen is. My brother and I measured so we'd know how far we could throw."

Bryn shook her head. "I'm sure your mother loved that."

"Growing up around knives and swords, no one seemed to care as long as we didn't upset the customers."

"What other knightly things did you do growing up? Did you find any underwater caves in the lakes around Dragons Bluff?"

"No, but not for a lack of trying." He frowned and flipped pages in the book until he came to a map. He laid the book out flat for Bryn to see. "We did spend time searching for treasure."

The drawing showed a main street in a small town. Nearby, there was a group of stone buildings fenced off and guarded by knights. "Is that supposed to be a castle, or the Institute?" Bryn pointed at the drawings of the stone buildings.

"I always thought it was a castle." Valmont traced his finger down a path. "But after being on campus, I can see this resembles the Institute, and that looks like the library." He tapped the building with the treasure chest drawn on top of it.

Bryn pulled the book closer. "Is this one of those knowledge is a treasure analogies, or is there a story that goes with this map?"

"If I remember correctly, *A Knight's Errand* goes with the map."

Bryn turned pages until she found the correct story. "Do you remember what it's about?"

"A knight goes to collect a payment that was due to the dragons of his village. He rescues knights from an evil dragon, or something like that."

Bryn and Valmont read the story together. When they finished, she turned back to the map. "So the knight rescued people from evil dragons, here." Goosebumps broke out on Bryn's arms as she pointed to the Institute. "What does that mean?"

Valmont sat back and rubbed his chin. "I guess it means the people who wrote this book didn't love the Directorate or the Institute. Maybe that's why your library doesn't house these books."

Bryn's heart sped up. "Do you think we'll find some clues in here about things the Directorate doesn't want us to find? Clues about hybrid dragons who aren't evil?"

"Maybe." He reached into the bag and pulled out the remaining books and laid them on the table. "If there are clues of some sort, we should probably start with the first book."

Half an hour later, Bryn had read her fill of gruesome fairytales in which someone was always stabbing someone or gouging out their eyes. "Why are these so violent?"

"Aren't all tales violent, like the Brothers Grimm?"

"I grew up on the Disney movies, not the gory original versions." Bryn's eyes teared up as she remembered evenings spent with her parents in front of the television, munching on popcorn. She took a shuddering breath.

"Come here." Valmont opened his arms and pulled her into a hug. "I'd ask if there was anything I could do, but I know the answer already."

"Just having you here makes it better." And that was the truth.

He kissed the top of her head and then released her from the embrace. "Do you have any more ideas about the books?"

The tomes lay scattered on the table. She lined them up one through five. There was some sort of pattern stamped into the leather on the covers, but she couldn't quite make it out. Turning her head to the side, she tried again. "Do the covers go together like a puzzle?"

Valmont leaned closer and ran his fingers over the embossed leather. "I've never seen all the books at once. Normally we only had access to one at a time." He performed the same head tilt maneuver. "It seems like they should form some sort of pattern, but I can't see it."

"Let's call Clint and Ivy. They're the artists. They probably know how to see it differently than we do."

. . .

Clint and Ivy knocked on the terrace window half an hour later and came inside.

"You look so much better." Ivy hugged her friend. "Now what's this art puzzle you want us to look at?"

Bryn hadn't thought it wise to say too much over the phone. As they walked into the living room, she explained the situation. "Before you look at these books, you need to know the Directorate would not approve of us even having them."

"Books? What books?" Clint asked as he picked volume one up off the coffee table and studied it. "You never asked us to look at any books. Is that how we're going to play it?"

"Exactly." She explained the origin of the tales and how they thought there might be a map to things the Directorate didn't want them to find. "I'm hoping for some sort of secret message." And that's when she realized she hadn't told Clint and Ivy about having proof other hybrids existed. She still wasn't sure she should drag them any deeper into her quest.

Clint flipped volume two open and then spread it out flat so the front, back cover, and spine were one smooth piece of leather. "What if we turn them all like this?"

Ivy helped him open all the books and lay them flat. Then they shuffled the covers around. Bryn and Valmont sat back watching them move the tomes around like they were part of one of those slider puzzles where you move the pieces and line them up to make a picture.

"The top branches are missing." Ivy walked around the coffee table.

"Branches?" Bryn asked.

"You have to stand off to the side to see it," Ivy said.

Bryn joined her friend. From this angle, the imprints in the leather book covers lined up to create a tree trunk and some branches.

"Are there more books?" Clint asked.

"I don't know," Valmont said. "What would a tree mean? I can understand a road map, but a tree?"

"Wait a minute." Ivy moved the books so they were two across and three down and then walked around the table in a circle. "Nope. I've got nothing."

Clint squinted like he was concentrating. "This is going to make me crazy."

"Glad I could share the insanity," Bryn said.

In an odd maneuver, Valmont stepped up onto the couch. "If it's different angles we're wanting, we should consider all of them. Think outside of the box."

Ding, a light went off in Bryn's brain. "A box is like a treasure chest."

"Are we shouting out random facts now?" Clint asked.

"No." Bryn went over to the art displayed on the shelves by the library table and grabbed a small hinged box made of black and white marble. "Maybe the books can be placed together to form a cube."

Ivy shook her head. "A cube has six square sides. Open like this, the books are rectangles."

Miss Enid's warning flashed in Bryn's mind. "These are old, we need to handle them carefully."

"So we shouldn't duct tape them together to make a pirate chest?" Clint pretended to be serious.

"Probably not." Valmont hopped down off the couch and picked up book one and book two, fitting the covers together like different sides of a box. "If we're on the right track we should be able to see something when we fit these together the right way."

"But if it's a three-dimensional object, it can't be a map," Ivy said. "You'd never see all the sides at once."

Clint rubbed his temples. "This is giving me a brain cramp."

Chapter Eleven

Skipping two days of classes seemed to have multiple consequences, like extra homework and people staring at her like they had when she'd first come to school. She hadn't missed that level of scrutiny and wasn't happy to have it back.

"What is everyone's problem?" Bryn asked as she walked on the treadmill in Basic Movement.

Valmont ran on the treadmill next to her, not breaking a sweat. "We are a curiosity."

"I wish we could fly today." Something inside of her ached to shift and take flight, but Mrs. Anderson refused to let her fly until she had clearance from a medic.

"After classes today, why don't we find Medic Williams and ask her for a note, so you'll be able to fly tomorrow."

"Or we could go flying tonight." Bryn increased the speed on her treadmill to a jog.

"Sorry, I'm siding with the authorities on this. If you need more time to recover, then that's what you'll have."

She glared at him.

"That look doesn't work on me." He grinned. Then the

corners of his mouth turned down.

"What?" Bryn checked the area for whatever had made him frown. Jaxon stalked in their direction. Great.

When he reached her, he smacked the button to turn off her treadmill. "You need to joust or do something to show everyone you aren't weak."

Valmont turned his treadmill off and moved to stand at Bryn's side. "You need to work on your manners."

Jaxon didn't even acknowledge Valmont. "I'm trying to help you."

"Why?" It was a serious question.

"Because I don't like being associated with anyone who is weak," Jaxon snapped.

Now she understood. "You went from caring and concerned to a self-centered asshat in one sentence."

"You do realize your opinion of me means nothing." Jaxon stepped closer. "Go do something to prove you're not spineless."

He'd crossed a line. "I could start by blasting you across the room."

"You could try," Jaxon said. "But you wouldn't succeed."

The desire to shoot a fireball at his head had flames crawling up the back of her throat.

Valmont put his arm around her shoulders. "He's an idiot, but he knows how his Clan thinks. Let's go practice with broad swords."

"Fine." Bryn let Valmont guide her toward the lockers where the equipment was kept.

Valmont squeezed her shoulders. "You do realize, when you face off with Jaxon, you won't be doing it alone."

She wanted to argue but knew that would hurt his feelings, so she nodded in acknowledgment. Why did it feel like she was lying to him?

Valmont opened several lockers until he found what he

wanted. Pulling a set of rapiers from the locker, he frowned. "Are these toothpicks the only blades they have?"

Bryn chuckled. "Jaxon and his friends have trained with those since they were five. I think your broadsword is a much better weapon."

"Agreed. But for the Bryn-is-still-a-badass show, I guess we'll use these."

"I like the sound of that. It would look good on a T-shirt." Valmont pointed toward the ring. "After you, Ms. Badass."

"Does that make you Mr. Badass?" Bryn asked.

He grinned. "I think it does."

Once in the ring, Bryn faced off with Valmont, which felt weird. "I'm not sure we can—" He came toward her swinging his sword in a wide arc. She blocked it with her sword. "Hey!"

"Showtime." Valmont's eyes darted to the side.

A crowd was gathering. Fan-freaking-tastic. Ignoring the crowd, she shoved Valmont's sword back, forcing him to retreat. He came at her, and she blocked. She swung at him, and he dodged the blow. Faster and faster, they dueled. The sound of wooden sword clacking against wooden sword played out like a song. The fact that she hadn't been able to touch Valmont with her sword both irritated her and made her proud. Her knight had skills.

His sword whizzed by her shoulder. Too close. She focused on pushing him back. Sweat ran between her shoulder blades. He held his ground, giving little. She raised her sword and brought it down with all her might, he blocked and *crack* half his sword was gone.

She stopped wide-eyed. Valmont held out his stubby sword. "I think you won."

The crowd around the ring drifted away. Jaxon caught her eye and gave a nod of approval. She reined in the instinct to roll her eyes or flip him off. Instead, she gave a curt nod back.

When she made eye contact with Valmont, his jaw muscle

was clenched. "What's wrong?"

"I hate that Jaxon was right."

Bryn laughed. If that didn't prove they were meant for each other, nothing would.

Ivy bounded over toward Bryn as she and Valmont climbed out of the ring. Clint trailed along behind his girlfriend with a sappy grin on his face.

"Are you going to stagecraft tonight?" Ivy asked.

Stagecraft meant Nola and Zavien. She couldn't let Valmont think Zavien still bothered, her, because he didn't. She was over him, romantically, but Nola and her flowing flowery dresses still annoyed the crap out of her.

"Of course I'm going. I can't leave Rhianna to paint substandard scenery by herself." Unless Rhianna wasn't coming back. Scenery falling from the rafters had injured Rhianna's spinal cord, which resulted in the limp, which had ended her marriage contract to Jaxon. "If she's coming back... should I ask her if she's going?"

"You're going whether she does or not, right?" Clint said.

Bryn nodded.

"Then I wouldn't call her out on it in front of Jaxon. You know he'll have a strong opinion one way or another."

"And he does love to hear himself talk," Valmont said. "If Rhianna isn't there tonight, I can help you paint."

"Cool." It might be immature, but Bryn couldn't wait to see the look on Zavien's face when she walked in with Valmont.

When they reached the theater, there was a sign taped across the door.

Clint flicked the piece of paper with his finger. "No more stagecraft until the theater is repaired? Couldn't they let us know before tonight?"

"Maybe they thought it would be ready in time," Bryn said.

"It's weird." Clint ruffled his Mohawk. "Why didn't someone send out an email explaining it was canceled?"

Not having to deal with Nola was a relief, so Bryn wasn't complaining. "Want to come back to my room and hang out?"

"It's not nearly as much fun now that Jaxon won't be there to irritate," Clint said.

"We could call and invite Rhianna to join us. I'd bet anything Jaxon would insist on coming with her," Valmont said.

"Please, an evening without Jaxon is fine with me." Bryn grabbed her knight's hand. "Let's go."

Back in her room, Clint and Ivy sprawled out on the floor while she and Valmont sat on the couch.

"So, everything is good between you two now?" Clint pointed at Bryn and Valmont.

Ivy whacked her boyfriend on the shoulder. "We had a plan. What part of, 'don't badger Bryn for answers' did you not understand?"

"That's such a girl way of doing things. Guys straight-out ask." He grinned at Valmont. "Fill us in."

"Do you mind?" Valmont asked.

"Go ahead." Better for him to fill in the blanks, because she wasn't sure what to say. Something, like, "Valmont will stick by my side no matter what, because he doesn't want to kill me." That wasn't fair.

Valmont scratched his chin. "You know that old saying 'Sticks and stones may break my bones, but words can never hurt me?' It turns out, if you're bonded to someone, words can hurt worse than any weapon. We found that out the hard way."

Rather than comforting her, his words piled on the guilt.

"So you guys are stuck together now, like forever?" Clint asked.

Ivy whacked him harder on the shoulder. "Why would you say that? They aren't stuck together. They like each other. They *want* to be together."

Time to jump in with both feet, because at this point there was no turning back. "Ivy's right. This is a good thing. Kind of like when your marriage contract to Ivy is approved, you'll be together forever, but you won't feel like you're stuck. Right?"

"That's what I meant in the first place." Clint leaned back on his elbows. "Girls are so sensitive. Back me up here, Valmont."

Valmont moved closer and put his arm around Bryn's shoulders. "Clint, it might be time to change the subject."

"Good idea." Ivy pointed at the stack of black leather books on the table. "Have you made any progress discovering a secret map?

"No." Bryn glared at the books. "Every time I line them up differently it seems like I'm on the verge of finding something, but it never comes together."

• • •

The rest of the week flew by without any incidents, but by Friday night at dinner Bryn felt claustrophobic. "I realize we didn't go to Dragon's Bluff every weekend before the attacks, but knowing we can't leave the campus makes me feel caged in."

Valmont's mouth set in a thin line. "Believe me, the shopkeepers in Dragon's Bluff aren't happy about the situation, either. Last I heard, revenue had dropped by 40 percent."

"That's not good." Bryn pushed her plate away. "I wonder if we could organize a group trip to Dragon's Bluff to increase sales."

Ivy leaned forward in her seat. "It might be time for you to play the Grandma card."

Would her grandmother help organize a shopping trip? "I don't know if my grandfather would approve."

Clint pointed across the room. "Maybe you could have Rhianna organize something. She could set it up with Jaxon's mom like you did with the Back to School Gala."

"Good idea." Bryn stood. "Come on, Valmont, let's go visit Rhianna and her eternally crabby boyfriend."

"As your knight, I'm supposed to guide you away from evil, and yet here you are, asking me to lead you straight toward it."

Bryn laughed and grabbed his hand. "Come on. It will only take a minute. And if he's really obnoxious, you can run him through with your sword."

"Define 'really obnoxious,'" Valmont said. "Because I'm not sure I'd recognize it given his normal behavior."

Joking with Valmont eased the odd weight of guilt she was carrying around on her shoulders.

Jaxon glared at their approach, while Rhianna gave a small wave. They stopped at the table, and all conversation ceased.

"I do love the warm reception I receive in your presence," Valmont addressed Jaxon. "You always make me feel so welcome."

"I'm sure that's due to the fact that your social skills are on par with Bryn's. What do you want?"

"I know this will disappoint you, but I wanted to speak to Rhianna," Bryn said, "not you."

"Why don't you come by her room, this evening," Jaxon said. "Alone."

Bryn pointed at Rhianna. "Did you lose the power of speech, or is Jaxon being a Westgate?"

Rhianna looked like she was trying not to laugh. "My voice is fine. What did you want to talk about?"

"Valmont mentioned that the shopkeepers revenue in Dragon's Bluff has dropped off since we aren't allowed to visit anymore. I was wondering if you thought there might be a way to organize a sanctioned trip so a large group of students could visit together. Safety in numbers, and all that."

"That's an interesting proposition," Rhianna said.

"It's an idiotic idea," Jaxon said. "Whoever went would be setting themselves up as targets."

"Maybe the merchants could come here to the Institute instead," Rhianna said.

"I like that idea." Valmont's single dimple appeared.

"No," Jaxon said. "That wouldn't be allowed."

"I don't believe I was asking your permission," Valmont said. "In the future, you might have the power to decide who is allowed to do what, but you don't have that power now."

Jaxon's eyes narrowed. "Fonzoli's just reopened. It would be a shame if a health code violation was filed, and the restaurant had to be shut down."

Valmont leaned toward Jaxon. "Given your pregnant mother's fondness for our food and the fact that she cries at the drop of a hat, you'd be hurting her more than anyone else."

Rhianna gave a theatrical sigh. "Can't we all agree to be civil?"

Both males continued the stare-off.

"Bryn, why don't you call your grandmother, and let me know what she says," Rhianna suggested.

"Sounds good." Bryn tugged on Valmont's arm. "Come on. Clint and Ivy are waiting for us."

As they walked away, Valmont whispered to Bryn, "One of these days I'm going to wipe that smug expression off his face."

"No. You're not. Because my grandparents would have a fit, and I'd have to deal with the fallout."

"Fine. Can I accidentally elbow him in the face?"

Bryn laughed. "As long as you make it look like an accident."

. . .

"I think a campus fair is a wonderful idea," Bryn's grandmother's voice came through the phone loud and clear and far too early on a Saturday morning.

"Really? Because Jaxon pitched a fit."

"He's male. He doesn't understand. I'll set up a meeting with some of the merchants, and I'll call you back when we have a plan."

Bryn hung up the phone and dialed Rhianna.

"Hello?" Rhianna sounded groggy. Crap. She should have waited to call. It was eight in the morning on a Saturday.

"Sorry. Want me to call back later?"

"No," Rhianna said. "Hold on."

Through the phone, she could hear someone griping. The voice sounded suspiciously like Jaxon. Bryn shivered. This was information she did not need to know.

"All right," Rhianna said. "I'm back. What did your grandmother say?"

Bryn repeated what her grandmother said. "It looks like it might actually happen."

"I didn't have a chance to call Lillith last night."

"Because you had company?" Bryn teased.

"I've no idea what you're talking about," Rhianna said in a perfect upper-class Blue tone.

"Right." Bryn yawned. "I'll let you know when I hear anything else."

By Sunday morning, Bryn's grandmother had organized a

Merchant's Fair day for the next weekend. Merchants would set up stalls in different locations on campus. Fonzoli's would sell pizza, and the Snack Shack would bring caramel popcorn. All week there was an excited buzz on campus as students discussed what they wanted to buy.

· · ·

"I'm going to eat my weight in caramel corn," Clint said the morning of the Fair.

Bryn's mouth watered. "Maybe we can buy extra bags and stash them in our rooms."

By the time the booths were set up Saturday morning, there were lines at every stall. Valmont grinned and waved at all of the friends and acquaintances he hadn't seen in weeks because he'd been guarding her. Great. One more thing for her to feel guilty about.

Their first stop was Fonzoli's booth. Valmont's family greeted him with open arms, literally. Bryn stood off to the side feeling awkward. None of his family gave her dirty looks, but they weren't overly thrilled with her presence, either. At least his grandmother wasn't there to give her the evil eye.

Soon, the Fonzoli's booth was swarmed with students forcing his family back to work. "We'll visit when the crowd dies down," Valmont promised his mother, kissing her on the cheek.

"Come this way." Valmont placed his hand on Bryn's lower back and steered her toward a stall displaying jewelry. Talia, the owner of All That Sparkles, greeted him with a hug.

"Valmont, it's been too long."

"I've been otherwise occupied." He pulled Bryn close. "I assume you two have met."

"Yes." Bryn had met Talia when Zavien bought her the dragon locket she used to hide her protection charm. Since she no longer needed to hide the small key-shaped charm, and she'd chucked the dragon locket in a drawer at her grandparents' house, maybe she'd buy a new piece of jewelry. To support the economy, of course.

"What's the prettiest piece of jewelry you brought here today?" Valmont asked.

Oh, crap. What is he doing?

Talia pointed to a display of bracelets. "These are my newest products." She picked up a silver bracelet, which wrapped around in a circle twice, and slid the bracelet on her own wrist, spiraling it around. "There are no clasps, and it warms to body temperature, giving each person an individual fit."

Valmont picked up a different version of the bracelet, which had silver and gold woven together. He slid the bracelet on Bryn's wrist, twisting it around until it lay correctly. "What do you think?"

She wanted to say he didn't need to buy her anything. Due to her grandparents' wealth, her bank account was far healthier than his. One look at the hope on his face melted her heart. "It's beautiful."

"And so are you." He leaned down and pressed his lips to her cheek.

The kiss was brief, and to anyone else it would appear innocent, but the sensation of warm lips pressing against her skin didn't fade. The guilt and fear she'd felt since she'd become sick due to the bond faded away. "Thank you. I love it."

"You're wel—" His eyes narrowed, and he pointed at something in the sky. "What's that?"

Specks flew in a V formation in the sky. Her stomach dropped. "Please tell me those are geese." Should she panic? Other students were also staring at the sky.

"Take cover or take flight," a male voice yelled.

Bryn shifted and whipped her tail around so Valmont could climb onto her back. Even without the saddle, he settled perfectly in place. She shot up into the air along with the other students. Pumping her wings, she climbed, trying to gain a height advantage over whoever was approaching.

The incoming dragons slowed their flight, stretching out their wings and treading air like a swimmer treads water, holding their place and not coming closer, to show they weren't a threat.

Four of the Red guards approached the strangers and lead them to the ground. So, maybe they weren't attacking anyone. Bryn settled to the ground and Valmont hopped off her back. She wasn't sure if she should shift back to human form yet. At least, not until she knew who these dragons were.

The strangers shifted. Three men and two women nodded at the guards. They had the ivory skin, dark hair and dark eyes all Black dragons shared. Their leader, a man with wild eyes and leaves clinging to his hair took a step forward. "We come in peace." He grinned. "Actually, we came to shop."

The lead guard scowled. "Next time you want to visit the campus, you need to enter through the check point at the back gate."

"My apologies." The wild-eyed male gave a slight bow. "We did not mean to distress you."

Right. That's exactly what they meant to do. The members of the Radical Revisionists, who lived in the forest in dragon form most of the time, liked nothing better than to play with people's minds.

"Shift back," a voice near Bryn spoke in a commanding tone.

She shifted to human form and then realized Jaxon was the person who had issued the command. Now she wished she hadn't done it. A smart-ass comment was on the tip of her tongue, until she noticed how stiffly Jaxon stood, like he was ready for a fight.

"Do you recognize them?" he asked.

"I know who they are." How could she forget when it was one of their members, Alec, who had tried to kill her, along with Jaxon and his mother.

"Then you know to stay away from them." He turned his attention to Valmont. "Be wary."

And then Jaxon melted back into the crowd.

"What was that about?" Valmont asked.

The official Directorate-sanctioned story had stated Alec had suffered an aneurysm while addressing the Directorate. Bryn and Medic Williams had tried to save him but failed. A far cry from the truth that Bryn had fought Alec while saving Jaxon and his mother, before Zavien had finished Alec off. What could she tell Valmont? She didn't want to lie to him.

"I'll fill you in later when we're alone. The gist of the story is those dragons are not to be trusted."

He nodded and stepped between her and the wild dragons who were coming their way. Not everyone seemed as creeped out as Jaxon had been. Something about the newcomers, the feral look in their eyes and the almost feline grace with which they moved, signaled they were different. The faded low-slung jeans and black T-shirts they wore made them look like a rock band. Around her, the other students acted in one of two ways. Some avoided the wild dragons, while others were drawn to them. The avoidance plan fit her fine.

The booth for the Snack Shack selling caramel corn was at the far end of the field. "Let's go get some popcorn," Bryn said.

Valmont followed her lead. Clint and Ivy were already in line at the booth.

"I'll buy some for all four of us if you'll go snag a table," Clint said.

"Good plan." Valmont put his hand on Bryn's lower

back and steered her to one of the picnic shelters with the protective metal roofs.

The sweet scent of the caramel corn made Bryn's stomach growl.

"Does Clint know you'll need your own extra-large bag?" Valmont asked.

She laughed. "He should know me well enough by now."

"Time for caramel corn." Ivy plopped down next to Bryn.

Clint set a large container of popcorn between Valmont and Bryn.

She inhaled the sweet, salty scent. "They should make that into perfume."

"I'm surprised they don't have it at that smelly lotion store you girls go to," Clint said.

"It's called Bath and Beauty," Ivy said.

"Nope. It's now officially called the Smelly Lotion store." Clint grabbed a handful of popcorn and shoved the entire thing into his mouth.

Ivy pretended not to see him. Instead, she took a piece of popcorn, tossed it up into the air, and caught it in her mouth.

Valmont threw two pieces of popcorn in the air and caught both of them in his mouth.

"It's on." Ivy threw three pieces of popcorn and managed to catch all of them.

Valmont pointed at Bryn. "Do you want to play?"

"You're asking me if I want to do something which might result in me not eating food." She arched a brow at him. "I'm pretty sure you know the answer to that question."

Ivy and Valmont battled it out, until he tried to catch five pieces but one bounced off his nose.

Ivy threw her arms into the air. "I am the grand national popcorn catching champion."

"We should have that printed up on a T-shirt," Clint said.

For the rest of the afternoon, Bryn relaxed and enjoyed

shopping with Valmont and her friends. She kept an eye out for anyone who might be a hybrid, although she had no idea how she'd recognize them. When it was time to close up the booths, she spotted Rhianna and Jaxon in a heated debate.

"Uh-oh." She pointed at the blond couple. "What do you think that's about?"

"Rhianna can hold her own with him," Valmont said. "But if you'd like me to go over there and stick my nose in where it doesn't belong, I'd be happy to do that, too."

"Since he doesn't love you, how about I stick my nose in and you play back-up," Bryn said.

"It's not like he loves you, either," Valmont said.

"I'm siding with Bryn on this one," Clint said. "On a scale of irritated-to-I-want-to-shift-and-bite-someone's-head-off, Valmont, you rank higher on the scale."

"Do I get a T-shirt for that?" Valmont asked.

"Sure." Bryn headed over to where Jaxon and Rhianna stood toe-to-toe. Both were red-faced and Jaxon's jaw muscle was twitching double time.

When she sidled up to Jaxon, he glared at her. "Go away. This doesn't concern you."

She ignored him. "Rhianna, are you all right?"

"I'm fine, but he's delusional."

Jaxon pointed at a bracelet Rhianna wore. "It's inappropriate for you to wear a gift from another male."

"I told you." Rhianna held out her arm to show off the silver charm bracelet. "Garret said all the injured students are wearing them as a symbol of solidarity. See." She pointed at the small crystals hanging off of it. "Blue, red, black, green, and orange."

Laughing would probably result in Jaxon killing someone, but Bryn couldn't help smiling. "Jaxon, if Garret bought bracelets for everyone, there's no need to be jealous."

In slow motion, Jaxon turned and gave Bryn a look that

could've melted steel. "It's not about petty jealousy. It's about loyalty and respect."

Rhianna's eyes narrowed. "It's not like I'm wearing diamonds from another male. It's a symbol which happens to be a piece of jewelry."

"I don't care if it's a wooden bead on a piece of string. Wearing something from another male is disrespectful."

"You're being ridiculous," Rhianna shot back.

Jaxon's eyes narrowed. Frost shot from his lips as he spoke. "Let me make this simple. If you insist on wearing that bracelet, we're through."

Rhianna sucked in a breath like he'd slapped her.

And all of a sudden, this became way too serious. There had to be a simple answer.

"What if it wasn't a bracelet?" Bryn said. "What if she put it on the strap of her book bag, like a decoration to show she's a member of a club?"

Neither Rhianna nor Jaxon spoke. They just stared into each other's eyes. Rhianna blinked like she was trying to hold back tears. "I'll put it on my bag as a decoration. Does that work for you?"

"I'd rather you throw it in the trash, but I can live with it on your book bag."

Rhianna unclasped the bracelet and slipped it in her pocket. "Then that's what I'll do, but you can't hold the threat of abandonment over my head every time we argue."

Jaxon pressed his lips together in a thin line and nodded in agreement. She held out her hand to him. "Let's go."

After a moment's hesitation, he took her hand, and they walked toward the Blue dorm.

"You should become a negotiator," Valmont said. "That was brilliant. Jaxon is still an idiot, but that was brilliant."

"The thing that's making me crazy," Bryn said, "is I can kind of understand where he's coming from."

"You're not serious." Valmont pointed in the direction Jaxon had gone. "He's a manipulative, insecure control freak."

It was Blue dragon logic and the fact that she understood Jaxon's thought processes scared the hell out of her.

Chapter Twelve

Sunday morning Bryn woke tangled in her blankets and breathing like she'd run a mile. Kicking and wiggling, she shucked off the blankets and headed for the shower. As the warm water sprayed over her body, she tried to remember what she'd dreamt about which had left her so twitchy. Something about the Black dragons from the forest and a group of militant hybrids hunting her across campus, killing anyone who got in their way. A lump came to her throat as the all too realistic image of Ivy laying on the ground, gutted, in a pool of her own blood, flashed in her mind.

She washed her hair twice, hoping it might help scrub the disturbing images from her brain, but it didn't work. Maybe one of the Green dragons could create a selective memory-erasing drug. That would be awesome.

By the time she made it to the living room, she smelled coffee. She peeked around the corner. Valmont waved and held a cup of coffee toward her. "I wondered when your nose would wake you up."

"Thank you." She accepted the coffee and sat across from

him. He seemed at ease this morning, so she relaxed back in her chair, took a sip, and sighed in satisfaction. At the moment, life was good.

Valmont drummed his fingers on the table. "There's something we need to discuss."

"No." She set the cup of coffee down with a thump. "Whatever it is, just no."

"It's not bad. I think something is bothering both of us."

"Can it wait until after I finish my coffee?" Just a few minutes of caffeinated bliss. That's all she asked for.

"Sure."

Once she was done, she scooted her chair back a bit, in case what he said really set her off. "What's up?"

"I think we're both a little freaked out about the whole bond thing."

She nodded. *Where is he going with this?*

"I need you to listen to my words and really hear what I'm saying. Don't jump to any conclusions. If what I say isn't clear, ask questions. As your knight, I will never leave you. I will never want to stop being your knight. But, the fact that you could get sick if we get in an argument terrifies me."

He was worried about her health. She relaxed back in her seat. "To avoid any fatal illnesses, how about I promise to understand that we may fight but you will never abandon me, like Jaxon threatened to do to Rhianna yesterday. That's where some of this is coming from, isn't it?"

"The look on her face when he threatened to end things with her…" He shook his head. "I was about thirty seconds from punching him."

"I'm quite familiar with that feeling."

"Did you see the look on her face?" Valmont asked. "At first she was sad, but then she looked angry. I bet if he tried to pull that crap again, she'd call his bluff."

"The sad part is, he wasn't bluffing."

"You think he'd really leave her?"

She nodded.

"Why would he do that? He obviously cares about her."

"As much as he's capable of caring about anyone. If Rhianna ever crosses him, or he feels like she does, he'd walk away and never look back." And then she might die in a car accident.

"I've lived around dragons my whole life, but some of their logic makes no sense to me."

"At least you've had time to take it all in. I was dumped into this world without an instruction manual. For some of this crap, there is a steep learning curve."

Valmont stood and held out his hand. "Come here."

She stood and took the hand he offered. He led her over to the couch, where he sat down, and pulled her onto his lap. It felt natural. She laid her head on his shoulder and let the sense of warmth and security surround her.

"This feels right." He ran his hand through her hair.

"It does feel right." His fingernails grazed her scalp, making her shiver. "No matter what weird stuff happens, promise you'll always be there for me."

"I promise."

Medic Williams's warning played on a loop in the back of her mind and kept her from relaxing completely. Keeping the information from Valmont felt wrong. "While you were picking up food the other day, Medic Williams lectured me about reining in my feelings for you. She said I shouldn't have gotten so sick so quickly."

Valmont was silent.

"I don't know what she expects us to do." Bryn brushed hair out of her eyes. "Any ideas on how to handle all this?"

He ran his hand up and down her arm. "I don't have a clue."

At least they were on the same page. "So we forge ahead

like everything is normal?"

"Define normal."

"Good point. I guess we move forward and hope for the best."

He yawned. "Sorry. I didn't sleep much last night."

"We could take a nap," she suggested.

"That sounds good, but you still need to fill me in on what happened with those wild Black dragons."

"First off, I signed papers saying I would never speak about this, so you can't tell anyone. Ever." To emphasize how serious this was, she added. "Clint and Ivy don't even know the truth of what happened with Alec."

"You can trust me not to share," Valmont said.

"Okay. Here's the short version. Alec drugged and kidnapped Jaxon and his mother. He planned to kill me, too. We fought. I rescued Jaxon and Lillith. Zavien finished off Alec."

Valmont stared at her like she'd spoken in a foreign language, and then words burst out of him like water from a ruptured pipe. "Why in the hell would the Directorate cover that up? People need to know the Black dragons in the forest are dangerous."

Bryn sighed. "Jaxon's Uncle Merrick, who is also a member of the Directorate, said if Alec's friends knew he died by our hand, they'd come after us. They probably suspect that's what happened, but they can't prove it."

"But—"Valmont's mouth hung open for a moment before he snapped it shut and rubbed his chin. "How many times has the Directorate changed facts to suit their purpose?"

"I think it's how they do business. Not that it's right." Bryn snuggled up against him. "I have this fantasy where I find a community of nice hybrids, and I become their voice on the Directorate."

He wrapped his arm around her, pulling her closer.

"That's a nice dream. Speaking of dreaming, I think it's nap time." Valmont scooted lower on the couch and propped his feet up on the coffee table. "Does that work for you?"

"Yes."

Bryn lay there listening to the comforting rhythm of Valmont's heartbeat, but her mind wouldn't stop spinning. She trusted Valmont not to share her secrets. What did that make him? A good friend? A confidant? They were more than that. She cared for Valmont, and she knew he cared about her, but after the relationship debacle with Zavien, she didn't trust her own instincts. The irony of the situation hit her. She'd been sure of her love for Zavien, but due to the arranged marriage laws, they could never be together. She liked Valmont, but wouldn't go so far as to say she loved him because it was all so new. Due to the bond, and no matter how she and Valmont truly felt, they could never be apart. Fate had one hell of a sense of irony.

. . .

Monday morning at breakfast, Bryn checked to see if Rhianna had the solidarity bracelet on her book bag. She did. The crystal charms twinkled and caught the light on the black leather strap of the bag. It probably showed up better there than it would have on her wrist. Maybe she'd start a trend.

"What are you looking at?" Ivy asked.

Bryn turned back around to face her tablemates. "I was checking on Rhianna. It looks like she has the bracelet situation under control."

Clint shook his head. "Someone needs to knock some sense into Jaxon."

"I volunteered," Valmont said. "Bryn said no."

Everyone at the table laughed. Bryn forced a smile even though she wanted to tell them this wasn't something they should talk about in public. Oh, crap. When had her grandmother invaded her head?

"New topic," Bryn said. "Was there any news in the Black dorm about when Stagecraft will start again?"

"Yes, and people aren't happy about it. The Directorate made a statement about the Arts not being a high priority," Clint said. "Maybe it's not a high priority for them, but to my Clan it is."

"Did they forbid you from fixing the theater building?" Valmont asked.

"What do you mean?" Ivy asked.

"Just because they aren't going to fix it, doesn't mean it can't be fixed by someone else." Valmont sipped his coffee. "Right?"

"Could we work on it without their permission?" Ivy asked.

"Let's find out." Clint stood and walked over to a table of Black dragons. He spoke with them and then they all started talking at once. Half of them stood and approached other tables of students and the pattern repeated like ripples in a pond.

Clint returned to his seat with a sly grin on his face. "I think we started something."

Across the cafeteria, students of Red, Black, and Green Clans shared information between the tables. "They're leaving out the Blues," Bryn said.

"Let's see how long it takes a Blue to ask someone what's going on," Ivy said. "I bet Jaxon sends Rhianna over here to find out."

"No. He'll want the information first hand," Bryn said.

Valmont tilted his head and studied her. "It's scaring me that you understand how he thinks."

"It terrifies me," Bryn said. "Blame my grandparents."

"And here he comes." Clint sat back and threw an arm

over the back of his chair, like he was totally relaxed and didn't see anyone approaching.

Jaxon came to the table and stood glaring at Clint. "Are you going to tell me, or are you waiting for me to ask?"

"I'm waiting for you to ask." Clint raised an eyebrow in challenge.

"Fine." Jaxon spoke in a tone like he didn't really care. "What did you tell the other students that they are passing around?"

"Some of us would like to see the theater building repaired. Since the Directorate doesn't have the time or the manpower to do the job, we're going to do it ourselves."

Jaxon shook his head. "You can't do that."

"Why not?" Bryn asked. "It's not like the Directorate banned anyone from fixing the building. They said they weren't going to do it. The students would be helping."

"The Clan who paid to have the building built will be the one to restore it," Jaxon stated like it was law.

"They'll restore it with their own hands, or they'll pay the other Clan members to restore it?" Ivy said, "Because those are two different things."

"The Blue Clan will fund the repairs at the appropriate time," Jaxon said. "Then the work will be contracted out to professionals who won't screw anything up."

Jaxon would hate what Bryn was about to say, and that knowledge gave her a big warm fuzzy. "If you're worried about the design of the building, why don't I call my grandmother and ask if she'd like to help with the planning. That way a Blue would be in charge."

Jaxon reached up and rubbed the bridge of his nose. "Bryn, do you remember when I said all the irritation in my life leads back to you?"

"I do."

"That truth still holds." He turned and stalked back to his

table.

Valmont high-fived Bryn. "Well played."

"Your grandmother trumps Jaxon's Directorate rhetoric." Ivy laughed. "I love it."

After classes, Bryn called her grandmother and explained the situation. "So what do you think? Can you use your influence to sidestep the Directorate and help us restore the theater building?"

"I'm proud of you, Bryn. You're learning how to play the game."

"Thank you. You should have seen the look on Jaxon's face."

"I'm sure it will be similar to the look on your grandfather's face at dinner tonight when I tell him about my plans. For this to work, I need you to spread the word among the students that the Women's League is sponsoring the repairs for the theater."

"I can tell people at dinner."

"No. Start right after we hang up. Call someone from each dorm and ask them to spread the word."

"No problem."

Bryn called Clint and Ivy, who promised to pass the word around their dorm. Then she contacted Garret who promised to take care of the Green and Red dorms, since he had contacts from his support group.

"Thank you, Garret. I wasn't sure who to call."

"One side effect from the support group is being more comfortable with members of other Clans. Maybe working together on the theater building will encourage more cross-Clan friendships."

The image of the dead boy who was half Red and half

Black dragon flashed in her mind. "That would be great, but let's not advertise that aspect. My grandfather doesn't approve of cross-Clan interaction and we don't want to draw his attention."

After she finished her phone calls, Valmont took one look at her face and said, "In your head, you're mentally taunting Jaxon."

"I am." Bryn grinned. "And I'm doing one hell of a victory dance."

• • •

Tuesday night, Bryn, Valmont, and the rest of the Stagecraft students sat in the auditorium listening to her grandmother talk about the planned restoration.

Dressed in a pale lilac suit, her grandmother stood in front of the empty space where the stage should've been, gesturing at a placard with designs for the new theater. "We've chosen to go with a theme featuring colors from each Clan interspersed throughout. The curtains will be navy. The carpet will be a pattern featuring black, orange, and red. The seats will be forest green."

"Are we going to be doing any of the work?" Clint asked Bryn.

"I don't know." Given her grandmother's personality, she'd probably hire a staff to take care of it.

"I'm sure some of you are wondering what you can contribute." Bryn's grandmother seemed to zero in on Clint. "The answer is simple. You can contribute what you wish. If you'd like to help with painting or installation of the new stage, you can show up here Thursday evening and offer your assistance to the workers I've hired. If you'd rather wait to see the finished product, that's fine, too."

"That last part," Valmont said, "was directed at the Blues."

Bryn glanced around. "I don't think there's a single Blue here." Neither Zavien nor Nola were present, either, which was weird.

"Maybe the Blues are boycotting the whole thing," Ivy said.

And miss the opportunity to boss others around? Bryn didn't think so. "They'll probably show up Thursday once the plans for the theater get around."

"Thank you for coming and being such attentive listeners," her grandmother said in a way that made Clint and Valmont slide lower in their seats. "Refreshments will be served in the back of the room. Please feel free to socialize."

"I'm going to say hello." Bryn popped out of her seat and headed for her grandmother with Valmont in tow.

"Your design is beautiful," she told her grandmother. "It reminds me of the fall leaf decor of my bedroom."

"Thank you. That was my inspiration." Her grandmother nodded at Valmont. "How are things going between you two?"

"Fine." Valmont's cheeks colored. "I'm sure you heard about our bump in the road, but I can assure you nothing like that will happen again."

"Good." She gestured toward the back of the room. "Let's have a drink."

Punch in hand, Bryn and her Grandmother stood off to the side, while Valmont watched from a few feet away.

"Did I make a mistake in appointing him your bodyguard?" her grandmother asked.

"No." Bryn sipped her punch while she tried to figure out what to say next. "The nature of the bond has changed since we fought in battle together, and it's taken some getting used to."

"What do you mean?"

So much for an easy explanation and glossing over the

details. "Honestly, I think it heightens our emotions. I have abandonment issues, and he is insecure. When you put both of those together, it's complicated."

"All relationships are complicated. What you need are some ground rules. The first rule, should be that your relationship cannot cross the line into anything beyond friendship."

That didn't seem fair. "I don't think it can help crossing beyond friendship. When we fly together, it's like we're one person. The feelings that come away from that are hard to ignore."

"Ignore them you must. Anything else will be inappropriate, and you'll be setting yourself up, and I do mean both of you, for disappointment. I'm sure you've heard the lineage check with Jaxon came back compatible. It's only a matter of time before the Directorate approves your marriage contract. That means you will marry Jaxon."

If she'd eaten any of the cookies from the buffet, they would've come back up. "We don't know that for sure."

Her grandmother placed a hand on her shoulder and stared into her eyes. "You promised me once that you would never run away."

"I did."

"And do you intend to keep that promise?"

"I do." What was her grandmother trying to say?

"Then you will marry Jaxon and you will do so with a smile on your face."

"So those are my choices? Marry Jaxon or break my promise to you? Because both of those options suck."

Her grandmother brushed Bryn's hair back off her forehead. "The second option would suck more than the first."

Bryn laughed. "I can't believe you said that."

"You're a bad influence." Her grandmother leaned forward and kissed her on the cheek. "You have years before marriage to Jaxon becomes a reality. While you're here at the Institute you should enjoy your friends and spend time with your knight. After you're married, you may not see much of each other."

Wait a minute. That was a load of crap. She'd still be friends with Clint and Ivy. The Blue Clan may not approve, but that was too bad. Better to tackle the bigger issue now. "Why wouldn't I spend time with Valmont? He'll continue to be my knight after I'm married."

"That wouldn't be appropriate."

"Is that what this comes down to, appearances? Jaxon plans to carry on with Rhianna after we're married, so why couldn't I continue my relationship with Valmont?"

"Part of the marriage vows include protecting your spouse above all others. Jaxon would provide all the protection you need. Having a knight after marriage would make him appear weak."

"Not this crap again."

"Bryn, I told you once before if you plan to stay in our world you must respect our ways. And not that I approve, but you wouldn't necessarily have to sever all ties with Valmont. He could remain a confidant, but you must release him from the bond before your wedding."

Bryn felt like she was falling down a well. "I'm not sure I can."

Her grandmother glanced toward Valmont. "In a way, it will be a good thing. If the bond is heightening your emotions, after you break the bond, they will go away. If it's not the bond keeping you two together, you'll know that, too."

Bryn's field of vision seemed to narrow. She clutched her paper cup of punch so tightly it crumpled. Lukewarm punch spilled over her fingers and dripped onto the carpet.

Valmont was by her side in an instant with his arm around her shoulders. "What's wrong? Do we need a medic?"

"No." Bryn leaned into his warmth. What she needed was a miracle.

"What were you discussing?" Valmont's tone toward her grandmother was respectful, but wary.

"Her impending marriage and what it will mean for the two of you," her grandmother said.

"I don't understand. Did you tell her about the turkey baster plan?" Valmont asked.

Bryn choked back a laugh. "Of course not."

Her grandmother crossed her arms over her chest and waited. "What on earth is he talking about?"

"Don't," Bryn warned Valmont. There was no way her grandmother would find the scenario appropriate or funny.

"Fine." He cleared his throat. "You can tell her when you're ready."

Like she'd ever be ready to share that information with her grandmother. "Can we talk about something that doesn't include Jaxon?"

"Of course." Her grandmother seemed intrigued but didn't push the issue. "There is a Valentine's Day party coming up. Since your petition has not yet been approved, you may attend the dance with whomever you wish. Once the petition is approved, that will be another story."

"But Jaxon said people date even after their petitions are approved."

"People might, but Sinclairs do not."

It was on the tip of her tongue to point out she was a McKenna, not a Sinclair, but that would hurt her grandmother's feelings, so she bit back the words and went with something less inflammatory. "This is something Jaxon and I should probably discuss before it happens." They had discussed it, sort of. The memory of Valmont kissing her and declaring he wouldn't give her up made her cheeks color, but it also made her sad. He hadn't kissed her like that since before she'd been ill, and she wasn't sure he planned to do it again.

"That would be a wise move. You wouldn't want to start off on the wrong foot."

She didn't want to start off on any foot with Jaxon.

"Mrs. Sinclair," Valmont's voice was pitched low, like he was trying to keep his emotions in check. "I care a great deal for Bryn. Whatever happens between her and Jaxon, my feelings will not change. I will uphold my oath until the grave. Nothing can change that."

Bryn leaned into him, loving the reassurance of his arm wrapped around her. She wanted to tell him not to worry, that they were a package deal, but if she followed her grandmother's way of thinking, she would have to set him free from the bond before her marriage. Her heart hurt just thinking about it.

"I have faith in you, young man. I'm sure you'll do what's best for my granddaughter."

Chapter Thirteen

After her grandmother left, Valmont wrapped his arms around Bryn and kissed the top of her head. The gesture should have been reassuring. What did he mean by it? Big brothers kissed their little sisters on top of the head. While it was affectionate, it didn't seem like something a boyfriend would do to his girlfriend. Then again, she didn't have much experience with the whole boyfriend scenario, so what did she know?

On the walk back to the dorm, Valmont kept his arm around her shoulders. "What did your grandmother say to upset you?"

Bryn glanced around. Other students walked on the sidewalk a few feet away from them. God forbid they overhear anything. "Let's wait to talk until we're back in my room."

"Is it that bad?" he asked.

"It's not good."

In her head, she'd always thought that even if she had to marry Jaxon, she'd still have her knight. She hadn't realized she'd be required to release him before the wedding ceremony.

Not that she couldn't still have a relationship with Valmont, but would he want one?

This whole arranged marriage thing was all so backward and archaic. Why couldn't Jaxon just marry Rhianna? They wanted to be together. An odd thought invaded her brain. If she were injured, or less than perfect, Jaxon would have to find someone else to marry. A limp would almost be worth not having to spend the rest of her life in a sham marriage. But that would not be honorable or loyal, and she cared about those things now, damn it. She was stuck like a fly in a web.

Once they reached the privacy of her dorm room, Valmont said, "What's wrong?"

A mild headache beat in Bryn's temples. "My grandmother shared something with me that sucks, big time."

Valmont pointed at the couch. "Step into my office."

She plopped down on the couch, where he joined her. "Whatever it is," he said, "we'll deal with it together."

How would they deal with it? As a couple? As best friends? There were too many balls in the air right now and she was sure they were all going to come crashing down on her head at any moment. What she needed was some reassurance about his feelings. "I'll tell you, if you kiss me."

Valmont's lips pressed together in a thin line. For every second he waited the beat in her temples increased.

He took her hands in his. "Bryn—"

Not this again. "Damn it, Valmont. I need some proof you care about me as more than a friend. If you don't, what I have to tell you won't matter, anyway."

"I'm trying to do the right thing." Valmont closed the distance between them and placed his hand under her chin so he could stare into her eyes. "But you're making it difficult." In slow motion, he leaned down and brushed his lips across hers. "Tell me what's wrong."

"If that's how you want to kiss me, nothing's wrong."

Was she being rude? Yes. But she needed more from him, some sign he wanted her. Then again, maybe the small, brief, I-want-to-kiss-you-about-as-much-as-I-want-to-kiss-a-dead-frog was the message he intended to send.

"Bryn, we discussed this."

Flames banked in her gut. "No. You made a decision without me. You decided to treat me like a little sister."

His eyes narrowed. "What are you talking about?"

Anger felt better than feeling sad and pathetic, so she decided to go with it. "That kiss and the other one where you kissed the top of my head…those were affectionate, and nice, but they weren't the same as the kiss at Rhianna's."

"I told you—"

"I know, 'blah blah blah, I'm being honorable.' I don't want honorable." Smoke shot from her nostrils. "I want you to really kiss me, and if you can't do that, then don't bother."

One minute he was glaring at her, and the next minute, she was flat on her back. Valmont's weight pressed down on her. His mouth moved against hers. She clutched at his shirt holding on to him as the kiss grew, fueled by the magic of their bond, full of hunger and longing and need. It felt like they were flying, soaring through the air except in this weird role reversal her legs were wrapped around his back.

A growl reverberated through her chest, and Valmont froze. He pulled away with a questioning look on his face. "That was a good growl?"

Good God, how can he form coherent sentences? She nodded, not trusting what might come out of her mouth if she tried to talk. Probably gibberish or some embarrassing, hormone-fueled comment about how pants were overrated.

He pressed his mouth to hers in a languid, lingering kiss. Warmth filtered through her body, and her grip on his shirt relaxed. Without breaking the kiss, he shifted back to an upright position pulling her with him, so she was sitting on his lap. Staying tangled up with him like this forever seemed fabulous.

When he pulled away from her, she sighed in equal parts frustration and satisfaction.

"Was that the type of kiss you had in mind?" he asked.

"Yes." She laid her head on his chest. "That is exactly the type of kiss I've been missing. I wasn't sure if you still wanted me."

He huffed out a breath. "Hello…knight…trying to do the right thing."

She laughed. "Stop that. Don't do the right thing. Kiss me while you still can." Oh, crap. She hadn't meant for that to come out.

"What do you mean?" Valmont asked, his light, happy tone gone.

Damn it. Back to sucky reality. She put her forehead against his. "My grandmother told me that before I marry Jaxon, I'll be expected to release you from the bond."

Valmont closed his eyes and exhaled. "Without the bond, I will still want to be with you. Is that what you were worried about?"

"Yes." She gave a small laugh to try and break the tension which had sprung up between them. "I wasn't sure you still wanted me now."

"And did I reassure you?" he asked.

"Mostly." She pressed her lips to the side of his mouth. "Maybe you can show me again."

"Just my luck to be bonded to a slow learner," he deadpanned. And then he pulled her in for another kiss.

· · ·

After Mr. Stanton's class Wednesday morning, Ivy yanked Bryn into the girl's restroom. "What's going on with you and

Valmont?"

"Just a minute." Bryn glanced under the stall doors for feet to make sure they were alone. Once she realized they were, she jumped up and down. "Valmont kissed me and things are complicated but wonderful."

"Thank God. For a while there you two were weird around each other and since you weren't *sharing*, I didn't know what was going on."

Bryn rolled her eyes. "It's hard to share when the guy you're talking about is in the room with you. I wish I still lived in your dorm."

"We should have a slumber party. I could stay the night. We could invite Rhianna. It would be fun."

That sounded like an awesome idea. "Too bad Jaxon would never go for it."

"She doesn't need his permission." Ivy headed for the door. "Come on. Clint and I need to go to history class."

Bryn headed toward the library with Valmont. He didn't say much on the walk over. Once they were tucked away at their usual table on the third floor, he winked at Bryn. "You shared, didn't you?"

"Maybe." Her face heated. "Maybe not."

"Nope, I'm pretty sure you shared about how fabulous I am." He ran his hand back through his hair.

Bryn reached over and mussed up his hair. "It's sad that you're so insecure."

"You should compliment me more often, to help with my self-esteem."

"I'll get right on that." She grabbed the Proper Decorum book from her bag. "But first, you're going to help me memorize what fork is for which course when some idiot decides to put six of them on the table."

"Why would you ever need six forks?" Valmont asked.

"I've no idea."

They'd been working for twenty minutes when a pair of students who looked to be in their college years came toward them. Both had the freckled skin and auburn hair of Red dragons. Bryn ignored them, expecting them to walk on by to wherever they were going. Valmont closed the book, stood up next to Bryn, and placed his hand on his sword.

"Hello," the Red female said, "I'm Eve. This is Adam. We wanted to talk with Bryn."

"Adam and Eve?" Valmont's eyebrows went up. "Did your parents have an odd sense of humor?"

"She's not my sister. She's my girlfriend, and those aren't our real names." The boy grinned. In a flash, his hair changed from red to black, and then it changed back. "Those are our hybrid names."

Bryn's mouth fell open for a moment. This was what she'd been searching for. At a loss for words, she pointed at the chairs across from her. "Have a seat."

"Not to be rude, but keep your hands flat on the table where I can see them." Valmont unsheathed his sword and held it at the ready. "You can never be too careful."

Eve gave a nervous laugh. "Just so you know, we had nothing to do with the attacks on the school or Dragon's Bluff."

"If you say so." Valmont didn't relax his stance.

"You're Black and Red?" Bryn said.

Eve nodded. "We're trusting you not to turn us over to the Directorate."

"I wouldn't," Bryn said, "unless you gave me reason to."

Adam glanced around. "We have friends watching out for other students, but we shouldn't talk about this here. We'd like to meet with you somewhere later tonight."

"No," Valmont said.

Bryn's knee jerk reaction was to snap at him, but he was only trying to protect her. She glanced at her knight. "What if we picked the place to meet?"

He frowned. "We still couldn't be sure they wouldn't bring reinforcements."

Adam leaned forward. "I get it. People tried to kill you, but if anyone outed us, the Directorate would charge us with war crimes we didn't commit and throw us in jail without a trial. You're not the only one who needs to be careful."

What he said made sense. There had to be a place where dragons of different Clans could meet without raising as much suspicion. And then she had it. "You could help rebuild the theater, and we could talk there. No one would think it was weird to see us together."

"That might work," Eve said. "Especially since Adam is planning to be an architect."

"And what area do you study?" Bryn asked.

"I'm working on my accounting degree." She reached over and laced her fingers through Adams. "But we're a couple, so no one would be suspicious if I went with him."

"Okay then." Bryn was dying to ask questions about who their parents were and where they lived, but it wouldn't be smart to talk here. "We'll see you at the theater building later this week."

After the pair walked off, Valmont re-sheathed his sword. "That was interesting. What do you think they wanted?"

"I don't know. But if my grandfather ever finds out I know about them, things will turn ugly."

"Is it worth talking to them?"

"Absolutely." Discovering there were hybrids that were peaceful made the world seem like a more balanced place.

It was physically painful not to tell Clint and Ivy about Adam and Eve. Bryn felt like a can of soda someone had shaken up. After their last class she convinced her friends to grab carryout from the dining hall and have dinner in her room.

Once they were all seated at the study table in her front room, she let loose with the details about the other hybrids. "And of course you can't tell anyone about this, and you can't let Adam and Eve know that you know, but what do you think?"

Clint shook his head. "I don't like it. How do you know they're hybrids. How do you know they aren't just good with Quintessence like you?"

Bryn slumped in her chair. Should she tell them about the hybrids in Dragon's Bluff? "Theoretically, let's say I may have proof other hybrids exist."

"You've developed a real *sharing* problem." Ivy glared at her.

"If I share with you and someone else finds out you know things you're not supposed to know, then the Directorate can come after you. So, if I don't share, it's to protect you, not to exclude you."

"Friends share," Ivy said. "End of story."

Wow. Ivy is mad. "Okay. From now on, I'll share."

"Good." Ivy opened her carryout container and dug into her chicken and dumplings. "Update us on everything we need to know."

She didn't feel good about this, but she told them about the dead bodies in Dragon's Bluff. "I swear. Even though I know the Red-Black hybrid boy attacked the town, and that is unforgivable, his face with those dead milky white eyes was the saddest thing I've ever seen."

Ivy looked at the dumpling on her fork and put it back in the container. "Maybe I should have asked you to share after we ate."

"Let's say we believe Adam and Eve. Now we know there are hybrids on campus," Clint said. "In the big scheme of things, what does that mean?"

"It means not all hybrids are dangerous," Bryn said. "And

maybe it means Directorate Sanctioned Arranged Marriages aren't necessary."

"I love that idea," Valmont said, "for obvious reasons, but to play Devil's Advocate, if the dragons that attacked the campus and Dragon's Bluff were all hybrids then the bad seems to outweigh the good."

"Maybe," Ivy said, "it's a certain combination of Clans that creates aggressive or violent hybrids."

"No, that doesn't work," Bryn said. "If we believe Adam and Eve are good, they are the same hybrid mix, Black and Red, as that boy I saw in Dragon's Bluff."

"Maybe it's like with the rest of the population," Valmont said. "Some people are good and some are not."

Clint walked over and picked up one of the *Days of Knights* books Bryn had left stacked on the library table. "We still don't know how these tales fit into the system."

"They may not fit into it at all, except as a way to needle the Directorate," Valmont said.

Clint lined the books up in various patterns. "Wait a minute. That looks like a staircase."

Bryn gazed at the area of the leather book cover. "You're right." She grabbed another book. "This one has the same pattern."

"Are they stairs going up or stairs going down?" Ivy asked as they crowded around the table.

Bryn shuffled the books until a pattern came into line. There was a building, with a star on top of it. Underneath the building stairs went down for two stories. "This makes it look like there's a secret staircase leading down to a basement somewhere."

"I don't think any of the buildings on campus have basements," Ivy said.

"The dorms don't." Clint scratched his head. "Maybe some of the other buildings do."

"We should start with the library," Valmont said.

"Why?" Bryn asked.

Valmont shrugged. "Isn't that where people go for answers?"

It was as good a logic as anything she could come up with. Checking the time, she said, "We have about ninety minutes until curfew."

"Let's fly over and see what we can find." Ivy headed for the window, which led out onto the terrace. The rest of them followed. Once they were outside, Bryn shifted. When Valmont settled between her wings, she felt the now familiar rush of power and connection from the bond.

"Whoa," Ivy said. "You're glowing."

"That's normal," Bryn said.

"Since when?" Ivy sounded ticked off.

"Did I forget to share?" Bryn asked.

Ivy dove off the terrace without responding. Clint followed his girlfriend.

Bryn dove after them. "It's not like I didn't tell her on purpose."

"I'm sure she knows that," Valmont said as they flew toward the library. "But she wants to be included in your adventures."

"Even if she's safer not knowing some things?" Bryn asked.

"Yes," Valmont said as they soared toward the library.

They landed, shifted back to human form, and entered the building.

Miss Enid waved at them from the front desk.

"Do you want to ask her about the basement, Ivy?" Maybe if she included Ivy more, her friend wouldn't stay mad.

"Sure."

They gathered at the desk, and Bryn let Ivy lead the conversation.

"We have a question about the buildings on campus," Ivy said, and she asked about the basement.

Miss Enid shook her head. "Not that I'm aware of. There are some storage vaults below ground here and at some of the other buildings, but no true basements. Why do you ask?"

"Bryn told us about the shelter at her grandparents' house. We wondered if the Institute had anything like that here."

"Unfortunately no, but that would be a good idea."

"Could we see the vaults?" Ivy asked.

Miss Enid shook her head. "No one can access the vaults without approval from the Directorate. I have to fill out a form to request access to the keys."

"What do they keep down there?" Ivy asked.

"Mostly old books and artifacts, which are too delicate to be displayed year round," Miss Enid said. "Research material the general public would have no interest in. Things of that nature." She picked up a stack of books. "If you'll excuse me, I need to return these to their rightful places."

"Thanks for the information," Ivy said, and then she turned to Bryn with a smile on her face. "Now that we know the vaults exist, we need to figure out where they are."

"Good idea." Bryn smiled back. Huh, Valmont had been right. Ivy just wanted to be included. Having friends on her "adventures" would probably make things easier on her, too, as long as she could keep them out of danger. "There have to be doors to the vaults on the first floor somewhere.

Valmont looked left and then right. "This place is huge. How do we know where to start?"

"We could start with the blueprints." Bryn headed toward the file cabinets. She knew where they were kept since she'd tried to find the plans for her grandparents' mansion.

"Sounds like a boring place to start," Clint said. "I'd rather skulk around like we're in a spy movie."

"Fine. You and Ivy can skulk, while Valmont and I check the blueprints. We'll meet at the entrance to the library in half an hour."

The blueprints showed vaults underneath the corners of the building, but no entrance points. No stairs and no outside doors. Bryn turned the paper over, thinking maybe she'd missed something. "There have to be doors somewhere."

"I'm guessing they don't want to advertise the entrance." Valmont took the blueprint from her, folded it back up into a neat rectangle, and re-filed it in the appropriate slot. "Let's head for the corner of the building and see what we find."

They ended up in the far back right corner of the building and stopped at a mahogany door with huge iron hinges and a plaque, which read, *Maintenance*.

"Do you think this could lead down to the vaults?" Bryn asked.

Valmont ran his fingers along the edge of the door. "These hinges look like they predate the modern architecture of the building."

"So they built the library around something that was already here?" That was an interesting thought. "I don't suppose we can just turn the knob and walk in?" Bryn placed her hand on the knob and turned to the right. Something clicked.

"It can't be that easy," Valmont said. "And if it is, there is probably someone or something on the other side of the door waiting to jump out at us."

Applying light pressure, Bryn tugged on the door testing to see if turning the knob had opened it. It didn't move. What had she expected? "Yeah, that would have been too easy."

The sound of Valmont unsheathing his sword had Bryn

spinning around with a fireball in her hand. All she saw was her knight staring at the door in awe. "What's wrong?"

Valmont pointed at the door with his sword. "The words. You don't see them?"

The dark wood of the door shone in the light, but its surface appeared as blank as it had always been. "No. What do you see?"

"Only those who have given their all may enter. Those who have taken everything must give to see," Valmont recited.

"Well that's not creepy or ominous at all." Bryn stared at the door until her eyes watered. Nothing. "What does the writing look like?"

"It's calligraphy, like in the books." Valmont held the sword in his left hand and reached for the doorknob with his right. He gripped the doorknob and turned it to the right. A click sounded, but when he tugged on the door nothing happened.

"Maybe there's a clue in one of the tales we haven't read," Bryn said.

"We finished the first book. I guess we need to read the other four." Valmont checked his watch. "We better go. We don't want to be caught out after curfew."

The giant wall clock behind the front desk displayed the time. "Crap, we have fifteen minutes to get back to our dorms."

They should have watched the time more closely. Where were Clint and Ivy? "Should we wait for them?" Bryn asked.

"We don't have time." Valmont glanced around. "I don't see them. They probably headed back already."

Bryn didn't feel right about abandoning her friends but it wasn't like she could yell in the library at closing time without causing a scene. If cell phones weren't banned on campus, she'd be able to find her friends right away.

"We better go." Valmont grabbed her hand.

"Wait." Bryn snatched a piece of paper off Miss Enid's

desk and wrote. "C&I We left. Call me." And set it up like a tent. "They'll know what it means. Hopefully, no one else will."

They darted for the front doors and exited the building. Bryn shifted, Valmont climbed on her back, and then she shot into the air, flapping her wings with powerful downward strokes, flying faster than she'd ever flown while carrying a passenger.

"No one else is out," Valmont said.

"We'll make it." Being incarcerated without food or water for twenty-four hours wouldn't kill either of them, but it would infuriate her grandfather. She knew, without a doubt, his reaction would be far scarier than the punishment.

Wind buffeted Bryn's wings as she came in for a landing on her terrace, knocking over both chairs.

Valmont hopped off her back and opened the window while Bryn shifted. As they climbed inside, Bryn could hear her heart beating in her ears.

"Why does it feel like I'm waiting for someone to jump out and yell, 'Gotcha'?" Valmont asked.

Goose bumps broke out on Bryn's arms. "I know what you mean." She grabbed his hand and led him to the living room. "I'm going to call Clint and Ivy."

"I'm sure they're fine."

Bryn dialed Ivy's number. The phone rang and rang.

"Crap." Bryn hung up. "What if they didn't make it back?"

"Maybe they flew to Clint's room."

"I don't have his number." Bryn paced the living room, hoping her phone would ring.

"Do you know anyone else's number in the Black dragon's dorm?" Valmont asked.

There was only one other number Bryn knew, and she didn't want to use it.

Valmont seemed to read her mind. "Zavien is the only

other number you know, isn't it?"

Bryn nodded. "He was my friend before the other stuff happened, so yeah."

Valmont huffed out a breath. "If Ivy doesn't call in ten more minutes, you should call him."

They sat on the couch and watched the time tick by.

"Damn it." This would be beyond awkward. She dialed Ivy's number one more time. No answer. Double damn it. "I guess I have to call him."

She punched in the number. When he answered, she had a strange sense of deja vu. "Zavien, sorry to bother you—"

"Bryn?" He sounded surprised.

"I'm afraid Clint and Ivy were out after curfew. Can you check their rooms? I only have Ivy's number."

"What were you doing out after curfew?" His accusatory tone made the tinge of sadness go away.

"We were at the library and lost track of time. And before you tell me how stupid I am, could you please check on them and call me back?"

Zavien sighed. "I wasn't going to call you stupid. It's just…I worry about you."

The present tense of the statement made her stomach go cold. "I'm fine. Please check and have them call me back."

"Okay."

Bryn hung up and turned to find Valmont. "Just so you know, I didn't love having to do that, either."

"I know." He walked over and flopped down on the couch. "Come here."

She joined him and cuddled against him. A sense of warmth and rightness settled over her. "There. That's better."

Valmont sat up, pushing her away in the process.

"What the hell?"

"Sorry, but look." He pointed at the books on the table. "There's an extra book."

Chapter Fourteen

"What are you talking about?" Bryn counted out loud and then leaned forward. "A sixth book. Why would someone break into my room and leave a book for us?"

"Good question."

Before her induction into the fine art of almost being blown up several times over, Bryn might have reached for the book. "Should we call someone to come look at it?"

Valmont stood and peered down at the tome. "If someone wanted to blow up your dorm, I doubt they'd go through the trouble of creating an exact replica to match a set of books you already had. Books no one was supposed to know were in your possession."

He was right. "Miss Enid, you, Clint, and Ivy were the only people who knew about the books."

"Miss Enid must've told the librarian in Dragon's Bluff who the books were for," Valmont said. "Maybe there was something in this book the librarian didn't want to risk falling into the wrong hands." He reached for the new book. As he flipped open the cover the phone rang, startling them both.

Heart racing, Bryn grabbed the phone. "Hello?"

"They aren't here." Zavien's worry came through the phone line loud and clear. "I checked both their rooms. No luck."

"Crap. Now what?"

"There's a chance they realized they were out too late and holed up somewhere."

That would be the best-case scenario. "If they were arrested, what would happen to them?"

"Incarceration overnight without food and water, to start."

"To start?"

"If the Directorate finds their behavior suspicious, they could be questioned and kept longer. Use your connections. Call your grandmother and tell her you're worried about them, because you were studying late, and you can't reach them. She should be able to find out where they are."

"Okay....thanks for helping."

"I'll always be here for you, Bryn."

What did she say to that? Of course he meant as a friend, but it was still awkward. "Thanks. I'll let you know if I figure anything out."

Bryn hung up.

"No luck?" Valmont asked.

She shook her head. "Time to call out the big guns."

She dialed her grandmother's number and Rindy, the all-knowing phone operator, answered on the second ring. "Sinclair estates, how can I help you?"

"Rindy, this is Bryn. May I speak to my grandmother?"

"One moment, please." The line went silent. Unease built up under Bryn's skin with every passing minute.

"Bryn? Why are you calling so late? Is something wrong?"

"I'm fine, but my friends might not be. I was hoping you could help."

"Which friends?"

Did it matter? Shouldn't her grandmother help, no matter what? "I was studying with my friends Clint and Ivy about an hour ago. Time got away from us. Valmont and I flew back to my room. I'm afraid Clint and Ivy may not have made it back before curfew. I called their rooms, but they aren't there."

"You must be more careful. Sinclairs abide by all Directorate-sanctioned laws."

Hello…this was about her friends. "I promise I'll pay closer attention to the time. Can you check on my friends, please?"

"I'll see what I can do without directly mentioning their names. If your grandfather found out you were associated with anyone who has been arrested, he would be most unhappy."

Like he wasn't a freaking ray of sunshine already. "Thank you. I'll be waiting by my phone."

After hanging up, Bryn filled Valmont in on what her grandmother had said.

"Well," Valmont picked up the sixth book, "there isn't much we can do until she calls. We might as well read."

They sat on the couch.

"Why don't I read out loud? You can close your eyes and listen."

"Thank you." She leaned back and waited.

Bluffstone was a village like any other village. There was a bakery, a blacksmith, and even a small bookstore. The people were happy until one day a dragon named Bain came to town and demanded they hand over all their gold.

Bryn opened her eyes. "That's different."

Valmont nodded and scanned down the page. "It says this dragon was unlike any others the villagers had dealt with. Bain was consumed with desire for gold and treasure to the point of insanity." He read a few more pages. "The gist of the story is the dragon associated with the village tried to reason with Bain. In the end, the knights of the village and their lead dragon killed him."

Bryn tried to make sense of the story. "Do you think dragons can literally go insane with greed, or is that a parable?"

"I don't know."

The shrill sound of the phone made Bryn jump. She answered, hoping for the best.

"Bryn," her grandmother spoke in a solemn voice, "two black dragons were arrested for being out after curfew, a male and a female. Since it's their first offense, they are being held overnight without food or water. They'll be released in the morning."

"Held where?" Bryn asked.

The dial tone was her answer. She hung up. Smoke shot from her nostrils. Clint and Ivy were arrested because of her. Guilt pressed down on her like a giant invisible hand.

"Not good news?" Valmont asked.

"They'll be released in the morning." Fire banked in Bryn's gut. Sparks shot from her nostrils.

"They wanted to help," Valmont reminded her. "And like us, they should have kept better track of time. But they'll be all right."

"I hate this." She punched Zavien's number into the phone and explained what she'd learned.

"Promise me you'll be more careful from now on," Zavien said.

She didn't owe him any promises about anything, but she didn't say that. Instead, she kept it short. "I will. Good night."

• • •

First thing in the morning, Bryn called Ivy. No one answered. She went to breakfast and scarfed down waffles, made two carryout containers, and hurried to the Black dragon's dorm.

She found Zavien standing outside Ivy's door, holding similar Styrofoam boxes.

"Looks like we both had the same idea," Zavien said. "But they aren't back yet."

"Did you try Clint's room?" Valmont asked.

Zavien nodded.

"Now what?" Bryn didn't know what to do.

"Go to class," Zavien said. "I'll let you know when they're back."

"No." Bryn leaned against the wall. "I'm waiting here until I see they're all right. And before you say it, I know I'm being immature. Deal with it."

Instead of yelling, Zavien's mouth turned up in the lopsided grin that used to make her heart flutter. "Now, there's the Bryn I remember."

Valmont cleared his throat. "We should go to class. Mr. Stanton might know what's going on."

"You're right." She set the boxes of food by the door. "Let them know I stopped by."

Valmont placed his hand on her lower back as they walked down the hall. Once they'd exited the building, she waited for him to say something. He was uncharacteristically quiet.

"Instead of stewing about it, why don't you say whatever is on your mind before we go into class," Bryn said as they walked across campus.

"I don't like how familiar he is with you."

Bryn sighed, reached over, and laced her fingers through his. "You don't have to worry about me having feelings for him anymore."

"I know, but does he still have feelings for you?"

That was an interesting question. "Even if he did, it doesn't matter because I don't have any for him." She squeezed his hand, hoping to emphasize the point.

"Good to know."

They entered the science building and made their way to Mr. Stanton's classroom. A new seating chart decorated the board. Clint and Ivy's names weren't on it. Fear jolted through Bryn's veins.

"Don't panic," Valmont said. "They could have the day off classes."

That was the best-case scenario. She approached Mr. Stanton's desk and waited for him to acknowledge her.

After scribbling his name on the bottom of a few reports, he glanced up. "Yes?"

"Do you have any information about Clint and Ivy?"

He gave a slow nod and went back to signing his name on the paperwork. "They will return to classes after lunch."

What did that mean?

"Please take your seat, Bryn. And if you want to help your friends, don't ask any more questions."

What the hell? Mr. Stanton was one of the good guys, so why was he warning her away? He had to have a good reason. "Thank you, sir."

. . .

By the time lunch rolled around, Bryn felt like she was about to crawl out of her skin with impatience. "Should we go to the dining hall for carryout and take it to Ivy's room?"

They crossed the threshold into the building and Valmont pointed at their usual table. "No, because they're here."

Bryn started to run, but Valmont grabbed her arm. "Low profile, remember?"

She settled for speed-walking, sliding into the seat next to Ivy and tackle hugging her friend. "I'm so sorry."

"Sorry for what?" Clint asked as he shoved half a dozen fries into his mouth.

Bryn pulled back from Ivy and noticed the annoyed expression on her friend's face. Ivy laughed, but it sounded forced. "What happened last night wasn't your fault. We're old enough to pay attention to the time."

"For Valentine's Day, Clint, maybe you should buy Ivy a watch," Valmont joked.

Okay. If he could play along, she could, too. "We should get our food."

"I'll go up with you," Ivy said. "I forgot ketchup for my fries."

Okay. What could she say in the food line that she couldn't say in front of Clint?

Bryn grabbed a plate and filled it with chicken tenders and fries.

Ivy followed along behind her. "I need to copy the notes I missed from Mr. Stanton's class. Can I come by before dinner?"

Since when did Ivy need to ask permission to come over? "Sure."

"Good." Ivy glanced around. "Have you ever had one of those days where you felt like everyone was watching and waiting for you to do something stupid?"

"Just most of my waking hours."

"Glad you understand." Ivy didn't make eye contact with Bryn as she squirted ketchup into a little paper cup that looked like a bucket for a mouse.

For the rest of her afternoon classes, Bryn did her best to make casual small talk with her friends in order to keep up the charade that nothing was wrong. What had the Directorate done to make Ivy not want to share? Terrible ideas flitted through her head—from brainwashing to lobotomies. Once classes ended, she had a hard time not running to her room.

Ivy showed up on Bryn's terrace minutes after Bryn made it inside.

Where was Clint?

Once inside, Ivy said, "I think someone stole my boyfriend and replaced him with a pod."

"Okay." Bryn pointed toward the living room. "This sounds like a conversation we should have sitting down."

Valmont closed and locked the window, and they reconvened on the couch in the living room.

"I know this sounds crazy, but that's not my Clint."

Bryn opened her mouth to speak, but Valmont beat her to it. "Why don't you start at the beginning? Tell us what happened last night "

"We never made it out of the library. Someone was following us, so we acted like we were trying to find someplace to be alone. Clint pulled me down an aisle and kissed me. We didn't even hear the guard sneak up on us. One minute we were kissing, and the next minute someone grabbed me and declared I was under arrest for breaking curfew. Clint told him we'd lost track of time. The guard didn't care."

Ivy rubbed at the red marks on her wrists. "He handcuffed us with those plastic zip ties and marched us up to the top floor of the library where—surprise—some of the Directorate members keep offices."

"I didn't know that," Bryn said.

"It gets better," Ivy said. "Ferrin Westgate was behind door number one."

"Aw, crap." Bryn did not like where this was going.

"Yeah, not who we wanted to see. He lectured us about breaking Directorate law and told us we were getting off easy this time. No real jail. They'd just lock us in study cubicles overnight."

The guard separated us and shoved me into one of those

tiny rooms. There wasn't a light or a chair or anything. Just a concrete floor. I used an emissary to see. I tried knocking on the walls to see if Clint would knock back, but I never heard anything. This morning a different guard let us out and told us to go clean up and then head to lunch."

"And that's when you noticed Clint was different?" Bryn asked.

Ivy nodded. "He didn't hug me. He didn't even hold my hand. Didn't ask how I was doing. Nothing. It was like he didn't care about me. He kept talking about how irresponsible we'd been and how it wouldn't happen again."

Valmont frowned. "Yeah, that doesn't sound like Clint."

"He walked me back to my room and kissed me on the cheek like I was his freaking cousin." Ivy created a small ball of lightning in her hand, which crackled and sent out forked tongues. "I have no idea what's going on. I can't shake this feeling I'm being watched. And I really want to zap someone."

Ivy let the ball of lightning flare up, doubling in size before she extinguished it. "So... thoughts?"

"Besides, what the hell? No." Bryn's mind raced. "We need someone on the inside who can give us some information. Since Mr. Stanton already told me to stop asking questions, who does that leave?"

"You could call your grandmother," Valmont said. "She knows how the Directorate operates."

"True. And I don't have a better idea. Ivy?"

"Call her."

Bryn dialed and told her grandmother she was worried about her friend's strange behavior.

"I'm sure you're worried about nothing," her grandmother said. "Why don't you call Jaxon and spend some time with him this evening. He always makes you feel so much better."

Had her grandmother turned into a pod, too? Or was she saying they couldn't talk about this over the phone?"

"You know what would make me feel better? Cherry pie from Suzettes. I wonder if they deliver."

"Pie sounds wonderful. Why don't we have dessert in your room this evening. I'll have the driver stop by Suzettes for carryout."

"That sounds like a great idea."

"I'll see you in an hour, Bryn."

Valmont walked over to the bookshelf and grabbed all six copies of *Days of Knights*. "I'll put these in my room."

Ivy glanced at the books. "Wait a minute. Weren't there five books?"

Bryn nodded. "There was an extra one when we came back last night. It has stories of dragons who went insane with greed and lust for power. It's different than the other ones."

"Definitely not a book the Directorate would want us to read." Ivy stood. "I'm guessing we'll tell your grandmother the same story we told the guard."

"That's my plan," Bryn said.

Chapter Fifteen

An hour later, Bryn's grandmother arrived. She wasn't alone. Her driver walked behind her, carrying a large picnic hamper, which he set on Bryn's library table before exiting the room.

Bryn smiled and hugged her grandmother. "Thanks for coming over."

"It's always nice to see you." Her grandmother opened the hamper and pulled out china plates and real silverware. "Valmont, why don't you help me set the table."

"Sure." He made fast work of the place settings and then cut and divvied out slices of pie to three of the plates. On the fourth plate he set an entire pie. "Bryn, can you guess which spot is yours?"

They all laughed. Due to the fact that Bryn used Quintessence to color her hair and do her makeup every day, she burned more than the average amount of calories, which meant she ate more food than most dragons. Valmont removed the whole pie and put a generous slice in Bryn's spot instead.

They all sat and Ivy recounted her story, in between bites

of pie.

"What do you think?" Bryn asked.

Her grandmother laid her fork on the edge of her pie plate. "Let's start with the easiest solutions first. Do you think Clint feels guilty he's the reason you were in trouble and maybe that's why he's acting strangely?"

Ivy shook her head. "Clint is…affectionate." She grinned. "If he's within touching distance, he's holding my hand or touching my hair or something. This morning he didn't touch me except to kiss me good-bye on the cheek, and even that didn't feel right."

"Perhaps he was sedated," her grandmother suggested. "If he was uncooperative when they questioned him, they could have medicated him in some way."

"You saying that like it's a normal occurrence concerns me," Bryn said.

"In the past, when witnesses have been uncooperative, medics were called in to help with the situation. While it's not common, it's not unheard of."

"But we weren't questioned," Ivy said, "except for in Ferrin's office."

Her grandmother's eyes narrowed. "Are you sure?"

What was her grandmother getting at? "Do you think maybe they questioned Clint, but not Ivy?"

"Ferrin would be more likely to question a male's allegiance or to think he might be the one behind some sort of espionage."

That was an interesting bit of information to file away for later.

Ivy stood. "If he was drugged, it would have to wear off eventually. Right? I'm going to check on him." She wrapped a slice of pie in a napkin. "I'll take him dessert as an excuse to go see him, which is stupid, because I shouldn't need an excuse to visit my boyfriend."

"Your young man may be keeping you at arm's length due to some threat made by Ferrin. If that is the case, he should be willing to tell you behind closed doors."

"Is there any way someone could impersonate Clint, act like a spy, and look exactly like him in an effort to gain information?" Valmont asked.

"None that I know of," her grandmother said, "but that doesn't mean it's not a possibility."

"So not the comforting advice I'd hoped you'd all give me," Ivy said.

"Call me later." Bryn stood and walked her friend to the terrace window, letting her out and then locking the window again.

Bryn's grandmother sat sipping coffee she'd brought from Suzettes. "Bryn, I know you probably realize this, but it is of the utmost importance that you are never caught out after curfew. Ferrin would use your arrest to shame your grandfather. The political ramifications would be terrible, and the damage it would do to your standing in our family would be irreconcilable."

"I understand." Bryn used her fork to swirl cherry pie goo around on her plate.

"Something else is troubling you," her grandmother said.

"How did you know?" Bryn asked.

Her grandmother pointed at the four pieces of pie left on the table. "If you were feeling yourself, there would be nothing left but crumbs."

Valmont chuckled.

Bryn snatched another piece of pie and took a bite. "There is something else, but it's a suspicion...nothing concrete." She ducked her head. "I think there might be other, peaceful hybrids at school."

"Why, exactly, do you believe this?" Her grandmother's tone was calm but wary.

"It makes sense. If there are crazy hybrids out there attacking the Directorate, then we know there are other hybrids and not all of them have to be violent. Right? My parents weren't crazy. I have a temper, but I'm not violent, and I don't have the desire to physically attack the Directorate. I'd be happy to argue a few points with them, but I don't have the desire to kill anyone because of politics."

"I suppose there is the chance other non-violent hybrids exist, but you shouldn't go looking for them. If you found them, you'd be duty-bound to turn them over to your grandfather, and I doubt he'd be inclined to believe they were innocent in the attacks."

"You're right." Bryn finished off her pie. "It would make more sense not to look for anyone, because finding them would only cause more problems."

Her grandmother reached over and touched Bryn's arm. "I'm glad you called me. Whenever you have questions, I will always try to help. I may not give you the answers you want, but I can help you avoid conflict with your grandfather."

Feeling the need to lighten the moment, Bryn said, "Plus, you bring pie."

Her grandmother laughed. "Yes, I do. Now I better go."

After a quick hug, Bryn let her grandmother out into the hall and locked the door behind her.

"So what do you think is going on?" Valmont asked.

"I have no idea." The phone rang, and Bryn grabbed it.

"It's me," Ivy's voice came through the phone sounding happier than she'd been earlier. "Clint says thanks for the pie."

"Is he acting more normal?" Bryn asked.

"He said he didn't get much sleep last night because Ferrin questioned him and gave him something to drink that made him fuzzy-headed."

"So my grandmother was right? Does Clint remember

what he told them?"

"Ferrin asked about the attack on Dragon's Bluff and about who you're friends with. Then the asshat talked about what a *shame* it would be if he had to void our marriage contract."

Fire banked in Bryn's gut. "What?"

Ivy growled. "That's why Clint was acting so weird today. He was worried they might be keeping tabs on us."

"What about the not touching you part?" Because that still seemed weird.

"Apparently, Ferrin lectured him on proper behavior in public," Ivy said, "and the Directorate frowns on public displays of affection."

Seriously? "Is Clint acting normal now?"

"Mostly," Ivy sighed. "I think they threatened him with more than he's admitting, because he's acting like he's afraid to tell me too much."

Bryn heard a voice in the background. "Hold on. He wants to talk to you."

"I know there's something not right with me today," Clint spoke in a low, even tone. "It feels like I'm sleepwalking and looking over my shoulder at the same time. All the smart-ass comments that normally play on a loop in my head are gone. Whatever was in that crap they gave me to drink…it has to wear off, right?"

"Yes." God, she hoped so. "Do you want to go see a medic? Or I could try to scan you with Quintessence."

"No." Clint yawned. "I'm exhausted. All I want to do is sleep. If I'm still not myself tomorrow, maybe then you can scan me."

Chapter Sixteen

The next morning, at breakfast in the dining hall, Clint appeared mostly back to normal.

"Feeling better?" Bryn asked as she poured syrup onto a giant stack of pancakes.

He nodded. "The smart-ass comments are back, but I have no desire to share them, which is weird."

Ivy reached over and brushed her fingers through part of Clint's Mohawk. "He's much better today."

"You thought I was a pod-person yesterday," Clint teased.

"You scared the crap out of me," Ivy shot back.

"Maybe," Valmont said, "that was the point."

Syrup dripped off Bryn's fork onto her blouse. "What do you mean?"

Valmont cleared his throat and spoke in a quiet voice. "Maybe they wanted you to see what you had to lose if you didn't obey their laws."

Bryn smacked her fork down on the table and spoke through clenched teeth. "That rat-bastard." She managed to keep her voice down, but just barely. "This whole thing was a power play. He wanted to show us what he could do if we went against him."

"Like giving me a chemical lobotomy?" Clint stated in a normal tone of voice. "And yes that statement should have come out angry, but I can't make that happen right now which makes this all the more terrifying." He took a deep breath and blew it out. "It's like Ferrin is controlling something in my head, changing my emotions and reactions, and it's pissing me off."

"We'll make sure you never wind up in a position where Ferrin will doubt your loyalty to the Directorate again," Bryn said. And she meant it. No matter what, she would never involve Clint and Ivy in her investigations again.

Ivy sighed. "I finally understand why you were afraid to share everything with us."

"I hate that you get it now, and this was the cost." Smoke drifted from Bryn's nostrils. "And I really hate that Ferrin seems more dangerous now than ever."

Students scraped chairs across the floor as they stood to head to first hour.

"The most important thing," Valmont said, "is that we're all okay and we now have a better and far more terrifying understanding of what lengths the Directorate is willing to go to assure compliance, and we will act accordingly."

• • •

The next day in Elemental Science, Bryn noticed another one of Mr. Stanton's seating charts on the board. Today she was grouped with Octavius, Rhianna, and Garret. It was probably the first time in a month she hadn't been grouped with Jaxon. Maybe fate was finally smiling on her.

"Class, today you will learn to work together with your fellow dragons using your different breath weapons to solve a problem." Mr. Stanton walked around the room and placed wooden boxes on the desks grouped together in sets of four. "Figure out the most effective ways to solve the puzzles. You want to open the boxes without destroying them or the object inside."

Valmont pulled a chair up to sit beside Bryn. Octavius nodded at them. Rhianna smiled in greeting. Garret immediately picked up the box and studied it from all angles.

"How do you know it's okay to turn the box upside-down like that?" Rhianna asked.

Garret paused. "Mr. Stanton turned the box over and around after setting it down which means whatever is inside isn't bothered by motion."

"I knew you'd have a reason," Rhianna said, "I didn't know what it was."

The corners of Garret's mouth turned up in an amused grin. "I am a Green. We rarely do anything without thinking about the repercussions first."

"Did you think about the repercussions of forming a mixed Clan group?" Octavius asked.

Garret set the box down. "Yes, both negative and positive."

This line of conversation was almost more interesting than the locked box. Bryn leaned close and spoke in a quiet tone lest Jaxon hear their conversation and throw some sort of hissy fit. "Which reaction have you seen more of?"

Garret traced his fingertips along the edge of the box before answering. "More positive, I think." He flashed a grin at Rhianna, who returned the expression.

The old fear that Rhianna might run off with Garret, stranding her with Jaxon came knocking at Bryn's subconscious.

"Back to the box," Bryn said. "Anyone have an idea?"

"There's a keyhole." Octavius pointed at the side of the box. "I could direct a small sonic wave into it and see if it sets off the locking mechanism."

"Has that worked for you before?" Bryn asked.

Octavius nodded. "Sometimes Orange dragons use keyless locking mechanisms which can only be opened by a particular pattern of sonic waves."

Garret set the box down with the keyhole facing the Orange dragon. "Interesting. I've read about such things, but I've never seen it done. Give it a try."

Laying his hand on top of the box, Octavius concentrated. Since his waves were invisible, Bryn didn't see anything, but she felt vibrations go through the desks. The box however remained locked.

"That would have been so cool if it had worked," Valmont said.

"Could the key be something hidden on the box?" Rhianna asked. "Like a recessed button of some sort?"

Garret waved at the box, indicating Rhianna was free to investigate. Funny how the Green dragon took charge when it was a puzzle of logic. Maybe that was innate to their Clan.

Rhianna inspected the box, running her hands over it. "I can't find anything."

"Could we make a key?" Bryn asked.

"Try using ice to fill the keyhole," Garret said to Rhianna. "Maybe by adding a bit at a time you can jimmy the box open."

Rhianna did as he suggested. When that didn't work, she shoved the box toward Bryn. "Your turn."

"What can I do that none of you can?" Bryn asked.

The sound of Valmont unsheathing his sword startled her.

"Calm down, I'm helping you assess your resources." He held up the sword. "Think of it as a giant lock pick."

Bryn laughed. "Why not?" She touched the tip of the blade to the seam where the lid met the rest of the box.

"Be careful," Valmont warned.

Too late, Bryn's hand stung as she received what felt like the mother of all paper cuts. She winced against the pain and pulled her hand back to inspect her thumb.

The sword glowed red as several drops of blood rolled into the keyhole and *click*, the box popped open.

"Your blood opened the box?" Garret sounded appalled and intrigued.

"So it would appear." Bryn wasn't sure how she felt about that.

"And the glowing of your sword, was that normal?" Garret asked.

"I've never noticed it before, because as Bryn's knight my job is to keep her from bleeding." Valmont grabbed Bryn's hand and kissed her fingertips. "Are you all right?"

A happy warmth flowed from her fingers to her heart. She felt her face heat. "Yeah, I'm good."

"Do you mind?" Garret gestured at the mysterious contents of the box, which were shrouded in black silk.

"Feel free." Bryn wasn't so sure she liked the box or its contents if it was after her blood.

Taking great care, Garret pulled away the silk cloth without touching whatever was inside.

"Another box?" Octavius's deep voice broadcast his displeasure through the room.

"Someone else can bleed on this one," Bryn stated.

"There's a button on the side." Rhianna pulled a pencil from her book bag and used the eraser to press the button.

Something gave an audible click and then a faint ticking sound emanated from the box.

Not good. Bryn pushed back from her desk, "Mr. Stanton," she spoke loud enough to gain his attention, "tell me that's not a bomb."

"No bombs," Mr. Stanton called out. "Just the puzzle mechanism."

"Not that I don't trust you," Valmont said, "but Bryn has a certain history when it comes to things that go *boom*."

Rhianna, Garret, and Octavius glanced at the smaller box nestled inside the bigger box which suddenly seemed ominous.

"Just to clarify," Garret glanced at the other students huddled in small groups, "is anyone else's box ticking?"

A quick glance around the room showed no one else had managed to open their box yet to reach the contents.

Garret slammed the lid shut on the big box. Rhianna blasted it with frozen flames encasing it and the entire desk in a giant block of ice.

Mr. Stanton sighed. "Students, while I understand your caution, I can assure you—"

Ka-Boom!

Shards of ice flew. Rhianna blasted more frozen flames creating a wall on one side of the desk.

Garret created a twister making the shards of ice turn back on themselves in a twisting motion. Bryn blasted flames at the shards of ice that escaped.

"On my mark, stop your wind," Octavius yelled.

Garret nodded.

Octavius held his hands out, palms down. He moved closer to the twister and angled his hands so they were facing each other. "Now," Octavius yelled.

The twister stopped, and it looked like invisible hands had crushed the ice and the desk into a tangled ball of wood. Bryn felt the wave through the soles of her shoes. The ball of wood ground together, pulverizing itself. The air pressure shifted. Bryn's ears rang and then popped.

Where the desk and puzzle box had been, there was what appeared to be a small mound of wet sawdust.

Silence filled the room, and then footsteps sounded as Mr. Stanton approached and knelt down to touch the remains of their classroom project. "I'd say you earned an 'A' for teamwork today."

Wait a minute. "That was the assignment?" Bryn asked.

"We did use our breath weapons to work together." Garret frowned. "I'm not sure of the ethical implications of trying to blow up a classroom full of students."

Mr. Stanton stood. "There was only a small charge in the box. It should have gone off like a balloon popping. Something you did increased the power of the explosion."

"Bryn's blood," Rhianna said. "Somehow it changed the charge, making it more powerful."

"What are you talking about?" Mr. Stanton asked.

Bryn explained how she'd cut herself on Valmont's sword and how the box had opened.

Mr. Stanton shook his head. "That was not part of the plan. Wind would have opened the box if applied in the correct manner."

"So the Quintessence in my blood increased the balloon pop to a small bomb?" Bryn waited for someone to correct her. They all just stared.

"So if I scratch myself and bleed, weird crap will happen?"

"Not all the time," Mr. Stanton said. "I think this was an odd set of circumstances, combining your knight's sword and the bond with your blood, but you probably shouldn't ever mess around with fireworks."

"Gee, thanks. That's comforting."

Thankfully, the rest of Bryn's day was explosion free. That night, Bryn and her friends headed for the theater to help with the repairs. The meeting with Adam and Eve weighed on her mind. Should she ask questions if the answers might endanger herself and her friends? The stakes to the behind the scene espionage games she'd been playing now seemed far too high.

"Twenty bucks says there isn't a Blue in the entire theater," Clint said, sounding a lot more like himself.

They hadn't talked about his pseudo-chemical lobotomy all day. Though he did seem 100 percent back to himself, which was a relief. Bryn hoped they could put the experience behind them, never to be repeated again.

"I'll take that bet," Valmont responded with a grin on his face. Did he know something she didn't?

When they entered the auditorium, Bryn checked hair color. There wasn't a blond in the vicinity.

"Pay up." Clint held out his hand.

"Why would I pay you, when I won the bet?" Valmont said.

"What are you talking about? There isn't a Blue in this room." Clint looked around the area.

"Bryn's grandmother is the Bluest of Blues, and she is standing right over there."

Clint drew himself up. "That was sneaky and underhanded, and damn it, I wish I'd thought of it first."

They all laughed. Bryn took Valmont's hand and tugged him toward the area where people were painting. "I never thought I'd say this, but I want to paint."

"Why?" her knight asked.

"It's what I do at Stagecraft. After all the weirdness that's been going on around here I'd like to have a little normalcy back in my life."

"I think you and normal are polar opposites," Valmont teased. "But, I kind of like it that way."

"Bryn, I didn't see you come in."

Her grandmother's voice had Bryn whirling around with a genuine smile on her face. "We're here to paint."

"You don't have to paint," her grandmother said.

"It's not like I'd stand around and watch other people work." Aw crap. Open mouth, insert both feet. "Besides. I like to paint. It's relaxing."

Her grandmother appeared unruffled. "Gardening has the same effect on me. Valmont, why don't you grab supplies from the foreman over there, while I talk with Bryn."

"I can do that." Valmont took off like a shot. And she would so give him crap for that later.

"He's such a nice young man," her grandmother said. "You're lucky to have a friend like him who is willing to look out for your best interests."

Where was this going? And then Bryn saw a few members of the Blue women's league standing nearby. Time to play her part, for her grandmother's sake.

"He is a good friend," Bryn said. "I feel safer knowing he's watching out for me."

When Valmont returned with paint supplies, he had Adam and Eve in tow. "Bryn, Mrs. Sinclair, this is Adam and his girlfriend Eve. I shanghaied them to help us paint."

Everyone did the mandatory round of polite greetings, and then Bryn's grandmother excused herself to check in with the foreman.

"Let's work over there." Bryn pointed to a section of wall away from where others were painting. It would give them some privacy, but not enough to ask the questions she wanted to ask. After everything that had happened with Clint, she wasn't so sure she wanted to go down this path anymore. Okay, she desperately wanted to learn about other peaceful hybrids, but now the shadow of Ferrin and the Directorate blotted out some of her curiosity.

Eve dipped a roller in paint. "Your grandmother is impressive. I kept feeling the urge to curtsey."

Bryn laughed. "I know what you mean. She is a force to be reckoned with."

For a few moments, they rolled paint onto the walls without speaking. Valmont caved first. "I now know where the phrase, 'this is about as fun as watching paint dry' comes from. Painting is boring."

"Where are you two from?" Bryn asked.

"We grew up in small town no one has ever heard of," Eve said. "We live next door to each other, so we've known each other since we were little. We're both only children, so we hung out together a lot."

They made small talk and painted for half an hour. Then Bryn set her roller down. "That's it. I need a snack."

"Sounds good to me." Eve dropped her roller in the mostly empty paint tray.

Adam stretched his arms over his head. "Looks like everyone had the same idea at the same time." He pointed at the cafe tables, which had been set up by the snack table. Most of the seats were taken. "I'll clean up. You three go grab seats."

"Good idea." Valmont kept his hand on Bryn's lower back as they headed toward the tables. The warmth of his hand was reassuring. Her grandmother may not approve, but it could be passed off as a protective gesture.

"I'll snag a table," Eve said.

Bryn laughed when she saw the refreshments. Real china plates and actual utensils were set out alongside a buffet of appetizers. Glass tumblers sat beside pitchers of tea and lemonade.

Valmont gave a low whistle. "Talk about a gourmet snack table."

"I'm sure my grandmother would say, if something is worth doing, it's worth doing well." Bryn piled two plates with mini quiches, crab cakes, and other golden brown bite-sized treats wrapped in fried dough. "I don't know what these are, but I'm sure they're wonderful."

Valmont followed behind her, filling two more plates. "I'll take care of the drinks."

Having a boyfriend with the skills of a waiter came in handy. Bryn sucked in a breath. Did she just think of Valmont as her boyfriend? He was, kind of. But now wasn't the time to ponder her relationship status.

When they returned to the table, Adam sat whispering to Eve.

Bryn set the plates in the middle of the table and passed out napkins and forks. "Everything all right?"

Adam picked up a mini quiche and studied it. "Everything is fine."

Valmont arrived, passed out drinks, and shuffled the food on the four plates until each one held the same assortment. "Snacks are served." He sat and sipped his lemonade.

"He's handy to have around," Eve said.

Adam popped the quiche in his mouth, chewed, and seemed to think about something. "I don't know what that was, but I want more." He glanced at the buffet table. "Do you think anyone would notice if we took the whole tray?"

"Bryn, I believe we've found you a kindred spirit." Valmont clapped Adam on the back.

"He lives for food," Eve confirmed. "And he loves to cook, which works out great since I screw up scrambled eggs."

Valmont tilted his head and narrowed his eyes. "How can you mess up scrambled eggs?"

Eve popped a crab puff into her mouth and shrugged.

This would be nice if Bryn could relax. It felt like she was waiting for a secret message or clandestine information. It didn't help that Clint and Ivy were seated a few tables away, staring intently like they were trying to read everyone's lips.

"You could invite your friends to join us," Eve said. "It's not like we're divulging deep dark secrets."

"No secrets?" Bryn said, playing it off as a joke. "That's

disappointing."

"Not much to tell," Adam said. "We grew up with a small group of Reds...exactly like us. Sparks is a tiny farm town with a main street, a few stores, and a couple dozen houses. There isn't even a McDonald's."

"Is it like Dragon's Bluff where everyone knows everything about everyone?" Valmont asked.

"Yes, and we're all related in one way or another, so you have to check lineage before you ask someone on a date." Adam playfully tugged on Eve's ponytail. "I had my parent's check Eve's lineage when we were five."

Bryn grinned and shook her head. "I can't imagine living someplace that close-knit. My parents and I were pretty much on our own." The familiar ache flared up in her chest. How different would her life have been if her parents had sought out a small off-the-map town with other dragons?

"Sorry about your parents," Eve said.

Bryn nodded. "Thanks." What else should she ask them? "Do you think you'll move away from your town when you graduate?"

"No," Eve said. "It's home."

"Are there other small towns with populations like yours?" She hoped they understood that she meant other hybrid towns.

Adam nodded. "There are several remote towns where everyone is related. I know of a few who live in the Green dorm and a few who live in the Black dorm."

Which meant there were towns for hybrid Green and hybrid Black Dragons. "I'd love to visit one of those towns, to see what they're like."

"I wouldn't try it without an invitation," Eve said. "Small communities like ours are sometimes suspicious of outsiders. Given who your grandfather is, I'm not sure you'd be welcomed."

At least now she knew there were other groups of good hybrids out there. "Thanks for talking to me about this."

"We needed someone to know that we aren't all bad, and you were the only dragon likely to believe us. Not to be rude," he stood, "but we should be going."

They said their good-byes and left.

"That was interesting." Valmont leaned back in his seat. "Do we have to paint more, or can we be done?" He gave her puppy dog eyes.

She laughed. "We can be done." Bryn waved Clint and Ivy over. "I'm going to say good-bye to my grandmother, and then we can go back to my room."

As she worked her way across the room, Bryn saw her grandmother arch a brow at whatever one of the women told her. Then she spotted Bryn and smiled. It was a genuine, warm smile, one she wouldn't have thought her grandmother capable of when they'd first met.

"Are you finished painting?" her grandmother asked.

"Yes. I wanted to give you a hug and say good-bye before I went back to my room."

The other women stiffened a bit, because public displays of affection weren't a Blue characteristic, which was too bad. Without seeming the least bit affected by her friends' reactions, Bryn's grandmother gave her a hug and even kissed her on the cheek. "Don't forget about Lillith's baby shower this Sunday."

This was news to her. Not that she didn't want to go 'cause she did. "Did my invitation go missing in the mail?" She was joking, sort of.

"No. You were included in the invitation, which came to our house. I thought Jaxon would have told you."

Bryn snorted. "He's a guy. I don't think baby showers are on his radar. But that doesn't matter. The shower should be fun."

An evil grin lit her grandmother's face. "As payback for his lack of manners, the next time you see Jaxon, tell him he's required to attend the shower, and it's at Suzette's."

Bryn laughed. "Should I have Valmont take a picture of his face as I deliver the news?"

"Yes." Her grandmother grinned. "On a serious note, I will meet you at your room, and we'll go down to the car together Sunday at eleven."

Good plan, since the last time she'd climbed into a car the driver had tried to murder her. And since he'd been killed during her rescue she still didn't have a freaking clue why he'd done it. But, now wasn't the time to dwell on that.

"I'll see you Sunday."

Bryn met up with her friends, and they headed back to her dorm.

"Did you find out anything you think is worth sharing?" Ivy asked from the corner of the couch where she sat with Clint.

Bryn couldn't help but notice that Ivy had lost some of her enthusiasm, which was kind of sad but totally understandable. Best to keep the information she shared simple.

She told her about Sparks, where Adam and Eve lived and the confirmation that other hybrid communities existed. "So, not much to tell, really."

"Let's cut the crap," Clint said.

"What do you mean?" Ivy asked.

"I know you're scared. Hell, we all have a far better respect for the Directorate and the lengths they'll go to in order to keep us in line, but that doesn't mean I want to fall in line and be a good little soldier. If there is information out there about other hybrids, I want to know."

"Are you sure?" Bryn asked. "I don't want to be

responsible for your marriage contract being voided."

"If you start to share anything that makes us uncomfortable, we'll stop you," Clint said. "That way *I* get to decide how in the dark I am, not Ferrin."

"Okay." Bryn wasn't sure Ivy felt the same way.

"Do you think Adam and Eve's entire town of dragons is like them?" Clint asked.

"How would that even be possible?" Valmont added.

"I don't know." Bryn closed her eyes and tried to figure it out. "What if some of the mistresses managed to become pregnant?"

"Their benefactors would have to be okay with that," Ivy said. "And I can't picture a Blue being okay with that at all."

"But we aren't talking about Blues. We're talking about Black and Reds, who seem far more…" Valmont frowned. "What's the word I'm looking for?

"More reasonable, less volatile, far better looking," Clint said.

Bryn laughed, happy to have the old Clint back. "Even though Reds and Blacks aren't as anal as Blues, I can't imagine they'd risk discovery."

Ivy bit her lip, like she was thinking hard about something. "Maybe they're dragons who have lived apart from the Directorate their entire lives. Maybe they snuck under the radar and lived in quiet communities. Adam and Eve told you about Sparks. Who's to say there isn't a bigger community of Reds and Blacks hidden someplace else."

"Once you have one hybrid dragon, and they marry and have kids, their children will be hybrids, and when those kids marry, their kids will be hybrids, so this could have started with one hybrid a long time ago," Valmont said.

"That sounds like one of those story problems from math." Clint laughed. "If one hybrid dragon has two kids and they marry and each have two kids and the cycle continues, then one day there might be enough of them to populate a town, or take on the Directorate."

"And the ones taking on the Directorate would be endangering the peaceful ones who attend school and try to blend in," Bryn said.

"Which is why your grandfather and his cronies can never find out about Adam and Eve," Clint said.

Chapter Seventeen

Sunday, Bryn was happy to find herself at Suzette's without Jaxon, watching Lillith and the other Blue women *ooh* and *ahh* over baby clothes. It made the normally cold and standoffish Blues seem far more human and likable.

And the pie was *awesome*. Bryn dug into her third piece of cherry pie, while her grandmother handed another gift to Lillith. It seemed her grandmother and Lillith had become friends, which was nice and terrifying at the same time. Nice because Lillith seemed like she needed friends, and terrifying because it implied to all present that they were working at cementing an alliance between the two families, aka the nightmare marriage between her and Jaxon.

Valmont stood on guard off to the side, with a polite smile plastered on his face.

"Isn't this adorable?" Lillith held out a tiny tuxedo.

A tuxedo for a baby? Seriously? There was even a tiny bow tie. Poor kid. If Clint thought penguin suits were uncomfortable now, what would they be like for a baby?

Bryn leaned over and spoke to the woman next to her.

"Can you really get a baby to wear one of those?"

"Of course." She seemed shocked by the question.

No wonder Jaxon and his friends acted so stiff and formal. It had been drummed into them since birth.

Lillith unwrapped Bryn's present next.

"Oh, Bryn, I love it." She held out the silver rattle with Westgate engraved down the side so everyone could see.

Warmth bloomed in Bryn's chest, somewhat filling the gaping hole left by her parents death. If she had to marry Jaxon, at least she'd gain Lillith as a mother-in-law. *Oh, holy hell, are there drugs in the cherry pie? How'd I think that without flinching?*

She smiled at Lillith. "I'm glad you like it."

"You know, if things turn out like we expect, you could receive one of these one day." Lillith beamed.

Bryn opened her mouth to object, vehemently and with great gusto and many obscenities, at the idea of giving birth to Jaxon's children. It was bad enough she'd thought about marrying him, but having his kids deserved a whole other level of freaking out. Then she realized every woman in the room was staring at her. She swallowed her, over-my-dead-body response, and said, "It is a possibility."

Her grandmother nodded, but Bryn didn't know whether it was a response to how Bryn had handled the situation or if she was nodding in agreement. She ate two more pieces of pie to quell the instinct to run screaming from the room.

After the last present was opened, the guests said their good-byes. Bryn found herself drafted into the role of hostess as she thanked everyone for coming. Lillith glowed, and her grandmother beamed almost as much. Valmont stood off to the side, with his lips set in a thin line. She didn't think it was the baby shower that annoyed him. Ever since Lillith had made the remark about Bryn receiving a rattle with Westgate engraved on it, Valmont's expression had seemed frozen, like he was trying not to show emotion.

She wouldn't be too happy about listening to him talk about marrying someone else and having children. Once the last person was gone, Bryn started to pack up the gifts.

"Don't worry about that," her grandmother said. "We'll have everything packed and shipped to Westgate Estates."

Lillith clutched a small blue robe embroidered with snowflakes to her chest. "I'm holding on to this one." She held it out. "It's so cute."

And here came the tears. Lillith wiped her face. "Sorry."

"I'm surprised you managed to hold out this long," Bryn teased, in a good-natured way.

The sound of someone clearing her throat caught Bryn's attention. Valmont's grandmother stood in the doorway, looking as cuddly as a porcupine. She nodded at Bryn's grandmother and then spoke to Valmont in Italian and held her arms out like she was waiting for a hug.

His features softened. "I've missed you, too." He crossed the room and wrapped his arms around his grandmother.

Guilt hit Bryn between the eyes. She was the reason Valmont saw his family so infrequently.

"Come outside, Valmont, your grandfather wishes to see you."

Valmont had been given special consideration by being allowed into the back room. He'd had to swear never to divulge the secret that there was a second, more peaceful room in the establishment. He could've met his grandfather in the floral farce room, but being outside would probably be nicer.

Valmont glanced back at Bryn, his expression conflicted.

"Go visit. I'll be fine in here for a while." Bryn made shooing motions with her hands.

"Mrs. Sinclair?" Valmont said. "Do you mind?"

"Bryn and I will wait for you here," her grandmother said.

"Thank you." Valmont headed out the door with his grandmother.

Watching him ask her grandmother for permission to do something struck a nerve. It placed him in the employee position, which he wasn't. Actually an employee would be paid. He was volunteering. Crap. That idea made her feel worse.

"What's wrong?" her grandmother asked.

Bryn shrugged. "I know he doesn't mind, but I feel bad about taking Valmont away from his family."

"He is devoted to you, isn't he?" Lillith said. "After you marry, I guess he'll go back to his real life."

If anyone else had uttered those words, Bryn would have had the mother of all hissy fits. Since it was Lillith, and her intentions were never suspect, Bryn took a deep breath and pushed down the flames trying to crawl up the back of her throat. "That's one way to look at it."

Her grandmother raised an eyebrow in challenge. "How else would you look at it?"

Bryn sighed. She'd walked right into that one. "I don't like to think about a time when Valmont won't be there for me. Right now he's such a comfort."

"Once you're married to Jaxon, you won't need anyone else to look out for you," Lillith said.

"You have no idea how much those words make my head hurt," Bryn blurted out.

Both of her grandmother's eyebrows shot up.

"Please. It's just us. I can be honest. Neither of you are delusional enough to believe I find Jaxon's presence comforting."

"Reassuring might be a better description," her grandmother said.

"He would protect you from all threats," Lillith objected. "And that should be comforting."

She couldn't argue with a pregnant woman, especially one who might burst into tears at any moment so she said, "I never thought of it that way." There. She had finally found a use for the social double-speak her grandmother taught her to use when you couldn't disagree with someone.

On the ride back to school, Valmont was oddly quiet.

"How are your grandparents?" Bryn asked.

A sad smile tugged at the corners of his mouth. "They're fine."

Guilt rained down on her. "You could ask them to come visit you on campus," Bryn said.

He reached over, and despite her grandmother's presence in car, laced his warm fingers through hers. "Stop it."

"Stop what?" she asked.

"Stop worrying about me," Valmont said. "It's my job to worry about you."

Easier said than done.

· · ·

Monday morning Bryn was up and out of bed before her alarm went off. A strange sense of anticipation tingled under her skin.

"How much coffee have you had?" Valmont asked as she bounced in her chair at breakfast.

"My normal two cups. Why?"

"You're like a Mexican jumping bean this morning." Clint yawned wide enough for Bryn to see his molars.

"Wait a minute." Ivy looked over her shoulder at the tables where the Blues congregated. "Look at them. They're talking with their hands and laughing and fidgeting."

Valmont tilted his head and studied the Blues. "They're acting like normal people. And that's not normal for them."

"I've got it." A huge grin broke out on Clint's face. "It's

going to snow."

Just the mention of the word had Bryn bouncing in her seat. "What? How do you know that?"

Valmont laughed. "I should have guessed when you woke up before the alarm. I was too tired to think clearly."

What were they talking about? "I don't understand. Blues get wound up when it snows?" She observed Jaxon. He spoke with his hands, gesturing wildly in a manner she'd never seen before. "Yeah, that's not right."

"It's puppy weather." Clint sat up straighter like he'd made some sort of decree.

Valmont narrowed his gaze. "Please explain that so I can decide if I should be offended on Bryn's behalf."

Clint leaned in and spoke in a low voice. "It reminds me of how our dogs act when the weather changes. No matter how old they are, on the first cool day, they run around chasing each other and acting like puppies. Therefore, cool weather that hypes them up is puppy weather, and the first snow is puppy weather for the Blues."

Valmont grinned at Bryn. "I kind of like it."

"Puppies are cute, so it doesn't bother me." Bryn peered out the windows checking for white flakes. "I don't know how I'm going to pay attention to anything today. Will this happen every time it snows? My grade point average might take a nosedive."

"It's usually just the first snow." Valmont pointed to the windows. "And here it comes."

Bryn's breath caught as she watched fat white flakes drift through the air. She needed to go outside, to touch it, to glide, to exalt in the wonderfulness that was winter. Okay, that last thought was weird. Whatever. She thrust her book bag at Ivy. "Hold this for me." And then she was up and out of her seat and headed for the door.

Valmont followed along behind her, chuckling.

Bryn glanced back at him and stuck her tongue out. "Don't mock me. I can't help it. It feels like Christmas morning and my birthday and a shoe sale all rolled into one."

A dozen Blues made it outside before she did. When she stepped into the air and felt the snowflakes swirling around her skin, she shifted.

"Not without me," Valmont put a hand on her flank.

"Of course not." Once he was in place, she pushed off, flapping her wings and heading straight up into the sky. The snow was thicker the higher they went. The flakes skimmed along her scales like a caress. If the snow came down heavier, she wanted to roll in it on the ground. Wait a minute. Now she did sound like a puppy.

"Not too far," Valmont warned.

"Hang on tight." She twisted mid-air and dove toward the ground in a corkscrew spiral.

When she was a dozen feet from the ground, she banked right and zipped back up again altering her path to avoid the other Blues who had taken to the air. In the back of her mind, she thought about how it was strange that none of them were vying for territory or insisting they had the right of way. They were just enjoying themselves. Why couldn't it be like this all the time?

After a few more looping rolls and dives, Valmont said, "Clint and Ivy are walking to class if you plan to join them."

Nooooooo. "All I want to do is fly."

"Doesn't matter to me, but Mr. Stanton might mind."

Maybe Blues got a pass on the first snowy day. That would be the right thing for the Institute to do. Declare it a holiday, or a snow day, like they used to have at her old school.

No such luck. The Blues around her all headed toward the ground and shifted. Dang it.

"I reserve the right to pout about this." Bryn swooped low to the ground and flew toward the science building. She landed a few feet from Clint and Ivy, and crouching low, she used her wings to try and balance her landing. She tipped forward a bit and had to shuffle her feet, but all in all it wasn't an awful landing.

"Not bad," Clint said. "I was afraid you were going to do a face plant in the snow."

After Valmont dismounted, she shifted back to human form.

Ivy passed off her book bag. "Feel better?"

"Yes, but I'd still rather fly." Bryn entered the door Valmont held open for her. "I wonder if I could convince my grandmother that we need to declare the first snow day a holiday."

"You have my vote," Ivy said. "Any reason for a day off of school works for me."

Once they were seated in Mr. Stanton's class, the restlessness Bryn felt earlier dissipated. She still felt oddly cheery. Would snow always put her in a good mood? That would be a bonus.

The door to the adjoining classroom which was used as a storage closet opened, and Mr. Stanton came out accompanied by a man Bryn didn't recognize. He had the dark hair and dark skin of a Green dragon, but the look in his hazel eyes wasn't one of curiosity like most Greens. It was more like suspicion.

Were they having a guest lecturer? While Bryn studied the stranger, she realized he was taking note of every student in the room. One by one, he was making eye contact with each student looking them up and down. Not in a creepy, I-think-you're-cute way, but in an I-might-have-to-kill-you-if-you-annoy-me kind of way.

The sound of metal sliding against metal caught Bryn's attention. Valmont had drawn his sword. Gaze locked with the stranger's, he held the sword down to the side, like he was relaxed, but she could see the tension in the roped muscles of his neck.

The stranger grinned. "Don't worry, Knight. I'm not here for your dragon."

"I'm not worried," Valmont's tone was calm, even, and oddly threatening. "I'm giving you fair warning."

"You are delusional," the stranger said, "if you think your presence here concerns me."

Fire banked in Bryn's chest. Whoever this guy was, she didn't like him. "You have more than my knight to worry about."

"Bryn, calm down. Akbar is here by order of the Directorate. He is gathering information," Mr. Stanton said. "Nothing more."

"What sort of information?" Jaxon asked.

"I have a gift." Akbar continued to scan each student, studying them like he was waiting for one of them to mutate into a demon or something. "I can see what you don't want me to see." He pointed at Clint. "Say what you want to say. I can tell you have a remark to make which you think is clever."

Clint leaned back in his seat like he wasn't annoyed at being called out. "I've never met a Green who hoarded his intelligence. Some of them act annoyed or superior when they have to explain something, but none of them act...cryptic and judgmental and what's the word—stalker-ish, maybe?"

The atmosphere in the room shifted as the students seemed to realize Akbar could represent a threat.

"You never answered my question," Jaxon spoke in a superior my-father-is-the-head-of-the-Directorate tone. "Why are you studying us? What are you looking for?"

"A liar." Akbar continued to scan the students until he landed on Octavius. "And I believe I've found him."

A low growl came from Octavius's throat. It was echoed by his mate Vivian. Bryn and several other students also growled.

Akbar approached Octavius. "We need to talk. Come with me."

"Under whose authority do you demand my cooperation?" Octavius asked.

"The Directorate's," Akbar said.

"Then you should have papers," Jaxon said, "proving you are here on official Directorate business."

Akbar whipped around to face Jaxon. "I don't need papers."

Bryn stood. "If a Westgate says you need papers for Directorate business, then you need papers. Either show us the documents or get out."

Mr. Stanton stood there, not speaking, not intervening, not doing much of anything. What was wrong with him? Wait a minute. Was he smiling? Suspicion tickled Bryn's brain. "Teachers don't normally let guest speakers attack students. Is this some sort of test?"

Akbar's expression completely changed. His narrowed eyes widened. The hard flat line of his mouth softened and turned into a smile. "Well done, Bryn. And well done to the rest of you, too."

Clint raised his hand. "What just happened?"

Akbar leaned back against the desk and chuckled. "What happened is something I've been writing my thesis on. You all just proved it. Since the attacks, and since students were injured and have actually come back to school, Clan boundaries have softened. Your father, when he was a student here at the Institute," he pointed at Jaxon, "would never have stepped forward to defend someone from another Clan."

"You don't know that." Jaxon looked as pissed-off as ever.

"Actually, this study has been done for many years by different scientists, and the results have always been the same. Your father didn't object to a student being removed for questioning. No one did. None of them realized it was a test.

They assumed it was business as usual."

"Why did you pick me?" Octvious asked. He sounded as furious as Jaxon looked.

"You are a minority with the fewest Clan members to come to your defense," Akbar said. "So you were the perfect choice."

Octavius nodded like the answer satisfied him.

"Now if you'll excuse me, I have a thesis to complete." Akbar headed out the door.

Later that afternoon in Basic Movement, Jaxon came toward Bryn with a smile on his face.

"Is it me, or is that smile annoying as hell?" Valmont asked Clint.

"It's not just you," Clint responded.

Bryn moved to intercept Jaxon before a battle of words ensued. She'd had quite enough conflict this morning, thank you very much, so she walked over to meet him. "Hey, Jaxon. What's up?"

"What you said, this morning in Mr. Stanton's class, did you mean that?"

"I said a lot of things. What are you talking about?"

"That if I said something about Directorate protocol, I was right."

Where is he going with this? Bryn shrugged. "You've lived and breathed dragon politics since you were a kid. I figured you knew what you were talking about."

"It's good that you can acknowledge my superior intellect in these situations."

Bryn's mouth dropped open and then she laughed. Was he looking for some sort of ego boost? "Sure, you are superior in your knowledge of Directorate laws. Does that make you happy?"

He nodded. "Yes."

She crossed her arms over her chest. "I still fly faster than you." She couldn't let him get away with feeling too smug.

"I'm better with a sword." He tapped his chin like he was thinking. "That makes the score two to one in my favor."

What was he doing? "Sure. Two to one. Your favor. Go celebrate." With that, she turned back to Valmont, Clint, and Ivy who were standing by the treadmills.

Valmont stood stiff, shoulders back, staring at Jaxon with suspicion. "What was that?"

"He was all happy that I said he was the dictionary of Directorate law." Bryn shrugged. "I don't know what it was about."

"More like the douchebag of Directorate law," Valmont shot back.

Clint and Ivy laughed.

"No argument there," Bryn said. Although she couldn't help thinking that what Jaxon had done in Mr. Stanton's class showed he was a far better person than Ferrin, and for that she gave him a certain amount of respect, which seemed to annoy her knight.

"Are you worried I'll be wooed by his obnoxious holier-than-thou charm?" Bryn asked. "Because that isn't going to happen."

"Of course not," Valmont said, but there was an edge to his tone, which was only slightly less sharp than the blade strapped to his thigh.

Ivy clapped her hands. "Enough drama, people. It's time to joust."

A nervous, sick feeling pooled in Bryn's stomach. "I don't want to." She hadn't taken a turn on the joust since she'd been shish kabob-ed earlier in the year.

"A javelin through the thigh does have that effect on a person," Clint said.

"But," Valmont took her hand and pulled her toward the line, "sometimes you have to face your fears to overcome them."

"I don't suppose I could walk around my fears or ignore them?" She did a bob and weave maneuver to illustrate her point.

Valmont shook his head. "No."

"Damn." Bryn glanced at the pit with the foam blocks. Sweat beaded along her hairline as she remembered the wrenching ripping pain of the javelin driving through her thigh...all the way through. The image of the javelin tip protruding from her flesh featured in her nightmares on a regular basis.

Mrs. Anderson stood across the pit. "Bryn," she spoke in her loud teacher-voice, which rang throughout the gym, "I was wondering when you'd be ready to joust again."

Anyone who hadn't noticed Bryn turned to stare. Students already in line eyed Bryn like they expected her to cut and run or make some sort of argument. Both of those options sounded better than actually jousting again, but she'd be damned if she let them know that. Apparently, Blue dragon pride trumped common sense.

"Don't worry," Mrs. Anderson added, "I cleaned out the pits and replaced the foam blocks this morning. Nothing pointy is waiting for you if you fall."

"Good to know." She'd just have to make sure she didn't fall, ever.

Bryn climbed the ladder to the jousting platform, making sure to keep a calm expression on her face. This wasn't a big deal. She'd jousted dozens of times. Nothing bad had happened. The sharp pointy metal javelin through her thigh had been a fluke. It wouldn't happen again.

Once she reached the platform, she grabbed the jousting stick and did a few practice swings. Not a problem. She glanced at the foam pit below and fear banked the fire in her gut. She focused on snow and cold. Smoke drifting from her nostrils would give her fear away. Frost was a lot harder for any of those watching from down below to see.

"Are we jousting or not?" Her opponent, a Red female Bryn didn't recognize, called out from the other platform.

Bryn planted her feet hip-width apart for better balance. "Let's go."

The Red swung, and Bryn blocked before delivering a blow of her own. The other girl wobbled and then struck at Bryn's knees. Shuffling her feet, Bryn maintained her balance and swung at the girl's hips. They traded blow after blow, with neither of them making much progress or giving an inch.

The girl swung widely and clipped Bryn's temple, making her head ring. What the hell? That was out of bounds, and two could play at that game. Bryn thrust her jousting stick low between the girl's calves and yanked sideways, lifting the girl's left foot off the platform, causing her to pitch sideways, lose her balance, and take a header into the pit of foam blocks below.

From her perch, Bryn watched as the girl snarled up at her. For a second, it looked like her eyes flashed dark brown before returning to their normal shade of green. Bryn froze. Was this girl a Red-Black hybrid, or was it a trick of the light?

Bryn scrambled down the ladder and ran to the foam pit, but the girl was nowhere to be seen.

"That wasn't so bad, was it?" Valmont slung his arm around her shoulders.

Creeped out that she might have run across an unfriendly hybrid, Bryn leaned into his warmth for comfort and because it gave her a chance to whisper, "I think that girl may have been like me."

Valmont didn't respond right away. Maybe he didn't get it.

"Black and Red," Bryn whispered. "And none too friendly."

"Then we need to find her."

"I don't see her." Bryn scanned the gym, but there was no sign of the girl. "Can you spot her?

"No. Maybe we should ask Mrs. Anderson if she knows who it was."

A quick check with Mrs. Anderson didn't provide any answers. Bryn filled in Clint and Ivy.

"I didn't pay much attention to your opponent." Clint scratched his head. "In fact, I don't pay much attention to a lot of people. I file them away by Clan unless I know them. Why does that suddenly make me feel like a jerk?"

"I think the enemy is counting on us acting like that," Ivy said. "Since it's the way we've always acted."

"According to Akbar's experiment with Octavius, we're not acting the way dragons have always acted," Bryn said.

Clint touched his forehead. "Thinking big thoughts is making my head hurt."

Ivy bumped him with her hip. "Be serious. We need to figure this out."

"We're not going to figure it out here," Bryn whispered. "Let's meet in my room tonight to do homework and see what we can come up with."

• • •

After dinner, Clint and Ivy followed Bryn and Valmont back to their room.

"We're not really doing homework, are we?" Clint asked as Ivy pulled a notebook from her book bag.

"I am." Ivy fished a pen from the bottom of the bag. "I'm guessing you're going to stick with your standard wait-until-the-last-minute routine."

"How well you know me." Clint sat on the couch and put his feet up on the coffee table.

"Okay," Bryn sat on the other end of the couch while

Valmont stretched out on the floor, "let's make a list of ways the students are acting differently and what that might mean."

"Mean to whom?" Valmont asked.

"Good question." Bryn tapped her pen on the paper. "Some of this will tick off the Directorate. Some of it will tick off whoever has been attacking campus."

"If the Clan boundaries are softening, that isn't a bad thing," Valmont said. "Being friendlier toward each other doesn't hurt anything, right?"

"I wonder if Jaxon would agree with that statement." Clint stared up at the ceiling. "He helped Octavius, but if someone had told him his actions would undermine the Blues' status, I'm not sure he would have."

The instinct to defend Jaxon reared up inside Bryn. *What the hell is that about?* And why was Valmont studying her like he was waiting for her to do exactly that? Maybe she needed to throw him a bone. "I'm not sure, either."

Valmont's posture relaxed. *What is up with him? Is he jealous?* That was ridiculous. Then again, she was slated to marry Jaxon. If Valmont acted chummy with a girl he was supposed to end up with, she wouldn't love it, either. She'd have to be more careful around him. Being loyal to her knight was more important than being friends with Jaxon.

They talked in circles for the next hour while they finished homework. At eight o'clock, Ivy shut her notebook and smiled triumphantly. "All done."

Clint stood and stretched. "Good, then you can help me with mine."

Bryn laughed.

Ivy packed her book bag. "That's not how it works."

"I'm pretty sure it is." Clint grabbed her book bag and then held out his hand to help her to her feet. "Come on. It'll be fun."

"Right." Ivy rolled her eyes but let him pull her up and

lead her toward the terrace exit. "Goodnight, guys."

"Goodnight." Bryn locked the window behind her friends and returned to find Valmont had moved to the couch. She plopped down beside him. "Hey there."

"Hey." He sidled closer and put his arm around her shoulders.

Leaning into him was a habit now. It felt right. She closed her eyes and let the stress of the day drain away.

Valmont cleared his throat. "We need to talk."

Chapter Eighteen

So much for relaxing. "Why do I feel like this isn't going to be a fun conversation?"

"It looked like you were flirting with Jaxon today."

Laughter was the only logical response, and then she noticed the tight set of his jaw. "Sorry. The idea of flirting with Jaxon is beyond absurd." She grabbed his hand and gave what she hoped was a reassuring squeeze. "The only feelings I have for Jaxon are irritation and grudging respect."

"I hate him," Valmont spoke in a voice so quiet she barely heard him.

And the situation had gone from funny to tragic. "You have no reason to be jealous."

Valmont laughed, but it was a bitter sound. "You're going to marry him, aren't you?"

How could she answer that question? "There is the possibility I will *have* to marry him, but it won't be real. I will never want to sit and hold hands with him like this. I will never want him to kiss me. I will never care about him the way I care about you. Does that help?"

"It does." Valmont squeezed her hand. "But I still hate that you're going to be bound to him."

"Only on paper." How else could she reassure him? "I know it must be hard thinking about me being with him. The idea makes me nauseous, too, but don't let that distort what we have."

Valmont took a deep breath and then let it out. He raised his gaze and stared into Bryn's eyes. "And what do we have?"

And the moment was here. Time to step up and say what she felt and hope he felt the same way. Because if he didn't... She couldn't even think about that. It was too painful.

"What we have is something wonderful. Something worth holding on to. Something we shouldn't throw away based on insecurities and fear and the idiocy of the Directorate." She leaned in and brushed her nose against his. "You're my knight. I'm your dragon. No one can take that away from us."

Her heart thumped in her chest as she waited for him to respond. As every second ticked by, she feared she'd said too much.

"You're mine." His face was so close to hers she could feel the warmth of his breath as he spoke. He moved so his mouth lined up with hers and whispered, "My dragon." And then he kissed her. Magic flowed through their bond. The flying sensation zinged through her body, and she felt him draw back for a second before he wrapped his arms around her and pulled her close.

A knock on the door had Valmont jerking away from Bryn so quickly, it made her dizzy.

"What the hell?" Bryn shot him a dirty look.

He didn't seem to notice as he stalked to the door. "Who is it?"

There was no answer. Valmont put his hand on the doorknob.

"Don't." Bryn scrambled to her feet. "People have a habit

of wiring bombs to doorknobs around here."

"We walked through that door two hours ago."

"Yes, which would have given someone ample time to mess with it. Plus why would someone knock and then run away? The only reason to do that is to play a prank on someone or do something worse."

"You make a valid point." Valmont moved away from the door. "We could fly down and go in the front entrance, climb the stairs and see what's out there."

"We could." Bryn worked to phrase her next suggestion carefully. "Or I could call Rhianna. She's just down the hall."

"You know damn well Jaxon is probably with her and he would be the one coming to investigate."

"Maybe." Bryn tried to look like she didn't think that was the case even though she knew it was. What was the best diplomatic tact to take? "You choose. We can fly down and come back up the stairs to check it out, or we can make a phone call."

"No contest. We're flying."

Wow. She hadn't thought he'd go that route. Too late to second guess his male pride now. "Okay."

They climbed out the window to the terrace. Bryn shifted and whipped her tail around for Valmont to use it as a step. Once he was seated on her back, magic flowed between them, making her feel more connected to him and stronger because of him.

"Hold on." She launched herself off the terrace and up into the sky, reveling in the sensation of cool evening wind on her wings.

"The door is down that way," Valmont said.

The yearning to fly made the mystery of the door seem not so important. "Whatever is outside my door will still be there in a few minutes."

"Unless it's a bomb," Valmont said. "In which case the

entire building could be gone in a matter of minutes."

Well, crap. She couldn't argue his logic, but that didn't mean she had to be happy about it. "Way to ruin a perfectly good flight."

"You know I'm right."

Why did she have the childish urge to mock him by repeating what he said in a superior tone? That wasn't like her. It wasn't nice. Not that she was always sweetness and light, but this was Valmont. *Gah.* The desire to fly was messing with her head.

"Fine." She dived toward the ground and landed in the grassy area across from the dorm entrance. She dug her talons into the turf, in an attempt to steady her landing and ended up jolting forward ripping up hunks of sod. She really needed to figure this landing thing out. Valmont dismounted, and she shifted back.

Without commenting, Valmont helped her stomp the chunks of sod back in place and then they headed inside the Blue dorm. Heads turned, about a third of them acknowledged her with a quick glance and then went back to what they were doing. A few gave a polite nod. Mostly those who she'd healed after the attack over Christmas break. She mirrored their polite nods. The rest of the Blues stared through her. *Gee, that never gets old.*

She headed up the stairs with Valmont by her side.

"None of them make eye contact with me," Valmont said.

"I'm familiar with that game." Bryn laced her fingers through his. "Don't let them bother you."

"I really want to punch some of them."

"We're on the same page." They made it to the second landing and headed down the hall toward Bryn's door. On the floor, there was a plain white legal-size envelope like bills came in. Bryn nudged it with her right foot. "It's too flat to be a bomb, right?"

"I think so." Valmont leaned down for a better view. "Should I pick it up?"

"Us standing here staring at it isn't accomplishing anything, so, I guess you should."

He grabbed it and flipped it over. "No writing on the front."

Bryn stuck her key in the lock. "Let's get back inside."

Once they were seated at the library table in the living room, Bryn gestured at the envelope. "You want to do the honors?"

"Sure." He drew his sword and used it like a giant letter opened, slicing through the flap of envelope.

Bryn chuckled. "I'm not sure knights of old would approve of that maneuver."

"Sometimes when I'm bored, I find domestic uses for my sword. It cuts a mean slice of pepperoni."

The piece of notebook paper Valmont pulled out had three words scratched on it in pencil. "Don't trust them."

Bryn grabbed the paper and flipped it over like there might be more to the message on the other side. "Don't trust who? What kind of stupid message is this?"

"Why would someone give you this tonight?"

"I don't know." Bryn stalked over to the phone. "We need a Green." She dialed Garret and explained the situation.

"I'd love to help, but I won't make it there and back before curfew." Garret sighed. "If I could still fly it wouldn't be a problem."

Her heart ached for him, losing the ability to fly would be devastating. And then an interesting idea popped into her head. "Valmont rides on my back. Do you have a friend you can ask to fly you over?"

Dead silence met her comment. Crap. Had she offended him? Now what could she say?

Laughter came through the phone line.

"Garret?"

"I mean…it's just…it's such a simple solution." Garret sighed. "And I never would have thought of it."

"I guess that's one of the advantages of being an outsider. You think differently."

"I wouldn't say you're an outsider, anymore. Not after your grandparents recognized you." Garret was back to his analytical self. "About the note, do you feel like it represents an immediate threat?"

"No. It's more of an annoying mystery."

"I'd like to practice flying with a friend and take a few trial runs before I head off across campus. Why don't you bring the note to class tomorrow?"

"Will do." After saying good-bye, she hung up the phone with a sense of satisfaction. She may not have solved her own problem, but she'd given Garret a way to overcome a huge stumbling block in his life. Who could he talk into being his pseudo-flyer?

• • •

In the hall outside Mr. Stanton's classroom, Bryn showed the paper to Clint, Ivy, and Garret.

"That's nice and vague." Clint tapped the paper with his finger. "Couldn't they have given a name? How are you supposed to know who not to trust?"

"That may be the point." Garret held the paper up to the light and squinted at it. "I think this came from a student's notebook. If you look closely, you can see the indents of writing from the page in front of it. Someone give me a pencil."

Ivy grabbed a yellow number two pencil from her book bag. "Here you go."

Garret reached for the pencil with his good arm, which was still holding the paper and then froze. Pain flared in his eyes.

"I was going to shade over the paper to see the indentations, but someone with two functional limbs will have to do it."

Everyone stood still for a moment. Ivy reached for the paper in Garret's hand. "I'll hold the paper, you use the pencil."

Garret nodded and did as Ivy suggested. He traced over the back of the note with the flat side of the lead, shading in a large area. The outline of letters appeared in the indents made from the page on top.

"Can you see someone's name?" Bryn asked. That would make figuring this out a whole lot easier.

"No." Garret exchanged items with Ivy and held the paper up to the light. "These look like notes from an advanced economics class, which means the paper came from an older student's notebook. No one our age would be enrolled in this class."

Valmont tapped his fingers on the pommel of his sword. "And what does that tell us?"

"It tells us whoever sent this note isn't one of Bryn's immediate acquaintances. My best guess is someone wants to make you question who you can trust. The whole thing is probably baseless and meant to cause anxiety."

"Well, it worked." Smoke shot from Bryn's nostrils. "I have enough to worry about on my own. The idea of someone doing this just to mess with me really pisses me off."

"Can I keep the note?" Garret asked Bryn.

"Sure."

For the rest of the day, Bryn felt like she had to keep looking over her shoulder. Nothing strange happened. No bogeymen leapt out at her from dark corners. She almost wished someone would come at her. Her nervous system was on high alert, her muscles felt twitchy, and she was ready to fight.

When Ivy grabbed her arm and said, "Look," Valmont

drew his sword and Bryn produced a ball of fire in her hand.

It took Bryn a few seconds to realize Ivy was pointing at a poster for the upcoming Valentine's Day dance.

Ivy pointed at the fireball in Bryn's hand. "Overreact much?"

"Not funny." Bryn closed her fist, extinguishing the flames. Valmont re-sheathed his sword.

"Sorry, I didn't meant to startle you," Ivy clasped her hands together, "but it's a dance."

Ivy said this like Bryn would say, "It's a bottomless cup of coffee," or "It's a pie the size of a Mack truck's tire."

"A dance… Yippee," Clint deadpanned.

"Do not rain on my I-love-dances parade. It's a small price to pay for being my boyfriend."

Clint laughed. "You're right."

A nervous feeling settled in Bryn's middle. It felt like goldfish were swimming around inside her stomach. "Dances have never been very good for me."

"What are you talking about? I rescued you at the last dance." Valmont didn't sound pleased.

"Hello? Christmas Ball…death and destruction…ring a bell?"

Valmont ducked his head. "I thought you were talking about—"

"I wasn't," Bryn cut him off. Even though she *had* been thinking of Zavien a little bit. "So, will you fulfill your knightly duties by escorting me to the terrifying Valentine's Day dance?"

He pretended to think about it and then gave a wicked grin. "Can I pick out your dress?"

"You can help."

Harmony restored, they continued walking back to Clint and Ivy's dorm. When they reached the sidewalk outside the building, harmony was shot straight to hell at the sight of

Zavien walking hand in hand with Nola.

For a moment, both groups of people froze.

"Nice night for a walk, isn't it?" Valmont said.

Zavien opened his mouth, but nothing came out, like he was an actor who had forgotten his line. He cleared his throat. "It is."

"We haven't seen either of you around the theater during the rebuilding," Ivy said.

Nola shook her head. "I don't want to see it before it's complete. It's too distressing."

Okay, time to jump in and say something since everyone else was talking. "My grandmother's designs are beautiful. I think you'll love the theater when it's done."

"I'm sure we will." Zavien tugged on Nola's hand. "We need to go. Goodnight."

"Goodnight." Bryn and her friends echoed.

Talking to Zavien when she'd been concerned for Clint and Ivy's welfare was one thing. Making small talk with him and Nola was too freaking weird.

Bryn squeezed Valmont's hand. "That wasn't too awkward, was it?"

"I no longer want to run him through with my sword." Valmont grinned. "Jaxon, however, is another story."

Everyone laughed. Bryn felt like some sort of emotional slate had been wiped clean. Truth be told, she'd done all she could to avoid bumping into Zavien and Nola since they'd returned from Christmas break. It's not like she wanted to go on a double date with them, but knowing she didn't have to avoid them anymore was a relief.

. . .

Bryn sat on Ivy's couch with Valmont and looked around. It was weird how the room seemed cramped to her now. Good lord, she would *not* turn into an uppity Blue. She'd loved these rooms when she lived here. They might be half the size of her dorm, but they were fine.

"Bryn?" Valmont poked her on the thigh.

"What?" She blinked. "Sorry lost in thought."

"About?" he prompted.

"I was trying to figure out how we were going to shop for dresses for the Valentine's dance when we can't leave campus."

"That's what I said while you were in La La Land." Ivy laughed.

Now she really did take a moment to think about it. "I hate that my first thought is that a group of students going to Dragon's Bluff would be a target."

Valmont frowned. "Didn't Jaxon say something like that once before?"

"He did. I can't help but think having a dance makes a great target, too. Help me. There's something wrong with my brain. My Blue DNA won't let me have fun anymore."

"You've been through some rough stuff," Clint said. "That's bound to leave anyone a bit jaded."

"Listen up," Ivy said. "The dance will be fun. Shopping for dresses will be fun. I expect you all to get with the program."

"You're right," Bryn said. "But before we go running to my grandmother about shopping, let's see if someone else steps up to solve this problem. I don't want to wave my grandmother card around the same way Jaxon waves his my-father-is-speaker-for-the-Directorate flag in everyone's faces."

The next day, in the hall outside Proper Decorum, Rhianna gestured for Bryn to come speak with her.

"What's up?" Bryn asked, ignoring Jaxon who stood scowling a few feet away.

"I'm sure you're aware of the Valentine's Day dance."

"Yes, I saw the poster." Bryn crossed her fingers for luck

and hoped this was going where she wanted it.

"I've been speaking with some of the females in our dorm, and we all need new dresses."

Bryn didn't think "need" was the correct term, but whatever.

"I made a few calls, and we arranged for several of the boutiques in Dragon's Bluff to bring their inventory to campus this weekend."

"That's great." One thought plagued her. "Did you ask any normal stores to bring dresses?"

Rhianna tilted her head to the side. "I don't understand what you mean."

Crap. "I'm not sure if the girls from different Clans can afford to pay boutique prices rather than regular store prices."

Rhianna laughed, which seemed sort of rude and totally unlike Rhianna, and then she noticed Jaxon shaking his head at her like she was an idiot.

"What?" Bryn snapped.

"The difference between the boutiques and the stores on Main Street isn't necessarily the price," Rhianna said. "I mean there are some higher end items, but the real difference is the level of service."

"Oh." Bryn frowned. "You mean the way the saleslady fawns all over you and brings clothes to the dressing room instead of letting you pick things out on your own?"

Rhianna nodded.

Now she felt sort of stupid. In the human world, boutiques were expensive and trendy and out of reach for normal income families. Here, boutiques were snobby in the way they waited on you, but the prices were the same. That seemed oddly civilized. "What if a girl from another Clan went to one of the boutiques? Would the saleslady act the same?"

"Someone from another Clan wouldn't be let in the door," Jaxon said. "It's a service offered only to the Blues."

And the Blues were back to being the insufferable elite she knew them to be. Bryn opened her mouth to speak and decided she didn't want to start this argument because it was a no-win situation, but she couldn't let it go. "That's a whole level of absurd I don't want to get into right now."

Jaxon opened his mouth to speak but Rhianna cut him off before he uttered a syllable. "Please tell your friends and spread the word that we'll have dresses and dressing rooms set up in the Ballroom C at the theater building Friday night."

"Thanks. I'll pass the information along."

Chapter Nineteen

Bryn sorted through dresses on one of the two-dozen circular racks set up in the ballroom, waiting for something to catch her eye. Too short, too frilly, too sparkly, too revealing, too—

"I like that one." Valmont pointed at the dress she'd passed because the V-neck would come down to somewhere around her navel.

"Not going to happen." Bryn kept flipping. Too boring. Too ruffly. Too beige. And then she found it. A midnight-blue sheath dress with a silver choker-type collar. "This is my dress."

Valmont eyed the garment critically. Then he reached over and touched the side of the dress where the thigh high slit was located. "Works for me."

"You're such a guy." Bryn elbowed him.

"Guilty." He grinned, and his dimple appeared.

Kiss him, her subconscious screamed. But they were in public, so she couldn't do that. Which sucked.

"Look what I found." Ivy bounded toward Bryn holding a strawberry-red strapless dress.

"I love it." Bryn glanced around. "We need to find an open dressing room."

Small canvas tent-like structures had been set up all along one wall of the ballroom. Girls stood in line waiting for an open room. "I guess we play pick-a-line."

Ivy pointed to the closest one. "They're all about the same."

As they waited in line, Bryn checked out the dresses the other girls had chosen. She was grateful to see she liked her selection the best. Once they made it into the dressing room, Bryn changed as quickly as possible. The idea that the temporary dressing room could collapse and the entire room would see her standing there in her green bra decorated with pink flamingos made her cringe.

Ivy modeled her dress for Bryn. "What do you think?"

"That color is amazing on you." With Ivy's pale skin and dark hair, she looked like a fairy tale princess. Bryn finished fastening her dress and checked the mirror. "I swear, I still expect to see striped hair when I look in the mirror. This blond person staring back at me with the one red streak doesn't seem right."

"But the dress is amazing," Ivy said. "Should we show the guys?"

"I don't know. There were a lot of girls in line behind us."

"You're right." Ivy changed out of her dress and back into her clothes. "Plus, this way there's still a little mystery."

When they emerged from the dressing room in their normal clothing, Valmont frowned. "Didn't it fit?"

"It did."

"Then why didn't you show us?" Clint asked.

Bryn gestured at the girls still waiting in line. "We didn't want to hog the room."

"And this way we remain women of mystery," Ivy added.

Clint smiled and shrugged like it was no big deal.

Valmont's lips pressed together in a thin line, but he didn't say anything. After parting ways with her friends, Bryn and Valmont returned to her dorm room where she headed straight to her armoire to hang up her new dress. For some reason, Valmont followed behind her like he was waiting for her to do or say something. But she didn't have a freaking clue what he wanted. "Is something wrong?"

He stared up at the ceiling. "I'm trying to figure out how to say this without starting a fight."

Great. She was never going to another dance again. Crossing her arms over her chest, she waited.

"Who are you wearing that dress for?"

What was he talking about? "I don't understand the question."

He reached into her armoire where the copper dress from the fall dance still hung. "Did you buy this dress with someone in mind?"

"Ivy forced me to try on a dress even though I didn't think I was going. I loved it, so I bought it."

"So you didn't buy this for Zavien?"

Seriously? "I bought the dress because I liked it. Zavien didn't have anything to do with it." Liar, her subconscious screamed. "This dress," she touched the navy-blue dress, "was bought to attend the Valentine's Day dance with you. So this dress should rank higher on whatever weird boyfriend rating system you're using."

Valmont froze. "Did you just call me your boyfriend?"

And now the situation had reached a whole other level of crap-tastic-ly awkward. She ducked her head. "That's kind of how I think of you."

One thousand one, one thousand two, one thousand three…she counted seconds while waiting for a response, which so far he wasn't making.

"Bryn?" Valmont whispered.

Her stomach twisted and pitched like she was riding a roller coaster. She was afraid to make eye contact, so she kept her head down. "What?"

His warm hand touched her chin and pressed up, signaling he wanted her to look at him. She met his gaze, which was far too serious, and it felt like the room shifted under her feet. She forced a laugh. "Forget I said that. I shouldn't have assumed you were interested in that title." *And why in the hell isn't he interrupting me and telling me he wants to be my boyfriend?*

"Remember what we said about how even if we have an argument or a misunderstanding that I'll still be your knight, so there's no reason to become sick?"

She nodded and backed away from him. "Yep. Not going to get sick, but you should go." Because she was going lose it and either cry or flash-fry him.

"You want me to go?" He seemed surprised.

Fire banked in her gut. She closed her eyes and took a deep breath. A memory reared up and made her laugh. "Jaxon once told me what I want is irrelevant. I guess he was right."

Valmont bristled. "Excuse me?"

"Don't even think about getting mad because I mentioned Jaxon. Some of the things he's told me have been painfully true. This happens to be another one of those times."

Valmont closed his eyes and rubbed the bridge of his nose. "How did we end up here?"

"You followed me into my room."

He looked at her likes she was being ridiculous. "No. I mean how did we end up in this situation, irritated with one another over something stupid, again?"

So, her thinking of him as her boyfriend was stupid. Flames crawled up the back of her throat. She took a moment and pushed them back down, but smoke drifted from her lips as she spoke. "You know what? Forget about it. I'll never refer to you as anything but my knight ever again. Happy?"

"No." He closed the gap between them and placed his hands on her shoulders. "I'm about as far from happy as I can be, because I can't ever really be your boyfriend."

"You can't? Why not?"

"Because every time we walk out that damn door, I can't be anything but your knight."

Bryn latched onto the light at the end of this dark murky tunnel. "Wait a minute. Are you saying you want to be my boyfriend, but you're mad because we can't act that way in public?"

"Of course that's what I'm saying."

"Thank God." She felt her body sag with relief. She moved forward and leaned her head against his chest. "I thought you meant you didn't want to be my boyfriend."

"How could you—"

She growled, and it wasn't a friendly growl. "You just traumatized me. So I suggest you shut up and hug me."

She felt his chest vibrate with laughter, but he wrapped his arms around her and whispered, "We need to work on our communication skills."

"Agreed."

• • •

The Valentine's Day dance seemed to provide the distraction students needed to avoid thinking about war and politics. Girls talked about their dresses. Boys griped about their tuxedos. All in all, the balance of normal teenage drama in the universe seemed to be restored.

So of course, Jaxon had to do something to mess the situation up. At least that's what she figured he was doing since he showed up at her door after classes.

Instinct told her she shouldn't invite him inside, but she couldn't leave him standing in the hall, either. "Hello, Jaxon."

She backed up so he could enter. "To what do we owe the honor of your presence?"

"There's something we need to discuss. Privately." He directed his gaze at Valmont. "Tell your knight to give us some privacy."

Where does he get off? "Number one, he's not deaf. And two, whatever you have to say to me you can say in front of him."

"No. I can't." Jaxon crossed his arms over his chest. "And I'm not leaving until we talk."

"That's a threat I'll actually respect." Valmont stood. "In the interest of getting rid of him, I'll wait in my room."

Bryn wanted to tell Valmont she didn't want to speak to Jaxon alone, but that wasn't a choice. Once her knight had relocated, she walked over and sat at the library table, gesturing that Jaxon should join her because she was tired of everything being on his terms. "What new drama is about to befall my life?"

"We need to discuss the dance." His tone was so serious, she wanted to laugh.

"Okay. What about it?"

His gaze darted to Valmont's door. "It's essential everyone believes your relationship with Valmont is appropriate."

She so did not like where this was going. "What exactly do you mean by that?"

"You must appear to be friends and nothing more." Jaxon was so adamant, she took a moment to analyze the situation. And it came to her. "Are you worried about how it will look if your, God-forbid-possible-future-wife, is out on a real date with someone?"

"Yes. Everyone knows our lineage came back a match. While I prefer to live in the land of denial, we still need to be aware of our behavior in public which means you cannot undermine my status by being seen as romantically involved with someone else."

A base drum started beating in her temples. "I get the whole I-must-appear-to-be-the-Alpha-male-to-protect-Rhianna routine. But that doesn't mean I'm giving up on having a fun night. Your ego will have to deal with it. Besides you'll be on a real date with Rhianna."

He opened his mouth to speak.

"I swear to God if you give me that no-one-cares-what-I-do-because-there's-a-double-standard line of bullshit again, I will blast you across the room."

His eyes narrowed. "I came here as a courtesy to you."

And now he'd stumped her. "How do you figure?"

"If I approached you in front of other students to speak about your knight and someone overheard, your grandfather would have Valmont thrown off campus so fast it would make your head spin."

What the crap was he talking about? "In case you forgot, it was my grandmother who asked Valmont to watch over me."

"Yes, but if your grandfather decided the situation was inappropriate, he could end it. He outranks your grandmother. Haven't you figured that out, yet?"

"No, he doesn't." Bryn smacked her hand down on the table. "If my grandmother wants something, she makes it happen. No matter if my grandfather agrees or not. In case *you* haven't noticed, the Blue females let the men think they are in charge, to save their egos. The women control things behind the scenes and don't brag about it."

"Or maybe," Jaxon placed both his palms flat on the table and leaned into Bryn's personal space, "the males let the females believe they have some influence in order to keep the peace."

If that was true, she was so going to get herself elected to the Directorate, if for no other reason than to piss Jaxon off.

"That's a nice little fantasy you have there, but it still doesn't change the situation. I'm going to the Valentine's dance with Valmont. We will behave however we want."

Jaxon pushed to his feet. "Just remember, if your grandfather gets wind of any inappropriate behavior, Fonzoli's might burn to the ground."

Fire climbed up the back of Bryn's throat. Sparks shot from her mouth as she spoke. "Are you threatening Valmont's family?"

"No. I'm warning you. I'm trying to explain the facts of life, which after all this time, you somehow still fail to grasp. Your grandfather is ruthless, and he will hurt Valmont if you give him reason to do so."

Bryn closed her eyes and focused on pushing the fire back down. "So even though you're an insensitive ass-hat, you're warning me away from behavior that might endanger Valmont's safety."

"Yes. So I suggest you keep the name-calling to a minimum, keep your knight in line, and try not to do anything that will reflect poorly on your Clan."

"The Blues aren't my Clan." The words slipped from Bryn's mouth before she thought about them. While she thought of her grandparents as family, the Clan at large didn't give her the warm fuzzies.

Jaxon's eyes narrowed. "Those words are treason. Never say anything so disloyal ever again. Not even your grandfather could save you, nor would he want to if anyone heard you utter such blasphemy. You should be grateful the Directorate afforded you such an honor. Otherwise you would be Clanless. It's not like the Reds offered to take you in."

Why hadn't the Reds offered to take me in? She'd never thought about it before. Maybe because her father's family was all dead, and she had no blood relation left to speak for her. Still, she hated to let Jaxon think he had the upper hand. "The Oranges offered to take me, so it's not like I was desperate for the Blues to step in."

"Fine. Run away and live with the Orange Clan. While you're at it, take your knight with you. If both of you disappeared, my life would be vastly improved."

Valmont's bedroom door popped open. He strolled out with a cynical smile on his face. "I'm good with that plan."

Hands on her hips, Bryn sighed. "While getting away from Jaxon sounds divine, I can't abandon my grandmother."

"She could come with us," Valmont said.

Like that would happen. Time to come back from fantasyland to sucky reality. "I'll try to restrain myself at the dance." She pointed at Jaxon. "Thanks for raining on my parade. Now, go away."

Jaxon slammed the door on his way out.

"I really want to hit him," Valmont stated with utmost sincerity.

"Get in line."

"What you told him, about the Blues not being your Clan, why did you say that?"

His tone was normal, but his disapproval came through loud and clear. "Seriously? Most of the Blues still hate me, and I'm pretty sure they'd do a happy dance if I fell into a rift and was crushed to death."

"Rhianna, Lillith, and your grandmother are good to you."

What the hell? "Why are you defending the Blue Clan and trying to make me feel like crap?"

"Family is important." Valmont ran his hand down his face. "Maybe I'm only saying this because I miss mine."

Rather than soothing her irritation his words fanned the flames. "To paraphrase, I'm disloyal, and it's my fault you miss your family. Thanks for a lovely evening." She stalked toward her bedroom.

"Bryn, wait." Valmont jogged across the room and stood between her and the bedroom door. "I'm sorry. I didn't mean to sound judgmental. I was stating a fact. I miss my family. You don't have to love the Blue Clan. If you ever find a group of hybrids to run off with, I will be by your side. For now, the Blues are your dysfunctional, snotty, elitist family, and I think you have to claim them as your Clan. As your knight, it feels like my duty to protect you by recommending you acknowledge this completely irritating, yet strong and possibly protective, alliance."

Where in the hell was this coming from? "Should I make a sign that says I'm proud to be Blue?"

He pointed his finger at her like he was about to give her a lecture, but then he stopped. "I need you to take a deep breath and listen to my words. As a knight, my job is to protect my dragon. Having my dragon aligned with an entire Clan of dragons makes sense strategically. This isn't me telling you to act a certain way. This is me recognizing a better battle strategy."

Her anger level went from a rolling boil to a soft simmer. "That makes sense. It still ticks me off, but it makes sense."

"So we're okay?" He didn't sound sure of himself.

"Honestly, I think we're both candidates for a psychological study on magical bonding making people a bit emotionally unstable, but other than that, we're good."

He hugged her to his chest. She inhaled his warm sunshine and leather smell, which allowed some of the tension to drain from her muscles. "I feel stupid worrying about the dance when we still don't know if there is anything worth investigating under the library."

"After what happened with Clint, and knowing Ferrin keeps an office on the top floor, I'm less inclined to go poking around," Valmont said. "The best option would be a teacher sanctioned trip to the archives."

"I do owe Mr. Stanton a research paper. Maybe I can talk to him about it."

• • •

Friday Mr. Stanton asked Bryn to stay late after Elemental Science. Once the last student had left the room, he waved her up to his desk. "You need to pick a topic for your research paper."

"About that. I heard there were vaults below the libraries. I'd love to see them."

He chuckled. "Most of the information down there is dry and literally dusty."

"Can I see for myself?"

"Given your personality, if I don't allow you access, you'll fantasize about sneaking in. So, here." He grabbed a piece of paper and scribbled a few lines on it. "Here is a list of topics for you to choose from which might give you an excuse to access the library archives. Talk to Miss Enid. She can arrange that for you. Don't blame me when you see how boring the information is. I helped Miss Enid catalog some of those files years ago, and it was almost coma-inducing."

"Thanks," Hopefully she'd find something more useful than information for a paper. She took the list and headed for the door.

Valmont read over her shoulder as they walked to the library. "Lineage checks, Clan population, and historical taxation? None of those sound interesting."

"Maybe Miss Enid can help us pick the least boring topic."

When they reached the front desk of the library, Miss Enid frowned at the note. "I'm sure you are aware that you'll need access to the vaults to research these topics."

Bryn nodded. "That was sort of the plan."

"And you know asking for access to the vaults will raise a

few red flags with the Directorate."

Valmont drummed his fingers on the desktop. "I want to see what's in the vaults, but not at the expense of Bryn's safety. Do you think pursuing this quest, for lack of a better term, will endanger her?"

"Knowing Bryn, she won't rest until she sees the vaults for herself. As her knight, I hold you responsible for making sure she isn't out after curfew."

Listening to them discuss her like she wasn't present was delightful. "I am standing right here, you know."

"I know you're here," Miss Enid said, "as does anyone watching the camera feeds on the top floor."

Bryn scanned the ceiling for a red light or a mirrored dome or any clue that a camera was present and recording her every move.

"You won't see them, but they will see you," Miss Enid said. "After Christmas, the Blue Clan claimed offices on the top floor and had surveillance security cameras installed throughout the library."

"Why?" Valmont asked.

"The more offices they have, the less likely people with ill-intent will be able to find them."

"To sum up, whatever we do in the library is being recorded and analyzed." Bryn frowned. "I still need to see what's in the vaults if you can make it happen."

Miss Enid typed on her computer. "I'll submit a form saying you would like to do a research paper on lineage checks. Given your impending union with Jaxon, no one will suspect you aren't interested in that topic." Her fingers flew across the keyboard, and then she hit enter. "Now we wait. I'll let you know when I have their answer."

It took three days for Bryn to hear back from Miss Enid about the vaults. "You can visit the vaults this evening for two hours," the librarian said from behind the front desk. "Are you wearing a watch?"

"I am." Valmont held out his wrist.

"Good. Follow me." Miss Enid signaled Bryn and Valmont should follow her to the offices behind the desk. They walked through a room with a copy machine and entered the back storage area, which housed damaged books waiting to be repaired. There was no other door visible.

"Here we are." Miss Enid smiled at Bryn and held out the key.

"Are we playing guess where the hidden door is?" Valmont asked.

"Look down." Miss Enid pointed at the floor.

Hinges and a keyhole on the floor were the only clue a trapdoor lay underneath. The edges matched seamlessly with the hardwood floor. Bryn took the key, knelt and placed it in the lock. She turned it hard to the right. There was an audible click, and then the trap door swung up and open, revealing a narrow set of corkscrew stairs.

Bryn stepped down onto the first step and then paused. "Valmont grab the key."

"You won't need it." Miss Enid retrieved the key and pocketed it. "The locks are meant to keep people out, not trap them inside."

"Are you sure?" Bryn asked. "The universe seems to have a strange sense of humor when it comes to messing with me."

"True." Miss Enid pointed down the staircase. "But the trapdoor is the only way in and out of this area."

"The blueprints of the library showed vaults under all four corners of the building," Valmont said. "Does this lead to all of them?"

"It leads to the area you're allowed to access." Miss Enid emphasized the *allowed* part. "Do not push your luck right now searching for something which may not exist. I applaud your quest for knowledge, but the Directorate is on high alert. Do not give them a reason to doubt your grandfather's loyalty."

It was on the tip of Bryn's tongue to say her grandfather had nothing to do with this, when she remembered her grandmother saying everything she did would reflect on them. "I'll be careful." That was the only promise she was willing to make.

"Let me go first." Valmont drew his sword. "As Miss Enid said, these are strange times."

He descended the stairs. As the sole of his boot hit each step, the rim of the next step lit up, providing enough light to see the step in front of him, but nothing of what lay beyond. The stairwell was so narrow Valmont's shoulders almost brushed the stone walls.

"Were people smaller when they built this?" Bryn asked.

"It's probably for defensive purposes. Any battles would be one on one. No group could sneak up on whoever was guarding the stairs."

"Good thing I'm not claustrophobic." The stairs curved back on themselves five times before they reached a stone landing four feet wide where a wall sconce shaped like a torch flared to life. "Nice theatrics." Bryn inhaled stale air that made her mouth taste like dust. "We should have brought bottled water."

"I doubt drinks are allowed in the archives." Valmont moved forward down the hall, which was wide enough for them to walk side by side.

The stone of the floor and walls were mortared together with something that sparkled, like ground-up diamonds. What was that about?

The hall ended in a large wooden door with iron hinges.

Valmont touched the hinges. "Look familiar?"

Bryn nodded. "Looks like the magical Maintenance door on the first floor. I don't suppose you see any weird cryptic messages."

"Not this time." Valmont grabbed the handle and turned, pulling on the door. It opened without making a sound. "I expected those hinges to creak loud enough for the entire campus to hear."

The lights in the room beyond lit up, revealing floor to ceiling bookshelves and glassed-in cabinets containing museum qualify artifacts.

Valmont pointed at a saddle with an intricate pattern of frozen flames created from embedded silver. "I want one."

"I'll remember that next Christmas." Bryn investigated the next glass case, which held a sword with the same frozen flame pattern etched onto the blade. "You might want to check this out before you make your list for Santa."

Valmont came to stand by Bryn and stared into the case with a longing that almost made her jealous.

"Would you like some time alone with your new girlfriend?" Bryn teased.

He backed up a step, shaking his head like he was trying to clear it.

"What's wrong?"

He pointed at the sword. "I'd swear there's some sort of magnetic pull from that sword, like it wants to find a new knight." He held his hand toward the glass. "Can you feel it?"

Bryn moved in closer and stared at the sword, putting her palm flat on the glass. "No. I mean it's beautiful, but I don't feel the need to possess it. Let's investigate the bookshelves and see if we can find the information for my paper and something about hybrids."

Valmont pointed at the old-fashioned mahogany card catalog. "Do we start there?"

"I guess." Fifteen minutes later Bryn had a newfound respect for anyone who'd done research before Google. "Why isn't lineage under L?"

"Did you try Directorate Lineage checks?"

"Yes, and marriage and laws."

"What does lineage check for, in the simplest sense?" Valmont asked.

Bryn racked her brain. "They talk about checking bloodlines." She moved over to the B drawer. Halfway through blood-related titles, which there seemed to be a disturbing amount of, she found "Bloodlines: Lineage Checks."

"Finally. This card says the books start with number 762 and go through 894."

"That narrows it down," Valmont headed for the bookshelves. After staring at a row of books, he sighed. "Did the card catalog tell you where the numbers were located on the books?"

"They're not on the spine, like normal library books?" Bryn moved to the closest shelf and grabbed a green leather bound book. The spine was bare. No title. No number. "It feels like the Directorate is mocking anyone who finds these books, like maybe you found our secret stash, but we removed all the titles to spite you." She flipped the book open to the first page, *The Best of Botany*. She slammed it shut. "There has to be an easier way."

When Valmont didn't respond, she glanced up. No knight. "Valmont?"

"Over here," he called from the other side of the ginormous card catalog. "You need to see this."

Chapter Twenty

Goose bumps broke out on Bryn's upper arms. "Why do I get the feeling this isn't a good thing?" She walked around the card catalog and found Valmont staring at the wall.

"Can you see it?" he asked.

"I'm going to go with no, since all I see is the wall."

"It's the same as upstairs. 'Only those who have given their all may enter. Those who have taken everything must give to see.'"

"And it's just written on the wall?"

"No. There's an outline of a door." He held his hand out to her. "Come here. I want to test a theory. I think the message refers to a knight and his dragon."

She moved closer and held his hand even though she didn't like how the description made it sound like the knight gave while the dragon only took. "Okay. Now what?"

He unsheathed his sword. "I think it want's your blood."

She did not like where this was going. "Like in Mr. Stanton's class?"

He pulled the hand he held toward the wall. "I'll hold the

sword. You touch it."

It went against her instinct to willingly touch the razor sharp weapon, but Valmont would do it for her, so she slid her finger down the edge of the blade, flinching as it sliced through her skin.

The sword glowed red as Bryn's blood trickled down the blade.

"Touch the wall right there." Valmont pointed at a blank piece of stone four feet off the ground with the tip of his sword.

A tingling sensation started on Bryn's scalp the closer her finger came to the wall. When she touched the stone, an electric shock made her wince. The smell of hot copper filled the air. And the wall was gone. In its place was a wooden door with iron hinges. "No way."

Valmont grabbed the handle and pulled. This door did creak from disuse. No lights came on, but the scent of dust and decay drifted out to them.

"I don't think anyone has been here in a long time." Bryn produced a fireball in her right hand and leaned in the doorway, scanning the area for anything dangerous.

A long wooden table took up the center of the room. Books were stacked on the table and spilled over onto the floor.

"Seems safe enough." Valmont crossed the threshold batting cobwebs out of his way. He pointed at a fat candle in a sconce on the wall. "Light that."

"Sure." Bryn lit the candle with her flame. The sound of creatures scurrying across the floor made her shiver. When something scrambled over her foot, she jumped backward.

"It's only a mouse," Valmont said.

She might be a kick-ass shape-shifting dragon, but a mouse crawling over her foot still gave her the heebie-jeebies.

Valmont laughed, like he knew what she was thinking.

"Shut up." As the flame on the candle grew, light filled the room. How was that possible? And then she saw it. The wall behind the sconce held a large mirror, which directed the light across the room to another mirror, where it bounced across the room again. "That," she pointed at the candle, "is ingenious."

"And probably a bit magical," Valmont said.

From the table, Bryn picked up a dust-covered book. Scrawled inside, she found names, with lists next to them, like a family history of greed, malice, and cunning. That was weird. Did the person who made this list consider those positive or negative traits? The elements symbol, a circle with the four triangles representing the elements, was drawn at the bottom of the page. Family names were written in under the different elements. If this was Directorate property, had there ever been a time when that symbol didn't mean treason? She tried to turn the page, but it crumbled beneath her fingertips. "Crap. Should we get Miss Enid to look at these? She might be able to preserve some of them."

"Are you sure you want to share the existence of this room?"

"If anyone else discovered it and found out we already knew, we'd be labeled as disloyal. We'll tell Miss Enid when we go back upstairs, but for now, we investigate. Sound good?"

Valmont checked his watch. "We have time."

The room held books in varying states of decay. A glass case on the wall contained leather bound scrolls. Another case held daggers. Using the tips of her fingers, Bryn picked up a scroll and gently laid it on the table. Touching the edges, she unrolled it, becoming more confident as the scroll unwound without breaking. "This is so cool."

She scanned the handwritten report detailing Clan members that were allowed to marry and those that weren't. "I wish this told us how they tested the bloodlines. There's a drawing of two dragons touching some sort of maze or plate."

"I might have found that." Valmont carried what looked like an oversize metal dinner plate. He placed it flat on the table so she could see it. "Careful, the rim looks razor sharp." A channel started on both sides of the plate and then turned into a maze, which met in the center.

"Do you think they actually bled on this and did some sort of scientific test?"

"Maybe." He cocked his head to the side. "Do you hear that?"

Bryn listened. "I hear the disturbing sounds of tiny scurrying feet which will probably haunt my dreams tonight. That's about it."

Valmont pointed toward the back of the room. "It's coming from over there."

Bryn followed him around the table to what appeared to be a box covered by a tapestry. He flung back a corner of the cloth to reveal another one of the glass display cases. Inside rested a sword etched and decorated with a red metal that created a design which looked like fire and some bluish metal embedded alongside it to resemble frozen flames.

"Holy crap." Here was physical proof hybrids had existed in the past. "No one would make a sword with both elements on it unless they were bonded to a hybrid dragon."

Valmont didn't respond. He was too busy running his hands over the case.

"What are you doing?"

"This has to open somehow."

"Are you sure that's a good idea?" Bryn asked. "There could be booby traps."

"Not against a knight who serves a Red-Blue Hybrid," Valmont said like he was 100 percent certain. "*Ah-hah.*" He pushed on something, and the side of the case swung open.

Bryn could feel something like Quintessence pulsing

from the case. "Be careful."

"It's meant for me." Valmont reached in and grasped the pommel, which was decorated with red and blue stones. *Whoosh.* Magic pulsed through the air like a wave.

With great reverence, Valmont removed the sword from the display case and held it up to the light. "Isn't it beautiful?"

The red and blue etchings seemed to pulse in the light.

"It is." Bryn noticed something else. "I think it comes with its own carrying case." She reached in and pulled out a black leather scabbard. Since Valmont didn't seem inclined to set the sword down, she buckled the black leather belt around his waist. "There you go."

"I'm not ready to put it away yet." He looked like a five year old with a brand new *Star Wars* light saber.

A thought occurred to Bryn. "We need to head upstairs and share this with Miss Enid."

"I'm not sharing my sword," Valmont said in a tone, which sort of sounded like he was joking.

"I doubt anyone will try to take it away from you. As for the rest of this," Bryn indicated the dusty old books and scrolls, "she's probably the only one who can read the books without destroying them." Something caught Bryn's attention. Amid the dust on the far wall, something twinkled. "What's that?"

Valmont turned to see where she was going. "What's what?"

"The sparkly thing." As Bryn walked toward it, the light winked out. "Where'd it go?"

"Where did what go?"

Had the sword scrambled his brain? "The light on the wall." Bryn hurried forward and scanned the items on the back shelf. There were boxes of paper and blank scrolls. Empty wooden boxes sat with their lids propped open.

A strange warmth started in Bryn's chest. Wait, not in her chest, on her chest. She pulled on the golden chain, which held the gold key with the red and blue stones. The key itself felt warm…far warmer than her body temperature.

"I think the key is attuned to something in here the same way you were attuned to that sword." Taking great care, she pulled the chain over her head and let the key dangle from it. Even though there was no breeze in the room, the key swung forward and to the right.

"It's like a magical magnet?" Valmont asked.

"I guess." Bryn advanced in the direction it indicated, taking care not to step on the books, which lay scattered about on the floor. It seemed to be leading her to a shelf, which held intricately carved wooden boxes.

"Before you try to open any of those, we should make sure it's safe," Valmont said.

"The same way you made sure that case was safe when you were trying to reach the sword?"

"Point taken." Valmont joined her by the boxes. "I believe this falls under the do-as-I-say-not-as-I-do rule. Which box does the key want?"

Bryn extended her arm, holding the chain out so that the key dangled in front of the boxes. It swung forward and landed on top of the box in the middle. Leaning in close, Bryn blew on the top of the box, scattering layers of dust. She used her sleeve to gently wipe away years of residue, revealing a keyhole surrounded by red and blue stones.

"This could be big," she told Valmont.

"It could, but be careful."

Afraid if she picked the box up it might fall apart, she placed the key in the box and gently turned it to the right. The lid slid sideways rather than opening like a normal treasure chest.

Nestled in blue silk, lay a thick gold cuff bracelet with red and blue stones. She picked it up and stared at it before attempting to slide it onto her left wrist. It didn't fit, so she tried her right wrist where it slid on and fit like a second skin. The metal of the bracelet felt cold, but then warmed to her body heat. Magic pulsed up her arm making her suck in a breath and then the bracelet stung her… It felt like two fangs had sunk into her wrist. She gasped as a wave of dizziness hit.

Chapter Twenty-One

One minute she was looking at Valmont in the secret room, and the next minute she was surrounded by darkness. "Valmont?"

She could hear him saying her name, but he sounded far away.

"If you want to wield the bracelet, you must survive the Trial By Fire," a disembodied voice spoke in Bryn's mind. "Prove your worth or burn."

Okay, she hadn't signed up for this. Time to put the psycho bracelet back in its box. She tried to move but was frozen in place. Crap. She tried to shift. Nothing happened.

Out of the darkness, she could see the bracelet. Red fire and Blue frozen flames swirled around within the gold and then shot up her arm, wrapping around and around and writhing like a red and blue boa constrictor that wanted to eat her whole. Her heart pounded as the fire and ice constricted. The twin flames worked it's way up her shoulder to her neck, tightening as it went, and then the snake reared back, flame fangs exposed before it struck, biting her carotid artery. Fire and ice shot through her veins, taking her breath away, but it didn't burn. "You are worthy," the disembodied voice said. "Wield the power well."

Fire and ice shot from her palm in a long thin stream and then froze in place creating a sort of sword.

"Wow." She felt the weight of the sword in her hand, like it was real.

And then she was back in the secret room with Valmont calling her name. "Bryn?"

"I can hear you now." She turned the sword, admiring the flames.

"You're all right?" Valmont stared at the sword.

She nodded.

"You're sure?" he asked. "Because flames are shooting out of your hand, and that's not normal."

"No, but it is cool." She told him about the voice and what it had said to her.

"What would have happened if a dragon with the wrong lineage tried it on?"

"According to the voice, he would burn."

"Makes me thing we should be a little more careful with what we find down here."

"Where's the fun in that?" she asked.

"Let's try a little test." He picked up a piece paper. "Hold still." He dragged the piece of paper over the blade of Bryn's sword. It sliced right through it like it was made of air. "Yep, it's a real sword."

"This is so cool." Bryn grinned at Valmont and struck a fencer's pose. "En garde."

He laughed. "I don't think there's enough room in here for a proper duel."

Wanting to try out her new weapon, Bryn backed up to the entrance of the room and swung the sword in figure eights. She misjudged the distance and clipped the corner of the table. The smell of burnt wood filled the air as the sword sliced through the oak table shearing off the corner.

She froze and stared at the table.

"Your sword burned through it?" Valmont retrieved the triangular piece of wood she'd sliced off. He turned it over in his hands. "Look, there are char marks where your blade made contact."

In a singsong voice, Bryn said, "My sword is cooler than your sword."

He snorted. "It is not." Drawing his weapon, he held it to the light. The red and blue metal glowed more brightly than it had before. "Stand back," Valmont said. "I want to try something."

Once Bryn was out of range, he positioned himself and swung his sword at the other corner of the table. The smell of burnt wood again filled the air as his sword burned through the table just like Bryn's had.

Valmont grinned. "You were saying?"

"Dang. I wonder if they are part of a matched set?"

"They could be." Valmont re-sheathed his weapon and then pointed at her waist. "Yours didn't come with a carrying case?"

"Uhm…no and I'm not sure how to turn it off." It's not like she could walk around holding a half flaming, half frozen sword. That was the type of thing people tended to notice.

"Open your hand, like you would to release a regular sword," Valmont suggested.

She opened her hand and the sword disappeared. A bit of panic filled her chest at its absence. She closed her hand like she would do to hold a regular sword, and it reappeared this time without sinking fangs into her wrist, which was a plus. "Again, wow."

"Agreed." He checked his watch. "Why don't you grab your key and we can show Miss Enid what we found."

Miss Enid stared at Bryn like she was a candidate for a psychological evaluation.

"I swear we're not making this up." Bryn pointed at Valmont's new sword. "Where do you think Valmont's shiny new friend came from?"

"Show her yours," Valmont suggested.

They were back in the room with the trapdoor, so it wasn't like anyone could see. "Watch this." Bryn held her arm out and pretended to pick up a sword. The sword came to life, making Miss Enid jump backward.

"Oh dear." She touched her forehead like she felt a headache coming on. "I don't understand how this is possible."

"The writing was on the wall," Valmont said.

Bryn choked back a laugh.

"I didn't mean that as a joke. Literally, I saw the writing on the wall."

Miss Enid paced back and forth. "We should alert the Directorate immediately before we go back down there. Otherwise they might think we're conspiring against them."

"Fine," Bryn released the sword so it disappeared, "but I'm not handing this over to Ferrin. I'm calling my grandfather."

One phone call to the Sinclair estates and her grandfather stalked into the library in record time. He didn't bother with social niceties. "Show me the room."

Okay. She'd show him her new bracelet *after* she showed him the room. It might make more sense then. She led the way down the stairs and over to the once again normal-looking wall.

"Is this some sort of joke?" her grandfather roared.

"It takes a knight bound to a dragon who is willing to bleed for him to open the door," Miss Enid said like this was a common everyday fact.

Bryn grabbed Valmont's hand, waited for him to touch his blade to the wall and then once again sliced her finger on the blade. Before she could touch the area where the door handle had been, her blood rolled down the blade and when it made contact with the wall the door appeared.

Her grandfather sucked in a breath. Good. She'd unsettled him. He'd done it to her often enough.

Valmont opened the door. Miss Enid turned on a battery-powered electric lantern, which flooded the room with light. "Oh my." She stared in wonder and then set down a canvas bag bulging at the seams with what she'd called a book preservation kit, which she'd insisted on bringing.

"Sometimes there are old spells set to guard items which might still have power. What did you touch?" her grandfather asked.

"The sword called out to Valmont, so we knew that was safe," Bryn said.

Her grandfather glared at Valmont. "That is Directorate property."

Aw, crap.

Valmont unsheathed the sword. The dual colored flames danced in the light. "Can you argue it wasn't meant for me? Especially since I'll use it to defend your granddaughter?"

"You may keep it," her grandfather said. "What else did you touch?"

Bryn pointed at the book with the crumbled pages. "I found that open and tried to turn the page, but it fell apart. And I opened that scroll."

Valmont pointed at the disc with the maze. "Be careful. The edges on that thing look sharp."

"Why were you down here in the first place?" her grandfather asked, sounding more curious than irritated.

"I'm writing a paper on the history of lineage checks."

"Strange topic choice." Her grandfather pulled a

handkerchief from his pocket and picked up the maze disc.

"There's still a lot I don't know about this world," Bryn said. "I thought that was a good place to start."

Her grandfather harrumphed like he almost believed her. "This is where your paper would begin." He held the disk out for her to see. "Hundreds of years ago, dragons who applied to marry would have grabbed the edge of this with their right hand, slicing through their palms and sending blood into the maze. If the blood combined well, marriage would be approved. If there was a negative reaction, the marriage was denied."

"But how can a metal plate tell you that?"

"The spell checks for traits such as greed, tendency toward violence, intelligence."

"So," Bryn said, "when you talk about bloodlines combining, you are literally talking about mixing together blood to see if the genetics will result in something undesirable."

"Exactly. And that is knowledge not all dragons are privy to," her grandfather said. "Calling me first, rather than turning this over to whatever Directorate member was the closest, leads me to believe you are ready to share in such knowledge and you will keep it to yourself. As will your knight."

A strange sense of pride and belonging flowed through Bryn. "Thank you. And yes, we'll keep this information to ourselves. There's one more thing I need to show you." She backed up a few feet and performed the grabbing maneuver, which made the sword appear.

Her grandfather stared open-mouthed. "How did you do that?"

She pushed up her sleeve revealing the bracelet. "This called to me the same way the sword called to Valmont. When I put it, on the sword appeared."

He blinked and stared then shook his head. "Miss Enid,

have you ever read of such a thing?"

"Only in legends. It's an elemental sword, created from the elements Bryn holds power over. The bracelet focuses those powers and forms them into a weapon."

"Forget diamonds, this bracelet is a girl's best friend," Bryn said.

Miss Enid pointed toward a bookshelf in the back of the room. "There are more boxes back there like the one Bryn opened, but I don't believe we have any other keys."

"Key? What key?" her grandfather asked.

Bryn held out her necklace so he could see the charm. How could she explain this without making it sound like a conspiracy? "When I first came to school, Onyx gave me a protection charm as a gift. He said he placed it on this key because it reminded him of me."

Her grandfather touched the small golden key. "Keys like this are not uncommon." He released the charm and pressed his lips together like he was contemplating something. "It seems like more than a coincidence your key opened a box containing a weapon. Especially since Onyx gave it to you. Do you know the legends?"

"I thought jewelry makers created the keys to be rebellious after the Directorate was formed and hybrid marriages were forbidden."

"That is partially true, but before there was any conflict with the Directorate, keys like this were worn to symbolize a dragon's ancestry."

Miss Enid retrieved the open box the bracelet came from. "For experiment's sake, try to remove the bracelet and return it to the box."

Bryn didn't want to, but one look at her grandfather told her it wasn't optional. "Sure." She grabbed the cuff and tried to slide it off. It didn't budge. Holding the bracelet with one hand she twisted the other arm. It didn't slide or twist or anything. It felt like it had fused with her skin. "*Umm…*we may have a problem."

Miss Enid stared at the box and then at the bracelet. "Try using your key."

"Where?" Bryn pulled the key from her blouse and touched the bracelet with it. A keyhole appeared between the red and blue stones. Reluctantly, she inserted the key and turned it. The bracelet opened a fraction of an inch and Bryn was able to remove it like a normal bracelet.

"For now, place it in the box," her grandfather said. "I don't believe it's something you should wear all the time."

"Does that mean I can keep it?" She'd been sure he'd claim it as Directorate property.

"Why don't we allow a few Greens, who I trust implicitly, to study it? Then you can have it back. Without fully understanding it, I'm afraid you could hurt yourself or others."

She didn't like that answer, but he made a valid argument. "I guess you're right. I'd hate to reach for a pencil in class and accidentally stab someone, but you should make sure no one tries it on." She told him about the Trial By Fire.

"That will make testing it a bit difficult, but I'm sure we'll figure something out. Now, is that all you have to tell me?" her grandfather asked in a teasing tone. "You're not hiding a giant flaming battle ax or a cannon that shoots daggers made of ice?"

"No." Bryn grinned, enjoying this side of her grandfather she'd never seen before, "but both of those would be cool."

"All right then. I will need to use you occasionally to open this door, unless we find a way to keep it open. If I call you out of class, you must come immediately."

"Yes, sir."

"Excuse me," Miss Enid said. "I'd like to perform a quick test which could help in that area. If all three of you would leave the room and close the door, I'll see if I can exit without your aid. If that works, we could leave a guard and a librarian inside the room to protect it and catalog it, plus you could come inside whenever you wish to visit."

"If you're not out of there in five minutes, we'll open it again," Bryn said.

"Thank you." Miss Enid gave a nervous laugh. "This is so exciting."

They exited the room, and the door disappeared. Then it reappeared as Miss Enid swung the door open.

"I am relieved that worked." Miss Enid turned to her grandfather. "Mr. Sinclair, I will start cataloging the artifacts, if that's all right with you."

"Good idea. I'll personally escort a guard downstairs to stay with you." His gaze drifted to Bryn. "It's past curfew. Stay with me, and I'll walk you both back to your rooms."

That was nice of him. When they emerged in the library on the main floor, her grandfather placed a few calls. "And now the fun begins."

Bryn wasn't sure why her grandfather looked so pleased with himself until Ferrin emerged from the stairs scowling.

"Explain yourself." He pointed at Bryn. "Why are you out past curfew?"

Bryn knew she was grinning like a smart-ass but it seemed unavoidable. "Perhaps, you should direct your questions to my grandfather."

"Is there a problem?" her grandfather managed to sound confused.

A pair of guards entered the front door of the library and walked toward them.

Ferrin growled. "There is plenty of security in the area. Why are your private guards here?"

"It's difficult to know who to trust in these troubled times," her grandfather said. "If you'll excuse me, I have work to do in the archives."

"I'm coming with you," Ferrin stated like he was hoping someone would try to talk him out of it.

"Of course you're invited to join me."

Bryn could practically hear Ferrin grinding his teeth in frustration at being relegated as a tag-a-long rather than being the one in charge. She had to clamp down on a giggle.

"Bryn, I'll ask you to lead us downstairs one more time and then I'll escort you back to your dorm. "

"Of course." She did as her grandfather asked, enjoying the look of avarice on Ferrin's face when he saw what she'd discovered.

"Perhaps you should have your granddaughter bleed on more walls," Ferrin said. "You never know what else we might find."

At this rate, she'd be a human pincushion.

Valmont leaned over and whispered to Bryn. "You don't have to be the only dragon with a knight. Then you wouldn't be the only one who could open doors."

Once her grandfather was finished lauding "his discovery" over Ferrin, he walked her back to the Blue dorm.

"We could fly," Bryn suggested as they walked across campus.

"Nonsense. We want to enter through the front door to see how many students have heard the news."

"How could anyone have heard about what happened half an hour ago?"

Her grandfather laughed. "Security guards watching the tapes will talk. Students who were in the library will be curious. Wait and see."

When they entered the Blue dorm, the first floor sitting area was oddly full for a Monday night after curfew. Bryn smiled at everyone who stared at her, just to be perverse.

"Would you like to come up to my room?" she asked when they reached the marble staircase, because truth be told, she wasn't sure what to do. She would have hugged her grandmother, but that didn't seem like an option with her grandfather.

"Thank you. Maybe another time. Valmont, I hope you enjoy the sword my granddaughter commissioned for you. Bryn, tell Jaxon I said hello." Her grandfather chuckled and headed back toward the front door.

"I get the part about saying you gave me the sword, but what was that other bit about?" Valmont asked Bryn as they headed up the stairs.

"I have no idea."

Jaxon standing outside her door, made her laugh openly. "My grandfather says hello."

"How nice of him." Jaxon jerked his thumb toward the door. "May I come in for a bit?"

"My vote is no," Valmont told Bryn.

"It's late, Jaxon. What do you want?"

"Don't play games. You know exactly why I'm here."

He could believe what he wanted. She unlocked the door. "After you."

He held his ground. "Ladies first."

Since when did he put me in that category?

"It's sort of my job to go first and make sure it's safe." Valmont drew his new sword, holding it out so Jaxon was sure to see it.

Jaxon sucked in a breath. "Where did that come from?"

"Early Christmas present." Valmont entered the room and flipped on the lights. "All clear."

Bryn and then Jaxon followed. As soon as the door shut, he spoke rapid fire. "Is it true you discovered a secret room in the library?"

"How in the hell did you hear that already?" Bryn sat at the table because she didn't want Jaxon to get too comfortable on the couch and decide to overstay his welcome, which would end in about thirty seconds.

"One of Rhianna's friends was in the library and saw your grandfather arrive. She knows the younger cousin of one of the security guards who watched the footage of the cameras in the library. Now, tell me what you found."

For once, she liked being the person in-the-know. Since arriving in the dragon world, she'd constantly been one step behind. "Something about the magic of the knight-dragon bond allowed us to discover a hidden room containing old books and scrolls."

"What about your bond allowed you to do that?"

"I'm not sure you should share this information with everyone," Valmont said. "It could be used against you or another dragon and knight."

She hadn't thought of that.

"I am not *everyone*," Jaxon said. "I'm…I won't say your future husband because God forbid that comes to pass, but I am the person who pulled you off a rather pointy javelin, so make with the details, now."

When he put it that way…she told him about finding the door, how they opened it, and what was in the room. And suddenly she was exhausted. "You have ten minutes to ask questions before I literally fall asleep sitting up."

In a surprise move, Jaxon reached for her hand, which was resting on the table. "Show me."

She turned her hand palm up so he could see the fine red lines that marked where she'd bled on Valmont's sword.

He pointed at Valmont. "That's why you don't want everyone to know. They could snatch a dragon and knight and bleed the dragon dry, hunting for hidden doors."

Valmont nodded. "We need to keep this information a secret."

"Secrets have a way of coming out. We need to lay a false trail." Jaxon sat back and ran his hand through his hair.

"Something close to the truth would be best." He stared up at the ceiling for a moment. "I know. Let's say both dragon and knight had to touch the sword for it to work like a key."

"Technically, that's true," Bryn said. "So it won't be hard to remember." She needed to include Valmont in this decision because it wasn't all about her. "What do you think, Valmont?"

"I hate that he thought of it, but I like it." He gestured toward the door. "Now that we have our stories straight, it's time for you to leave so Bryn and I can to go to bed."

Well, that sounded sort of wrong. Jaxon glared at Valmont as he let himself out. Was it because he'd been dismissed or was it because of the way Valmont had made it sound like they were going to bed together?

"Are you all right?" her knight asked.

"Tired, but good." Bryn stood and wrapped her arms around him in a hug. "It was an eventful day."

"That it was."

She looked up at him. "Are you okay?"

"I love my new sword, but I definitely do not like making you bleed."

And that's when she realized something. "I didn't heal myself after the cuts." She showed him her hand with the barely visible lines. "Do you think that's part of the magic?"

"I don't know. Blood-magic is messed up."

"Is that a real term?" Bryn asked. "Or are you improvising?"

"I've never heard it before, but it seems to fit. Now, enough big thoughts for the day. Come here." He tugged her toward the couch. "I'm not ready to let you go." He lay down, and she followed suit, using his chest as a pillow.

"My dragon," he murmured as he kissed the top of her head.

"My knight," she replied as she yawned.

. . .

At breakfast the next morning, Bryn noticed a certain trend. "And everyone is back to staring again. Lovely."

"It's your fault. You're the one who keeps doing weird things," Clint teased. "Finding secret doorways. Consorting with Directorate member's sons."

"What?" Valmont sloshed coffee over the rim of his cup.

Ivy chuckled. "There's a rumor Jaxon was seen leaving Bryn's room late last night."

"So." Bryn didn't get it. "It's not like I was alone with him. Valmont was there."

"Yeah," Clint snorted. "People are talking about it that way, too."

"Stop it." Ivy smacked Clint on the arm.

"What?" Clint rolled his eyes. "Number one, they need to know. Number two, it's ridiculous to think of those three together."

"Three? Oh, hell no." Valmont pushed away from the table.

And that's when Bryn got it. "Why…" Words failed her, but the look of utter disgust on Valmont's face made this seem oddly funny. If she laughed, he would not be pleased. She played it off as being mad. "Why would people think something so stupid?"

"Students are bored. Rumors are fun." Clint shrugged.

"Fun?" Valmont grabbed a butter packet and whizzed it at Clint's head.

"Hey." Clint ducked allowing the butter packet to sail over his shoulder onto the floor. "Don't fling dairy products at the messenger."

"You're enjoying this too much," Bryn shot back.

"I can't help it." Clint's grinned. "I'm dying to ask Jaxon if he's heard the rumors."

"Don't even think about it," Bryn warned. "There's enough strange crap going on without you adding to the situation."

"Fine." Clint shoved a piece of bacon in his mouth.

A roar reverberated through the room. Bryn whipped around to see Jaxon grab a Blue male she didn't recognize, pin his arm behind his back, and slam him face first into the table.

"If you ever repeat such a stupid rumor again," sleet shot from Jaxon's mouth with every word, "I will gut you."

"I'm sorry." The boy gave a fake laugh. "It was supposed to be a joke."

"Not funny." Jaxon yanked the boy to a standing decision. "Apologize. Now."

"I'm sorry." He rubbed his right arm and backed away slowly before turning and running for the door.

"Still wish you could've told Jaxon?" Bryn asked.

"On second thought, no," Clint said.

Chapter Twenty-Two

In Mr. Stanton's class, everyone gave Jaxon a wide berth. Whether it was his actions or the scowl, which seemed permanently etched on his face, Bryn wasn't sure. He avoided eye contact with her, which she didn't really mind.

"Class," Mr. Stanton spoke from behind his desk, "we are going to practice transferring Quintessence from one plant to another. On a theoretical scale, this mimics how medics heal. Later, if you choose to study Quintessential medicine, you will practice on one another. In my class, you will work with plants. We don't want anyone to sustain an accidental injury." He passed out small potted ferns.

Clint and Ivy sat at desks next to Bryn.

"I sucked at this the last time," Clint said.

"Watch me." Ivy touched the leaves of her plant. "I'm visualizing drawing the green color from the plant." The plants leaves darkened and turned brown. Then she touched the other fern. "Now I'm imagining pouring the green into this plant." The fern perked up, sending fronds out in all directions.

"You're really good at that." Bryn held her hand above the plant and concentrated. Nothing happened. She closed her eyes and focused on feeling power flow up from the fronds. When she opened her eyes, the plant hadn't changed.

"Crap."

"And you want to become a medic," Clint teased.

"You try it." Bryn pointed at his plant.

"Fine." Clint cracked his knuckles and then touched the leaves of his plant. Lightning crackled from his palm, shattering the clay pot and spilling dirt on the desktop.

"Looks like we both suck at this." Clint scratched his head. "Now what?"

Ivy held out her hand. "Give me your ferns."

Clint did as she asked. Ivy drew the life force from the donated plants and infused her fern with Quintessence, almost doubling it in size.

Bryn shoved her plants to Ivy and watched as Ivy transferred the Quintessence and caused the plant fronds to twist and bend so they curled back on themselves creating a heart shaped topiary.

"We should find out if you could help with the decorations for the Valentine's Day dance," Clint said.

After class, Bryn and Valmont headed toward the library. "How can I heal a person but not be able to do the stupid plant transfer?"

"You can't be great at everything. You have your gifts, and Ivy has hers."

He was right. "That's a mature way to look at it."

When they entered the library, a Red guard stopped them. "Miss McKenna, your grandfather would like a word with you. He's in the archives."

For a split second, she thought about accepting this directive at face value, but the moment passed. "I don't mean to be rude, but the last time I blindly followed one of my grandparents' employees, someone tried to kill me, so could you ask my grandfather to come upstairs?"

"I understand your concern, but I cannot leave my post." He pulled a cell phone from his pocket and dialed, explaining the situation to the person who answered. Then he passed the phone to Bryn.

"I require your assistance in the archives, Bryn. Bring your knight and that sword you commissioned for him with you."

"Yes, sir." She started to pass the phone back to the guard. "I don't suppose I could keep the phone."

"No." The guard plucked the phone from her hand and pocketed it.

"It was worth a shot." Bryn headed for the front desk.

"How do you know it's him?" Valmont asked.

"He said something only he would know."

When they reached the trap door, Valmont frowned. "I'm not sure if I should go first or guard your back."

His high alert status seemed a bit like overkill. "You can go first. I can roast anyone who sneaks up behind me."

"I don't like this." Valmont held his sword at the ready and descended the staircase. They reached the landing with no issues. A pair of guards stood in front of the open door. They waved Bryn and her knight through.

"There you are." Her grandfather waved her over to wall where the secret door should have been. "Open the door."

"How did it end up closed?" Bryn asked.

"The guard inside didn't come out at his appointed time." Crap. That couldn't be good.

Valmont held out his sword. Bryn gritted her teeth and slid her thumb down the ice-cold blade. Her blood rolled down the sword edge toward the wall and the door became visible.

One of her grandfather's guards yanked the door open.

Inside, the room looked much cleaner than Bryn remembered it. Books were shelved. The dust and cobwebs were gone. The glass cases gleamed. The old oak table had even been polished to a shine. It would have been an idyllic scene if only a guard wasn't lying on the floor foaming at the mouth. Bubbly spittle dripped down his chin as his body twitched and his eyes rolled back in his head.

"Call a medic," her grandfather ordered.

"I don't suppose he's epileptic?" Bryn said, knowing the answer.

"That is a human disease," her grandfather replied.

Maybe she could help. Bryn crossed the threshold into the room.

"Don't," her grandfather warned.

"I'm going to see if I can help with Quintessence," Bryn argued.

"Freeze." Valmont's fear sounded real. "Back up slowly."

Okay. The hair on the back of Bryn's neck stood up. Something was really wrong. She retreated toward Valmont. When she was back over the threshold of the door, she noticed he was staring at something beyond her in the room.

"What's going on?"

"Your knight has a keen eye." Her grandfather pointed at the wall next to where the man lay. Small silver darts were embedded in the bookshelf. "I'm guessing the poisonous darts that hit him are lodged in his back."

"Poisonous darts? From where?" She scanned the room and noticed an open display case. "Do you think he took something from the case?"

"Something not meant for him," Valmont said. "Do you remember what was in there?"

"Daggers," Bryn said. "I remember seeing them last night. They were etched with different elements like your sword."

"So the displays are booby trapped," Valmont said.

A chill ran down Bryn's spine. "We need to shut that case before someone else is hurt."

One of the guards stepped forward. "Sir?"

"It has to be me," Valmont said. "The artifacts are all meant for knights."

No way. "How do you know they were meant for a hybrid knight? What if that case held items only the knight of a Black dragon could touch?"

Valmont paused. "I hadn't thought of that."

Footsteps rang out from the outer foyer. Medic Williams dashed into the room.

"Stop," Bryn's grandfather said. "The room can be lethal."

Medic Williams looked around wide-eyed. "Good to know, but how can I treat the man if I can't reach him?"

"Do you think those darts could puncture dragon scales?" Bryn asked. "I could shift and grab him."

"No," both Valmont and her Grandfather shouted at the same time.

"Fine." Bryn held her hands up in surrender. "What's your idea?"

"I believe if we shut that case, the room will be safe." Her grandfather pointed at the medic. "Gently use your wind to shut that door."

The medic produced a small twister in her hand and stretched it out across the room, nudging the door closed.

A sound like gears grinding drifted through the room.

"Did that case just reload?" Bryn asked.

"Probably." Her grandfather waved his hand toward the man on the floor. "I believe it is safe for you to treat him now, although he might be past the point of help."

The man on the floor was no longer twitching. The spittle foaming from his mouth had turned a reddish pink. His eyes staring up at the ceiling were milky white.

"Damn it." She should have tried to help him.

The medic performed a quick examination and then rolled him over. "He was past help sixty seconds after these darts lodged in his back." She pulled a phone from her pocket and spoke to someone about body bags. The fact that she used the plural of the term made Bryn wonder if more deaths were expected.

"The dagger." Valmont pointed to silver knife etched with fire, which had been under the man's body. "Should I try to return it to the case?"

"Does it speak to you?" Bryn asked.

"It's whispering like the sword did. I think that means I can handle it without being attacked."

"The case reacted to someone removing an item. In theory, putting one back should be safe," her grandfather said.

"Or he could keep it," Bryn said. "Since he is attuned to it." She liked that idea a lot better.

Valmont retrieved the dagger and weighed it in his hand. "Mr. Sinclair, what would you like me to do?"

Her grandfather appeared pleased with Valmont's question. "Replace it in the case."

Not the option she would have chosen. Bryn bit her lip as Valmont found the mechanism that opened the glass. He replaced the knife and closed the door. No deadly darts appeared. Although the weird gear-grinding noise happened again.

A second medic appeared with the requested body bags. Bryn turned away. This wasn't something she wanted to witness.

Valmont walked around so he was facing her. He looked at his watch. "Basic Movement will end in ten minutes. We should go to lunch if your grandfather doesn't require your assistance."

Bryn turned to her grandfather. "Do you still need me?"

"You may go. I'll warn the guards that they aren't to

remove anything from the cases."

"How do you know the books are safe?" Bryn asked.

"We don't," her grandfather replied. "But Miss Enid wears gloves when she works with them."

That didn't seem like enough of a safeguard, not that anyone asked her opinion. If touching the books was safe, was the information inside of them harmless? The symbol she'd seen in the book before it had crumbled was the same symbol tattooed on the dead boy's wrist in Dragon's Bluff. To her grandfather, that symbol meant treason. The fact that Bryn had found a drawing of it tucked away in her mother's secret hiding place made her think it hadn't started out bad. Perhaps, it had once been a symbol of free-thinking. After the attacks on innocent people, though, it definitely meant something deadly.

"There's something I forgot to mention about one of the books. The one that fell apart when I touched it."

Her grandfather glanced at the medic. "Let's talk over here, so we aren't in the medic's way."

Worked for her. Valmont followed along, and her grandfather didn't object. Once they were across the room, Bryn said. "The page I tried to turn had the same symbol the dead boy had on his arm in Dragon's Bluff."

Her grandfather's eyes narrowed. "And why are you just telling me this now?"

"I wasn't keeping it from you. In all the excitement of finding the room and calling you to make sure you had a chance to investigate before Ferrin, it slipped my mind." That should earn her some bonus points. "Plus, it disintegrated so there wasn't anything to show you."

"It's good you remembered and that you shared the information with me."

Bryn breathed a sigh of relief. Interactions with her grandfather could be exhausting.

"You should go to class now."

"Can I ask you a question first?"

"I may choose not to answer, but you may ask."

"In the book, family names were listed by the different symbols of the elements. Was there ever a time when that mark didn't mean treason?"

"Originally it represented the elements, but a group of rebels repurposed it to mean dragons who fought against the status quo, against the Directorate."

"So that book wasn't necessarily bad?" Bryn asked.

"No. It was more than likely a ledger where family traits were recorded. I don't have to tell you not to share any of this information with your friends, do I?"

"No." That didn't mean she wasn't going to share with Clint and Ivy. One other thought bothered her. "What about Jaxon?" Not that she felt the need to share with him, but she knew he would ask. "He's persistent, and sometimes it's easier to share with him just to make him go away."

Valmont said something under his breath she didn't quite catch, but she bet it wasn't complimentary.

Her grandfather actually grinned. "It's good that you're coming to understand one another."

"You have no idea how frightening that concept is to me," Bryn said and then laughed because she didn't want to tick her grandfather off.

He patted her on the back. "In time you'll become formidable political partners much like your grandmother and I. Feel free to share with him what you wish, but I advise you to always keep a few details to yourself. Most of what happened here this afternoon will go into a report, which Ferrin and the other Directorate members will read tomorrow morning. So Jaxon will hear about this through his father."

"Is there always a bit of espionage between the Directorate members?" Bryn asked.

"It's what makes life interesting." He checked his watch. "I'll make your teachers aware of why you missed class. You'd best be on your way to lunch."

By dinner everyone on campus had heard of the guard's death, but they were divided on how he died: a giant ax beheaded him, a sinkhole opened up and swallowed him, or a sword from one of the cases slayed him.

"With every stupid rumor I hear, my opinion of my fellow students declines." Bryn sat in her dorm room on the couch with Ivy while Clint and Valmont sat in the wingback chairs. She'd waited for them to be alone to discuss what had really happened in the archives of the library. "Just so you know, you have two choices. I can share the real story with you, or you can be happily ignorant."

"Everyone knows a guard died. It's how he died that's in question," Clint said.

"Right," Ivy said, "so I think it's safe to tell us."

"Okay, here we go." She shared the manner of the poor man's death and the details about the lethal display case, but not the existence of the secret room or the bracelet.

Ivy pursed her lips in thought. "I guess the moral of the story is, if you come across a random display case, do not attempt to open it or remove any of the pretty, sparkly objects inside."

"I can't believe it was booby trapped with poisonous darts." Clint shook his head. "Who knows when those darts were placed in the case? What type of poison is good for decades like that? The whole thing is seriously messed up."

"Agreed." Valmont sat with his hand resting on the pommel of his sword. He glanced at Bryn. "Can I tell them about the sword you commissioned for me?"

Was he asking if he could share the truth with them? They already knew about the cases. "Sure."

Valmont drew his favorite new toy and held it up so the light reflected off the blue and red metal intricately worked into the sword, depicting frozen flames and fire. "I retrieved this from one of the cases."

"You could have been killed," Clint said.

"No. It was meant for me. I mean a knight like me who was bound to a Red-Blue hybrid dragon. I could hear the magic of it calling to me."

Ivy pointed at Valmont. "That is so cool. I know you met Adam and Eve, so you know there are hybrids on campus, but the sword is proof hybrids existed in the past, and it wasn't a secret. Do you know how old it is?"

"If the Institute wasn't on lockdown," Valmont said, "I could ask one of the metalsmiths in Dragon's Bluff to examine it."

It had never occurred to Bryn that someone in Dragon's Bluff was still making swords. Back in her old life she'd heard of people buying all sorts of ninja swords and throwing stars online but she'd assumed they had been made in a factory somewhere.

"Speaking of the lockdown," Ivy said, "I wonder if they'll lift it any time soon. There hasn't been an attack on campus in a while, except for the guard, of course, but that's kind of a separate thing."

A voice in Bryn's head urged her to speak. "If anyone is waiting to attack, the Valentine's Dance is the perfect opportunity."

"No. It's not." Ivy glared at her. "Repeat after me. The dance will be wonderful. We will all have a fabulous time."

Bryn rolled her eyes. "Fine. The dance will be wonderful. We'll all have a great time."

"Not exactly what I said, but close enough." Ivy grinned.

Later that night after her friends left, Bryn asked Valmont a question that had been bothering her. "Do you think someone will attack the dance?"

"They might," Valmont said. "They could attack at any time. On any given day they could attack the dining hall at lunch or gym during Basic Movement. Students congregate in groups all the time, so I don't think the dance is any more dangerous than sitting right here, right now."

"I'm not sure that makes me feel better." And then she remembered something she wanted to share with him. "Telling my grandfather about the symbol in that book today reminded me of something I found at Sinclair Estates." She went to her room and retrieved the legends books her mother had secreted away in the attic. Valmont would probably tease her about the books, which told stories of dragons from different Clans who fought side by side and fell in love with one another. The star-crossed romances were a big part of the books' appeal. And there were a few scenes she would be embarrassed to read if Valmont were in the room. A small part of her heart ached at the memory of her first kiss with Zavien. He'd teased her about reading the books, too. She'd refused to let him read them because he'd make fun of the romance. It was hard to reconcile the Zavien who'd saved her when she'd been poisoned with the one who'd lied to her about the dance and led her on, talking about a future he knew they'd never have. Anger, embarrassment, and guilt banked the fire in her gut.

Wow. She'd thought all of that was in her past, but her first kiss with Zavien was a powerful memory.

"Bryn, is everything all right?" Valmont called from the living room.

Her subconscious was playing whack-a-mole with her emotions. Other than that, everything was just peachy.

She returned to her knight, who would never leave her

side, even if he wanted to. Not that he wanted to, but her brain seemed intent on pointing out how strange her life had become.

Time to ignore her past and concentrate on the future.

Funny how *The Days of Knights* books hadn't featured more than a chaste kiss between a dragon and a knight. And that thought brought her to a full stop when she was within a few feet of the couch. What if they didn't include anything else because nothing more was supposed to happen between them?

"Bryn?"

She shook her head. "Sorry, weird random thoughts are ambushing me." She laid the books out on the table. "My mother had these stashed in a secret hiding place along with my father's picture." Bryn's breath caught and her eyes grew warm. Taking a deep breath, she laughed. "Sorry, I'm not sure why this is getting to me tonight."

"You never have to apologize to me for mourning your parents." Valmont grabbed her hand and pulled her to sit beside him on the couch.

He didn't need to know those weren't the only memories bothering her. She took a deep breath and blew it out. "Anyway, these are like the legends books Miss Enid gave me from the library which contain stories about a time before the Directorate when dragons were allowed to fall in love based on instinct rather than by Directorate-sanctioned arranged marriages. I've read other books, but I never looked through these." She ran her fingers over the cover of the closest book. "Not that I expect to find anything in them except dog-eared pages, but I thought you could be here with me when I look through them. It's not something I want to do alone."

"Of course. Do you want my help?"

It's not like she could tell him no. "Sure."

They each selected a book. Bryn flipped through the

pages, looking for random notes or drawings or doodles or any clue her mother had touched the pages.

Halfway through the sixth chapter, she noticed the page felt oddly loose. Maybe the binding was coming undone. Inspecting the book, she held it up to the light and saw what looked like the shadow of a handwritten note. "That's strange." She held the page between her thumb and index finger, rubbing them back and forth to see if she could detect any indentation on the page. Part of the page separated from the binding and opened like a leaflet.

"What's that?" Valmont asked.

"Good question." What had seemed to be one page was really a singular piece of paper folded in half. The outside held the typewritten story, but the inside portion, which was hidden, held handwritten notes, which Bryn read out loud.

"I'm not sure how much longer I can wait. Ferrin grows more obnoxious by the day, demanding we share every meal in the dining hall. It grows harder and harder to slip away to see Ian. There is the constant worry someone will discover us and turn Ian over to the Directorate. If that were to happen, I fear my father would have him thrown in jail."

"Do you think your grandfather would have had him thrown in jail?" Valmont asked.

"Yes." There was no question in her mind. "I can't believe my parents were brave enough to run away. Makes me feel like a traitor for working with my grandfather."

Valmont's lips pressed into a thin line. "I have a question to ask you, but I'm afraid of what your answer might be."

She tried to lighten the mood. "Should I repeat my grandfather's snooty you-can-ask-but-I-may-choose-not-to-answer response?"

He looked down as he spoke. "It's probably not fair of me to ask this, but if you still had family in the human world, would you choose to return to it, leaving everything behind?"

"No." The word shot out of her mouth without her even having to think about it. "I could never just walk away from you. Don't you know that?" She touched his cheek.

He lifted his head meeting here gaze. "Thank you. I was worried you'd run away in a heartbeat if you could have your old life back."

"Nope." She leaned closer and pressed her lips against his in a quick kiss and then leaned her forehead against his. "My knight. We're a package deal." A funny question popped into her brain. "If I had to leave, to run away, would you go with me?"

"I left Dragon's Bluff to come stay with you, didn't I?"

He had, and yet that wasn't the answer to her question. If war broke out and her grandparents sent her away, not that they'd do that, would he go with her? *Of course he would. What am I thinking?*

She sat back and smiled at him like her subconscious wasn't shooting out strange questions meant to drive her crazy. "I think everything that has happened over the past few days is finally catching up with me. My mind seems to be spinning in circles."

"It's my experience that most problems in life can be solved by one of three things: good food, good friends, or a good nap. I know you're always up for food, I'm here for you as your knight and your friend, and this couch happens to be my favorite place to take a nap. So you choose."

"I want to see if there are any more notes hidden in this book, and then I vote on taking a nap with my knight—with a snack later."

Bryn flipped through the pages of the book, holding them up to the light. Every other chapter, there was a hidden page which she never would have found if the first one hadn't been loose. Reading her mother's journal entries made her heart hurt. Every entry was about how much her mom loved her dad and the rising fear that someone might find out about them. The notes of Ferrin's obnoxious behavior proved the man had changed little over the years.

Valmont had held the pages of the other books up to the light, but no secret messages were revealed.

"Do you think my mom bought this journal somewhere and hid it among the other books?"

Valmont rubbed his chin. "The books themselves were frowned upon because they go against Directorate-sanctioned marriage. It makes sense the same people who produced them might create a journal where people could write down anti-Directorate thoughts."

"Maybe I'll ask Miss Enid if she's ever heard of any secret journals." Bryn hugged the book to her chest. "But showing my mother's secrets to the world doesn't feel right."

A sense of sadness rolled over her like a fog. "I think I'm ready for that nap now."

"Works for me." Valmont kicked off his boots and lay down on his side.

She lay with her back against his chest so his arm wrapped around her waist. His solid warmth was reassuring. It helped her feel less alone in the world, like he was her family now.

Chapter Twenty-Three

The next day in Basic Movement, Bryn noticed several students were missing. "Where is everyone?" she asked Ivy who stood next to her in line for the joust.

"I have no idea." Ivy pointed at a group of Blues. Her lips moved like she was counting how many students were present. She did this for each Clan and then scratched her head. "We're low on Greens. What does that mean?"

Was Ivy right? Bryn scanned the room and saw Jaxon doing the same thing. They made eye contact, and he frowned, and then he seemed to check the room one more time before heading in her direction.

Valmont huffed out an irritated sigh.

"Play nice," Bryn warned.

"We're missing half a dozen Greens," Jaxon said by way of greeting. "Where are they?"

"Good question." It's not like dragons took sick days.

The sound of the door to the gym opening and slamming shut drew her attention. Garret stalked in looking like he'd had a rough night. "Something's not right," Bryn said at the same time Jaxon said, "He'll know what's going on."

Bryn grabbed Jaxon by the bicep. "He looks like crap. How about we go with a soft approach instead of marching over and pummeling him with questions."

Jaxon's eyebrows came together in a way, which Bryn knew meant, I-don't-like-what-you-said-but-now-I-have-to-think-about-it kind of way. "Fine. Go play nice. I'll wait here."

"I'm going with you," Valmont said as he joined Bryn and headed toward Garret.

The Green saw their approach and changed course to intercept them. "We have a problem."

"You'll have to be more specific," Valmont said.

Bryn elbowed her knight. "Knock it off. Garret, what's wrong?"

"The Directorate is out of control. Last night a group of my Clan members and I were studying together in the library. We planned to exit the library half an hour before curfew, which would have given us plenty of time to return to our rooms. Someone ordered us rounded up like cattle. We were taken up to the top floor and questioned."

"Did they throw you in a study cubicle overnight?" Bryn asked.

Garret's eyes narrowed. "Yes, and worse than that, they made all the males drink some concoction and badgered us with questions for more than an hour. I don't know what they expected to find. It was absurd. Once they were done with the interrogation, they stuck us in the study cubicles. They released us about an hour ago and told us to clean up and go to class."

"I'm sorry. The same thing happened to Clint and Ivy not too long ago, except they were out after curfew."

"Well, we weren't." The air around Bryn seemed to churn as Garret's anger swelled. He pointed at Jaxon. "His father is to blame." He stalked toward his target.

Oh, hell.

"Please, let Garret kick his ass," Valmont whispered to Bryn.

Bryn dashed after Garret. Jaxon would pulverize him. Why did Valmont not realize that?

"He had no idea where your Clan members were, either," Bryn said as they reached Jaxon. "And I'm sure he wouldn't approve."

"Approve of what?" Jaxon asked, projecting cold upper-class snootiness.

"Just listen to him before you start to argue," Bryn said.

When Jaxon looked at her like he was about to rip into her, she added, "Please."

Garret repeated his story of unfair detainment and questioning.

Jaxon ran his hand back through his hair. "That makes no sense. At any point, did you speak to or see my father?"

"No, but it was his guards that did this," Garret seethed.

"Wait a minute. Ferrin actually interviewed Clint and Ivy when they were taken upstairs. Are you saying that didn't happen?"

"No. It was a bunch of Red Guards who work for the Directorate." A look of surprise and then fury crossed Garret's face. "If your father wasn't involved, then this could have been something else."

"A plot to turn the Greens, the smartest Clan, against the Directorate," Jaxon said. "Come with me. We need to make a call."

Bryn followed him over to Coach Anderson where he requested access to a phone. She led them to her office.

Jaxon dialed and then spoke to his father rapid fire. Bryn couldn't tell how the conversation was going from Jaxon's clipped responses. When he hung up, he faced Garret. "On behalf of my father, I apologize for your mistreatment last night. The men who detained you were not acting on Directorate's orders."

"How do you know that's true?" Garret asked.

"The Directorate was in session at Bryn's grandfather's house last night, and all members were accounted for since they were voting on several measures."

Garret growled and papers flew off Coach Anderson's desk as the air swirled around.

Bryn could tell Jaxon had more to say. "He's already angry. Tell him the rest of it."

"The rest of what?" Garret asked.

"Unfortunately, the real Directorate members would like to question you now. They plan to set up a late lunch in one of their private dining rooms. You'll be excused from classes for the rest of the day."

"And if I refuse their lunch?" Garret asked.

"I believe you know the answer to that question," Jaxon said. "Attendance is mandatory."

"We should go with him," Bryn said, and then indicated she meant herself, Jaxon, and Valmont.

The look Jaxon leveled at her showed what he thought of the idea.

"Great idea," Garret said. "Because I'm not going anywhere alone with anyone claiming to represent the Directorate ever again."

"Fine." Jaxon grabbed the phone. "I'll let my father know there will be extra guests."

Garret pulled Bryn off to the side. "Do you think your grandfather will be there?"

"I don't know."

Garrett's gaze flicked toward Jaxon. "Could you call and ask him to come? I respect Jaxon, but I do not trust his father."

"And you trust my grandfather?" Bryn asked.

"No," Garret said, "but I trust you, and you seem to trust

him."

"I do." That was an interesting realization. After Jaxon ended his call, Bryn called Sinclair Estates where Rindy the all-knowing phone operator redirected her call to her grandfather's cell phone. He told her he would be there.

Forty minutes later, Bryn entered a private dining room with a U-shaped table. Half a dozen Directorate members, her grandfather included, sat at the back of the U. Bryn, Valmont, Jaxon, and Garret sat on one side, while the four other Greens sat on the other side.

"Divide and conquer?" Garret said loud enough for Bryn and Valmont to hear.

Strangely enough, Jaxon chose the seat at the end of the U-shape farthest from the Directorate members. Bryn sat next to him, which left Valmont next to Garret.

"Why did you choose this seat?" Bryn asked.

"It allows me to observe the other Green's reactions to the Directorate's questions, and it gives me a clear view of how the Directorate handles the situation." Jaxon nodded toward his father who acknowledged him with the same cold nod.

Bryn waited to catch her grandfather's attention and gave a small wave. Miraculously enough, he smiled at her, so she smiled back. Then he went back to talking with a man she didn't know.

"What was that?" Jaxon asked Bryn.

"What was what?"

"Your grandfather is here on business," Jaxon said, "and you distracted him."

Seriously? "No, I didn't. I greeted him like he was family."

"And that would be proper if you were meeting him at a social occasion," Jaxon spoke to her like she was stupid. "This is business."

From her other side, Valmont muttered something about

Jaxon and his amazing ability to walk with such a giant stick crammed up a certain orifice. Bryn clamped her lips shut to keep from laughing and then turned to glare at her knight.

"I make no apologies." Valmont crossed his arms over his chest. "It needed to be said."

Waiters pushed carts into the room. The savory scent of steak filled the air, and Bryn's stomach growled.

As the waitstaff passed out plates, Ferrin stood. "It's my understanding you were falsely detained and questioned last evening. And I do see the irony in your presence being mandated here. Please enjoy lunch and then we'll discuss this situation."

Bryn inhaled her steak, and then wondered if she could ask for seconds.

"Don't even think about it," Jaxon said.

"Fine."

"I don't like that," Valmont whispered to Bryn.

"Don't like what?"

"The way you two seem to know what the other is thinking. Earlier in the gym you warned him not to do something and now he did the same to you."

"Oh." What did she say to that? "Maybe it's a Blue thing."

The plates were cleared away. Coffee was served.

"Now," Ferrin said, "we'd like to start with Garret. Can you walk us through the events of last evening?"

Garret launched into his tale about being detained and questioned. "They made us drink something and then badgered us with questions about the attack on Dragon's Bluff, which none of us were present for. Although that didn't seem to matter to them. Then they lectured us about obeying the curfew law which made no sense given that we hadn't been out after curfew." Garret blinked. "Now that I know you weren't involved, I think their main purpose was to make us hostile toward the Directorate."

"And why would they want that?" Ferrin asked.

"Isn't it obvious?" Garret sat back in his chair and looked at Ferrin like he was the one being interrogated.

"I have my own opinions," Ferrin said. "I'd like you to share yours."

"I think all of it—last night, the attacks on campus, and on Dragon's Bluff—are meant to set us on a path to a revolution. The attackers think if they can sway the students' opinion on the Directorate then maybe we can convince our parents to rebel, which would lead to a change in how dragons are governed."

"And is that something you're interested in?" Ferrin's question sounded more like an accusation.

Garret pushed his chair back and stood. "I lost the use of my arm because of those bastards. In what world would I ever side with them?"

Everyone froze as the tension in the room skyrocketed.

"And you tried to keep me from coming back to school because of my...how was it phrased in that wonderful letter... deformity. You suggested I not return because of my deformity." Garret spat the word. "But I'm here because I want to study and learn, and because I plan to create a prosthetic which will allow injured dragons to fly. I expect this creation to be fully funded and backed by the Directorate as recompense for what happened to me and my fellow students." He leaned on the table with his good arm, like the speech had taken a lot out of him. "Sorry, these are emotional times. And I hate that someone manipulated me and my Clan-mates last night. It worked, until I spoke to Bryn and Jaxon." He chuckled. "They are an oddly effective team."

Bryn's grandfather smiled at her. She shook her head but smiled back, and then she had a thought. "Could we, and by we, I mean the Sinclairs, fund Garret's prosthetics project?"

"That is something the Directorate must vote on," Ferrin

said at the same time her grandfather nodded and said, "Yes."

"You can't do that," Ferrin stated in his I-am-the-king voice.

"I believe this is more a case of my granddaughter asking to help a friend rather than an official bequeathal from a Directorate member." Her grandfather tilted his head toward Bryn.

"Yes. That's what I meant," Bryn said, working hard to keep an innocent expression on her face.

Ferrin's lip curled up in a snarl. "This is an official Directorate meeting. There will be no more personal matters discussed."

Bryn tried to look contrite but knew she failed miserably. She risked a glance at Jaxon but couldn't read his non-expression. She was 100 percent sure he'd agree that Garret's prosthetics plan should be funded, but he wouldn't speak against his father. What would happen on the day when Jaxon disagreed with his father's policies enough to speak up?

Dessert was served while the Directorate members questioned the other Greens. It was carrot cake, the same kind of cake Alec had infused with dragon bane to poison Bryn. Had Ferrin done this on purpose? There was not a chance in hell she would eat carrot cake ever again. He had to know that.

Jaxon's eyebrows came together as he studied the cake. His gaze flicked to his father, who was still questioning someone. Did he suspect his father had done this on purpose?

Bryn leaned over. "Is this supposed to be a snub of some sort?"

Jaxon pushed his cake away. "I doubt my father planned the menu, otherwise I'd say yes."

Wait a minute. "I'm surprised you'd admit that."

He smirked. "My father may respect your power and the Sinclairs in general, but he certainly doesn't like you."

"The feeling is more than mutual," Bryn shot back.

"Thank you all for coming on such short notice," Ferrin announced. "Feel free to finish your dessert, but we have pressing matters to attend to."

"Back in a minute," Bryn said to Valmont. She pushed her chair back, intending to speak to her grandfather.

Valmont stood with her. "Like you're going anywhere without me."

"It's across the room," Bryn said.

He placed his hand on her lower back and whispered, "I don't trust half the people in this room."

"On that we are agreed." She made her way over to her grandfather. "Thank you for agreeing to fund Garret's project."

"It's a worthy cause, and it will help generate some much needed good will. Plus, it annoys Ferrin." Her grandfather chuckled.

"Mr. Sinclair," Garret joined the conversation. "I echo Bryn's sentiments. Thank you for funding my project. There was another idea I hoped to discuss with you before you left."

Her grandfather checked his watch. "I must leave in ten minutes."

"This won't take long," Garret said. "Today, Jaxon and Bryn helped diffuse a situation which could have gotten out of hand. Having an open line with the Directorate would help ease student concerns. Would it be possible to appoint them as a sort of Student Directorate Council?"

"On that, we would have to vote," her grandfather said, "but I approve of the idea. We're headed back to vote on a few more items this evening. Before we adjourn, I'll open a discussion on this topic."

"Thank you, sir." Garret left them.

"Before I forget," her grandfather pulled a jeweler's box from his coat pocket, "here's the bracelet you wanted. It is irreplaceable, so be sure to read the instructions on how to care for it."

It must be her elemental sword bracelet. "Thank you." She felt a warm connection toward her grandfather. Something she had never expected to happen. Maybe it was because he'd stepped in and helped her friend, or maybe she was finally beginning to understand him. "I don't suppose hugging you would be appropriate?"

He paused like he was considering her request. "No." He placed his hand on her shoulder and squeezed. "But I am touched you would ask." He nodded at Valmont and left the room.

"I'm starting to like him," Valmont said.

"Me, too."

On the walk back across campus, Bryn noticed the Valentine's Day decorations had been added to the lampposts.

Valmont sighed. "One crisis averted. Next adventure, the dreaded Valentine's Day dance."

"According to Ivy, it will be fun." Bryn snorted to show what she thought of the situation.

"There is one problem we didn't consider," Valmont said. "I don't have a tuxedo."

"Oh," Bryn schooled her features to maintain an innocent expression, "I'm sure Jaxon has one you could borrow."

"That is so not funny." Valmont reached over and tugged on her hair.

She laughed. "No one said a tux was mandatory."

"Please, I already stand out like a Fruit Loop in a bowl of Cheerios. I'll call my father and have him pick something out for me. The shop should be able to deliver a package to the guards at the gate. We can pick it up after they determine it's not a bomb."

When they reached her dorm room, Bryn tried not to eavesdrop on Valmont's conversation with his father, but it was hard not to. The good news was Valmont laughed a lot as he talked to his parents. The bad news was Bryn hadn't thought to suggest he call them more often, though it wasn't like she kept him from using the phone. Maybe he called some nights after she went to sleep. There was no reason he couldn't call, except he spent all his time with her.

After he hung up, she held out the jeweler's box. "Want to read the owner's manual with me?"

"Sure." He joined her at the library table.

Snapping the box open, Bryn blinked at what lay inside. "That's not my bracelet." A platinum cuff bracelet decorated with sapphires winked at her from the blue silk lining.

Valmont pointed at the small envelope tucked into the lid of the box. "Maybe there's an explanation in the note."

Bryn retrieved the envelope and upended it, and a thick square of paper fell out. She unfolded it and read aloud. "We changed the exterior to better match current jewelry and to make it look like something a Sinclair might wear." So her gold bracelet hadn't been up to Sinclair standards? That was crap. "It will still operate as it did before. To turn on the new safety feature, which keeps the bracelet from activating, press the stones with your left palm. To activate it, wrap your left hand around the bracelet and squeeze."

Sounded simple enough. Bryn placed the bracelet on her right wrist and waited to see if it would sting her again. Nothing happened. Maybe the bracelet recognized her now. She squeezed it and then she pantomimed holding a sword. Fire and ice shot from her palm. "Thank goodness. I was afraid it wouldn't work."

She released the sword, and it vanished. Then she tried the "off switch" by pressing the sapphires with her palm. It worked. After playing with it a few more times, Valmont said, "Do you plan on wearing it all the time?"

"Is there a reason I shouldn't?"

"Kind of makes me feel obsolete."

Seriously? Are male egos so fragile? "Wrong. This is one more weapon in my dragon defense kit. I still need my partner in crime, or whatever you want to call yourself."

"So you still need me?"

"Of course. Do you think I want to face the Valentine's Day dance by myself?"

"True. And I'll be spectacularly handsome in a tuxedo."

She laughed. "Of course you will."

• • •

The day of the dance, Ivy came to Bryn's room so they could get ready together. Apparently, Ivy had interpreted this to mean she had free rein over Bryn's hair and makeup.

"Hold still." Ivy came at Bryn with an eyelash curler.

"Nope." Bryn batted the metal device away. "I don't trust those things. They feel like they're going to pull my eyelashes out by the roots."

"That's only if you put mascara on first." Ivy pointed at the bed. "Sit. Let me have my fun."

Ivy had put up with a boatload of crap to be her friend. "Fine."

"Don't blink." Ivy captured Bryn's lashes in the miniature vice and squeezed.

"As soon as you say don't blink, that's all I want to do."

Ivy ignored her. "There. Done." Ivy released her lashes and applied several coats of mascara.

Normally, Bryn would do all her makeup using Quintessence, but she didn't want to miss out on this girly bonding ritual, so she allowed Ivy to apply eyeliner way past the corner of her eyes. She could feel the liner swirling toward her hairline.

"Don't take offense, but what are you doing?"

"I am making you look artistic and mysterious and fabulous." After drawing on the other side of her face, Ivy sighed in satisfaction. "Valmont won't know what hit him."

Bryn jumped up and checked the mirror. Ivy had extended eyeliner in swirling curving lines, which gave Bryn the illusion of a mask and somehow scales. "You should so be a makeup artist."

Ivy laughed. "That's one of my options." She grabbed red liner and started drawing around her own eyes, doodling lines that turned into hearts. "What do you think? Too soft for my tattooed kick-ass chick image?"

"No," Bryn said. Ivy's wild hair balanced out the softness of the hearts. "I can't believe red eyeliner works on you."

"Any color works if you know how to use it."

A knock sounded on Bryn's bedroom door. "Are you ever coming out?" Valmont asked from the other side of the door. "Clint got here fifteen minutes ago."

Bryn checked her reflection in the mirror. The platinum cuff bracelet matched her outfit perfectly. And somehow the midnight blue dress made her look regal, like she actually was a Blue. That was a weird thought. "I think we're ready."

"Yes, we are." Ivy pointed at the door. "Let me go out first, I want to see Valmont's reaction."

Did she look that much different than she normally did? Sure, the fancy eyeliner gave her a mystery woman appeal, but it didn't change who she was. Still it would be fun to see his reaction.

Bryn followed Ivy into the living room. When Valmont glanced her way, she anticipated a sexy smile, or an appreciative glance. What she got was a wrinkled brow and a look of confusion. Her stomach went cold with disappointment. Well, crap. So much for sexy and mysterious.

"What do you think?" Bryn hoped to prod him into giving her a compliment or at least force him to say something to explain the strange expression on his face.

"Your dress is nice." Valmont's tone was wooden.

"Nice?" Bryn's tone rose a bit too high.

Valmont shot a glance toward Clint and Ivy. "Would you wait in the hall for a moment?"

"Sure." Clint grabbed Ivy's hand and pulled her to the door. The couple whispered to each other on their way out.

Bryn's irritation rose.

He cleared his throat. "Remember what we discussed. No matter what I say, I'm still your knight."

Unless what he said really pissed her off and she cremated him. "Still my knight. Got it. Go on."

He walked over and sat on the couch leaning back to stare up at the ceiling. "There's no easy way to explain this. You look ethereal, amazing, other-worldly."

"And those are compliments, so why do you look like you're about to go before a firing squad?"

He sat up and waved his hand toward her. "Those are good things, or they would be if I was in the same species. Tonight, well, you've never looked more desirable and you've never looked less human."

"In case you've forgotten, I'm a dragon."

"I know that. Most of the time you look like a girl and act like a kick-ass dragon. Tonight you look like you're someone I don't belong with."

What in the holy hell was he talking about? She pointed at him, "Knight" and pointed at herself, "Dragon. I thought you had figured that out by now."

He stood, shaking his head. "Forget I said anything. Let's go to the dance."

"Forget? Just like that?" Frost shot from her nose. "This was supposed to be a fun romantic night. But Ivy gets a little fancy with eyeliner and you freak out and tell me I don't look like your girl anymore and now you tell me to forget it?" Her voice grew louder with every word. "How in the hell am I supposed to do that?"

The door popped open. Ivy stuck her head in. "It's almost time. We should go."

"Stupid freaking dances." Bryn stomped out the door and down the hall, not caring if Valmont followed or not, though it wasn't like he actually had a choice to follow her, even if he didn't want to. He was still her knight and bound to protect her from whatever weirdness was headed her way.

Ivy fell in step with her while Clint drifted back to walk next to Valmont. "What did he say?" Ivy asked.

Smoke shot from Bryn's nostrils. "Apparently, I look like someone else tonight, someone he doesn't belong with."

"That's not what I said," Valmont objected from behind her.

Bryn stopped and pivoted around to face him. "Really?"

Valmont opened his mouth and then paused. "Okay. Maybe I said it, but I didn't mean it how you're taking it."

Clint scratched his head. "Try again, dude."

Valmont sighed. "You want to know what my problem is? Tonight, dressed up all fancy like this, you look like you belong with Jaxon."

Fire roared in Bryn's gut. Sparks shot from her nostrils. "Now is not the time for you to develop an inferiority complex."

"We'll see you at the dance." Clint grabbed Ivy's hand and tugged her down the hall toward the staircase.

"It's makeup, you moron," Ivy shouted back toward them as Clint tugged her forward.

"What she said," Bryn spat.

Valmont's posture stiffened and then he headed back toward her room. "How about we finish this discussion in private?"

She followed him back into her room, slammed the door,

and waited for him to explain why he was acting so strangely.

Valmont rubbed the bridge of his nose. "I'm trying to think of a way to say this so you'll understand. It's just that... being human doesn't make me inferior."

"I never said it did. You're the one with the problem."

He nodded. "You're right. I do have a problem. I'm in love with someone from another species."

Bryn sucked in a breath to retort, and then her brain registered what he'd said, "You're in love with me?"

"Of course I am," Valmont spoke in a quiet tone.

And they'd reached the relationship blast zone. Either she said it back to him or she blew his heart to smithereens. How did she feel about him? She cared about him and trusted him and needed him in her life. It felt like he was a part of her. She couldn't imagine a time where he wouldn't be there by her side, helping her face the world.

All of this led her to one conclusion.

Moving in close, she kissed him on the cheek and told him the truth. "I love you, too."

He exhaled what sounded like a sigh of relief and then turned to stare into her eyes. "You're my world. And the idea of you marrying Jaxon feels like acid on my soul."

"I'm not thrilled about it, either, but as long as you and I are still together, being legally tied to someone else doesn't have to change anything."

"You're sure about that?" There was doubt shining in his eyes.

The truth was, she didn't know for certain. She wanted what she felt right now to be real.

"Yes. I'm sure. Do you remember before, when you said even if I have to release you from the bond, you'd still want to be with me?"

"I did say that. But things have changed since then... what's going on between you and Jaxon...the way you know what the other one is thinking, like you have some sort of connection…I don't like it."

"Knowing what he might do and say is strange, but I think it's more about him being a Blue male rather than him being a male I have some sort of attachment to. I can predict what you'll say or how Clint and Ivy will react to something. Before, Blues were a mystery, but now I can predict how Rhianna, Jaxon, and even my grandparents will react. It's not Jaxon specific. It's more like I understand how Blues think, in general. Does that help?"

"Not really, but this might." He leaned in and pressed his mouth against hers. He tasted like mint toothpaste, and he smelled like soap and sunshine. His arms wrapped around her, pulling her close. Heat built between them. The sensation of flying flowed through her body and suddenly the dance didn't seem so important.

Chapter Twenty-Four

The phone rang, startling them both. Bryn answered and had to clear her throat before she could speak. "Hello?"

"Are you guys all right?" Ivy asked.

"Yes." She grinned at Valmont. "We talked it out."

"Good. If you're done talking, get your butt to the dance." Ivy hung up, making Bryn laugh.

"We've been summoned to the ball."

Valmont shook his head. "What is it with Ivy and dances?"

"I have no idea, but we better go before she comes to find us."

The teasing smile disappeared from Valmont's face. "We need to finish this first. You have no idea how terrified I was to tell you how I felt."

"Now that you know I feel the same way, are we good? Can we go have fun at the dance?"

"We can try."

Not the reassuring answer she'd hoped for.

Valmont led her down the hall, down the staircase, and out the front door. Music drifted through the air. Happy couples lined the sidewalk as they headed across campus and more ascended the steps outside the dining hall. And all of them, every single couple, were perfect reflections of each other. Dark skin with dark skin, blond with blond, everyone matched up according to Clan. She knew Valmont noticed it, too. "I hate all this color coding."

He snorted. "Me, too. Let's go show them you don't have to be the same to belong together."

They cleared the doorway, and Ivy appeared at Bryn's side. "Is everything all right?"

"Yes," Bryn said, hoping it was true.

"Good, now look." Ivy gestured around the room with enthusiasm. "Look at how absolutely magical everything is tonight."

Red and white hearts decorated the walls and floors like confetti that had been tossed in the air, frozen where it landed, and shellacked into place. "Cool decorations." Bryn inhaled a familiar Italian spice type scent. "Is that Fonzoli's food I smell?"

"Indeed it is." Valmont pointed toward the buffet. "We provided appetizers, lemon ice, and punch."

"Yum," Bryn said.

The tables had been pushed aside to make room for dancing. Music from a string quartet filled the air. Slightly out of place were the guards stationed at every entrance and exit. The fact that they wore tuxedoes in an attempt to blend in made them stand out even more.

Valmont pointed at the side doors. "If we're separated, we'll meet at those doors. The walkway they lead to is covered, so it will protect us from aerial attacks."

Bryn nodded in agreement. This is what life had been reduced to—hoping there wouldn't be an attack during a school function. "Kind of takes some of the fun out of the night, but I can't argue with your logic."

Valmont led her out onto the floor and oddly enough, only a few people gave them sideways glances.

"I think people are adjusting to your presence." Bryn placed one hand on Valmont's shoulder while he placed his hand on her waist. He clasped her left hand with his right. Soon they were swept along with the tide of the dancers.

"This is nice," Valmont whispered in her ear. "Normally, I have to be so careful about touching you in public." He applied pressure to her waist and pulled her closer. "Tonight I don't have to worry about that."

Valmont's arms around her felt right. Bryn allowed all the stress and worry she'd been afflicted with lately to drift away with the music as they danced through several songs.

Ivy and Clint found them after a song ended.

"You're having fun, aren't you?" Ivy asked in a know-it-all tone.

"I am." Bryn laughed. "And now that we've danced, I declare it is time to visit the buffet."

Valmont bowed. "After you."

In the buffet line, Bryn filled her plate with a little bit of everything, and then she followed her friends to the tables decorated with heart-shaped candles.

"It's funny. We eat here three times a day," Ivy said, "but it's never felt romantic before."

Clint put his hand over his heart like she'd wounded him. "Do I not sit next to you at every meal staring at you with adoration?"

Ivy laughed. "How could I not notice that?"

They ate and then they danced to a few more songs. All in all it was a nice evening, but Bryn couldn't relax. "This is fun, but I keep waiting for something bad to happen."

"I think the trick is to be aware of what is going on around you," Valmont said, "while you enjoy what you have."

Why does it sound like he's talking about more than the

dance?

When a song ended, Bryn noticed there seemed to be more guards in the room. "Speaking of being aware of your surroundings, am I imagining it—"

"No." Valmont straightened and put his hand on his sword. "There are more."

Bryn spotted Clint and Ivy dancing a dozen feet away. She waited to catch Ivy's eye and waved her over.

"What's going on?" Ivy asked.

Valmont pointed at the guards. "Reinforcements have been sent in, but we don't know why."

Bryn headed for Miss Enid, who seemed to be chaperoning the dance. "What's up with the new guards?"

"That is a very good question, Bryn. I have another one I'd like answered. Are they here to keep us in or someone else out?"

"Have you seen anyone leave?" Clint asked.

"No. Let me make a call." She pulled out her cell and dialed. After putting the phone to her ear, she frowned and dialed again. "That's strange… I don't have a signal."

Valmont's posture stiffened. "If the cell phones are out, this could be an attack."

Bryn headed for one of the guards wearing a tuxedo. "Did you call for reinforcements?"

"No."

"Were they sent because the campus is under attack?"

The guard looked left and then right before leaning down to speak with Bryn. "There was an incident. It could be nothing. We aren't taking any chances."

"Does your cell work?" Valmont asked. "Because Miss Enid's doesn't."

The guard pulled his phone from his inside breast pocket and held it to his ear. His eyes narrowed.

"Damn it," Valmont said. "We need to find a landline to

see if they're still working."

The guard put his fingers to his lips and whistled. Students turned to see what was going on. The quartet stopped playing. Bryn's skin tingled with the need to shift.

"This is only a precaution," the guard bellowed. "Cell phones are out. Please remain calm while we investigate. Do not leave the building."

"Have I mentioned that I hate dances?" Bryn said to no one in particular.

"It could just be a cell phone thing," Ivy said. "I bet that guard will come back and tell us everything is fine."

"I hope you're right." Bryn stared out into the darkness. Was something moving outside the main doors?

The guard came back and spoke to Bryn. "The landline is still functional. We are talking to guards outside who are investigating the situation. Everything is under control."

"Now what?" Bryn asked Valmont.

Valmont pulled her away from the guard. "Either we listen to the guards and wait here like sitting ducks, or we take the fight to them. I can't believe I'm about to say this, but let's ask Jaxon what he thinks."

And the evening kept getting stranger. Clint, Ivy, Bryn, and Valmont crossed the room and headed toward Jaxon.

"We spoke to the guard," Bryn said, "and—"

"Let me guess," Jaxon said. "They want us to sit quietly while the adults take care of everything."

"That plan sucks," Clint commented.

"Agreed." Jaxon pointed toward the back of the building. "The safest, most bomb-proof place would probably be downstairs in the kitchen."

"Unless the building collapses," Bryn stated the obvious.

"Excuse me." Rhianna stood and headed for the girls' restroom.

"Doesn't that break some form of girl protocol?" Clint

asked.

"What do you mean?" Ivy asked.

"I thought girls always had to go to the restroom in pairs," Clint said, "or small herds."

"Good point." Bryn elbowed Jaxon. "Do females in your Clan normally go to the bathroom by themselves?"

"Females in my Clan don't discuss bodily functions," Jaxon said.

Bryn rolled her eyes.

"And that's how Hermione got attacked by a troll," Valmont said.

"You read Harry Potter?" Bryn couldn't believe it. "I loved those books."

"I've had a lot of down time lately," Valmont said, "and Miss Enid recommended them."

Jaxon frowned. "If you're done with this ridiculous conversation, can we return to the fact that someone has cut off cell phone access?

Ka-boom. Lightning hit the building, and the power flickered. *Ka-boom, ka-boom-boom-boom.* The building shook and the power flickered and then blinked out. The only light came from the red and pink heart-shaped candles, which decorated the tables. The effect which moments ago had been romantic was now creepy.

"I don't suppose there is any chance we're experiencing an actual thunderstorm." Clint stood, trying to stare out the windows.

"Zero to none." Bryn squinted in order to see anything out in the darkness. Lightning flashed and zapped the ground, kicking up chunks of dirt and sod.

"That looked like one of your landings," Jaxon spoke without looking at her, but Bryn was pretty sure who he meant, and it's not like she could argue.

"Okay…let's see what we know: no cell phone access,

but the landlines work, the power is out," Bryn said, "and there are Black dragons attacking the campus but they aren't attacking us…yet."

"If they aren't attacking," Valmont said, "maybe they are distracting us from something else."

"Something happening someplace else on campus, or something going on here in this building?" Ivy asked.

The lights flickered back on.

"Okay," Bryn said. "They turned the lights back on. Does that mean they got what they came for?"

"They must have wanted something from another building," Valmont said.

A terrible idea settled in Bryn's mind but that was ridiculous. She didn't want to alarm Jaxon based on suspicion. "Ivy, let's go to the restroom."

"Sure."

Valmont followed along. When they were far enough away from Jaxon, he said, "You're worried about Rhianna?"

"I want to make sure she didn't fall victim to a troll."

Inside the restroom, there was no sign of Rhianna. "Do you think she went to a different bathroom?" Ivy asked.

"Any luck?" Valmont called through the door.

Bryn pushed it open. "No. Let's go tell Jaxon and see what he thinks."

"What do you mean she wasn't in the restroom?" Jaxon jumped to his feet and then stood on his chair scanning the room. "Damn it." He hopped down. Frost shot from his nose. "There are other restrooms. Right?"

"Yes, but she walked in that direction." Bryn frowned. "We can have Clint tell the guards while we search the other bathrooms."

A guard came toward Jaxon. "Someone called on the landline and asked us to give you this message. Rhianna needs you to bring a waiter named Zane to the library."

Jaxon paled. "Did you speak to her?"

"No. Is there a problem?"

"Yes." He explained how Rhianna had gone missing.

The guard frowned. "Why would they want the waiter?"

"Good question." Jaxon stared at Bryn.

Something in the guard's jacket beeped. He reached into his pocket and pulled out his cell. "That's strange. They appear to be working again."

"I should probably call my grandfather."

"No," Jaxon said. "I'll call my father. You go find this Zane person and bring him to the front door."

"I don't like this," Valmont said as they headed toward the buffet where a waiter was refilling pitchers of lemonade.

"I don't like it, either, but since it's Rhianna, we have to let Jaxon call the shots."

"Hello," the waiter gave a friendly smile at their approach, "did you need something?"

Valmont nodded. "Are you Zane, the new waiter my father hired?"

Zane held out his hand. "I am. Nice to meet you, Valmont. I've heard a lot about you."

Valmont shook his hand. "This is Bryn, my dragon."

"Nice to meet you, too." Zane looked at Bryn's face. "Something tells me this isn't a social visit."

Bryn opened her mouth to explain and then paused. "This is going to sound weird no matter how I explain it. Someone took our friend Rhianna, who is also Jaxon Westgate's girlfriend, to the library. Then they contacted us to say we needed to bring you to the library."

Zane's eyes narrowed. "What do you mean someone took her? And why would they want me?"

"We're not sure what's going on," Valmont said. "All we know is Rhianna needs your help.

"This is weird," Zane said, "but I'm in."

"I'm sure it will get weirder before the night is over," Bryn said. "Let's go."

Jaxon waited for them by the front door. "I called my father. The guards at the library haven't noticed anything unusual." He held his hand out to Zane. "I'm Jaxon Westgate. Thank you for agreeing to help."

Zane shook his hand. "Zane Freeman. Nice to meet you. Now what the hell is going on?"

"Good question. Let's go find out." Jaxon pushed the door open, and they followed him out into the cool night air. "Bryn you need to fill Zane in."

Valmont walked on one side of Bryn while Zane walked on the other. "Here's the abbreviated version. There is a certain kind of magic that responds to the Dragon-Knight bond. Valmont and I were able to open a hidden door when we both touched his sword. I'm guessing that is what these kidnappers are after. They want to make you Rhianna's knight."

"How can they do that?" Zane said.

"I imagine they'll set up a scenario where you rescue her," Valmont said, "which will activate the dormant spell in your blood."

"And then what?" Zane asked.

"For now let's focus on finding Rhianna." Jaxon quickened his pace. "I'm sure they'll tell us what they want soon enough."

When they reached the front of the library, everything appeared normal. Then Bryn noticed movement in the shadows.

"They're with us," Jaxon said. "Don't draw attention to them."

How did he know for sure? Not being the one calling the shots made her twitchy.

Inside the library, the guard who should've been stationed at the front door was gone. Did that mean he was in on it, or had he been sent on some sort of fake errand?

"Now what?" Zane asked, scanning the library.

"My guess would be that they've taken her to the archives," Bryn said.

"Where's Miss Enid?" Valmont asked.

At that moment, Miss Enid appeared from the doorway that led to the entrance of the archives. She glanced at Bryn and her companions but headed over to the front desk where she grabbed a marker, opened a hardcover book, and proceeded to write in it. And that wasn't normal.

Together, the group approached Miss Enid. "Your presence is requested in the archives," Miss Enid said.

Bryn could see what the librarian had written in the book in big black letters. *Send Help Archives*

Was the note meant for her or for whoever was watching the camera feed?

Miss Enid kept a blank expression on her face. "Go on down, Bryn. Your friend is waiting for you."

Okay...that was weird. Was Miss Enid afraid she was being watched by someone who could see her face, but she trusted whoever was watching the camera feed to read what she'd written in the book?

"There's a package for Zane by the steps," Miss Enid called after them.

Bryn led them back to the trap door in the floor, which stood open. A long package wrapped in brown paper lay next to the steps. Zane grabbed it and ripped off the paper, uncovering a sword in a scabbard.

Zane drew the sword. Light glinted off frozen flames etched into the blade. "Looks sharp enough." He returned the sword to the scabbard and buckled it around his waist.

Jaxon peered down the stairwell. "It's only big enough for us to go single file. Zane, they asked for you. Why don't you go first? I'll follow. Bryn can follow me, and Valmont can keep watch from behind, so no one sneaks up on us."

Zane drew his sword and headed down the stairs.

Bryn grabbed Jaxon's shirt so he didn't follow right away.

"Go slow," Bryn said as she activated her elemental sword, turning it on quickly and then releasing it to turn it off just as fast so Jaxon would be aware of her weapon. "I don't want you bumping into Zane. It's a long way down."

Jaxon's eyes went wide, but he nodded. "Good to know."

Bryn followed behind him. Valmont kept close on her heels and whispered, "You didn't want Zane to see?"

Bryn glanced back at her knight. "He seems like a good guy, but we don't really know him."

Valmont frowned but didn't comment. When all four of them reached the landing at the base of the stairs, Bryn was surprised to find the two Reds guards bound and gagged. Their eyes were closed, but from the way their chests moved up and down she could tell they were still breathing.

"We're here," Jaxon called out. "Let me see Rhianna."

A man with blond hair and a pale ivory complexion emerged from the room with Rhianna in his arms. She was bound and gagged. Her eyes were shut. A sheen of sweat covered her skin.

Chapter Twenty-Five

"What did you do to her?" Jaxon roared.

"She is merely resting." The man grinned. "As long as Zane plays his part, we will return her to you unharmed."

"We only need her to bleed a little," a man behind him with black hair and golden tan skin said.

If Bryn hadn't guessed what type of hybrid these two men were at first, her suspicions had been confirmed.

"You're Blue and Black?" Jaxon blinked like he couldn't believe what he was seeing.

"What? You thought only the lower classes mingled?" The man holding Rhianna laughed. "You have no idea of the extent of the hybrid population."

"Let her go," Bryn said. "Valmont and I can do whatever you need."

"Actually, little hybrid, you can't." The second man stated. "I need a Blue knight to retrieve my treasure. If your friends play nicely, we can all walk away from this unharmed. All I want is what is rightfully mine. Zane, this is where you come in."

"What do you want me to do?"

"It's not your turn yet. First I need Bryn and Valmont to open the door to the hidden room."

There should be a guard stationed in the room. Maybe he could help. "How do you know about the room?" Bryn asked as she moved toward it.

"We have eyes and ears everywhere."

"Did you attack Dragon's Bluff?" Valmont asked.

"Me, personally? No. Several of my friends gave their lives that night to prove to the Directorate they were no longer in control of this situation."

Valmont drew his sword but didn't move toward the door. "What if I show you that you are not in control of *this* situation?"

"We did not come alone. If we are not seen exiting the library at the appointed time, a contingency of our friends will destroy the dining hall, killing everyone at the dance. Now open the door."

Bryn could see the internal war that raged in Valmont's eyes as he joined her at the door. He placed the sword against the stone. She touched it, slicing her finger on it and watched as the drops rolled down the blade, hitting the stone. The door appeared.

Bryn put her hand on the doorknob.

"Tell the guard inside to stand down," the second man said.

Crap. Bryn pulled the door open. The Red guard looked at her in surprise. "What are you doing here?"

"Please do as these men say and don't try to fight." Bryn stepped into the room.

The man holding Rhianna entered the room and set her down in a chair at the table. "Why don't you wait outside until we complete our task?"

The guard looked at Jaxon. "What do you want me to

do?"

"Wait outside," Jaxon said. "We'll take care of this."

"I don't like this." The Red stepped outside, and the second man closed the door so anyone on the outside would be unable to open it.

The man who had been carrying Rhianna pulled a vial of clear liquid from his shirt pocket. "We dosed Rhianna with a slow-acting poison. Left untreated she will die by morning. Zane when you give her this antidote she'll recover. Since you will have saved her life, you'll become her knight."

Jaxon growled. "You better pray she makes a full recovery."

Zane stalked forward. "Give me that." He opened the vial and held the contents to Rhianna's lips, slowly pouring the antidote into her mouth.

"How will we know if she is okay?" Valmont asked.

Rhianna sucked in a breath, and her eyes flew open. She blinked in confusion and then coughed until she doubled over.

Jaxon pushed forward to wrap his arms around Rhianna. "It's okay. You're going to be okay."

"What happened?" Rhianna gasped, like she was fighting to catch her breath.

"You were poisoned, on purpose, so Zane would save you and become your knight," Jaxon said.

Zane kneeled down in front of Rhianna. "I am so sorry they did this to you. Are you all right?"

Rhianna stared at Zane for a moment. "Who are you?"

"I'm your knight." Zane spoke the words with such sincerity Bryn knew it was true. Forcing Zane to save Rhianna had activated the latent spell in his blood, turning him into her knight.

"Let's get started." The first man studied the wall on the right. "It has to be here somewhere." He went back to the threshold of the room and counted off five paces before staring at the blank wall.

"You." He pointed at Zane. "Come put your sword point here." He touched the wall at doorknob height.

"There's another door?" Bryn asked.

"We are about to find out." The second man pulled out a pocket knife and cut the restraints on Rhianna's wrists, then pointed toward Zane. "Touch the sword."

Rhianna rubbed her wrists and then Jaxon helped her stand.

"I don't understand." Rhianna swayed where she stood.

"Your blood will open the door the same way Bryn's blood opened the box in Mr. Stanton's room." Jaxon helped steady her.

"You don't need to come any closer." The second man pointed at Jaxon. "She can walk on her own."

"No," Jaxon said.

"It's okay." Rhianna grabbed the table for support and stood tall. "I can do this." Slowly, she made her way over to Zane. Never once did she let any discomfort show on her face.

Zane held his hand out to Rhianna. "The sooner we do this, the sooner it'll be over."

She reached for his hand and allowed him to place her pointer finger on the edge of the blade. In a quick motion she slid her finger down the blade. The blade glowed blue as red droplets of blood rolled down the blade to the wall. The outline of a wooden door appeared on the stone wall. The second man sucked in a breath and grasped the handle. The door creaked open on ancient hinges. He stuck his head inside, holding a ball of lightning out so he could see.

Light bounced around creating weird shadows. "This is it, cousin."

"Zane, look at your dragon," the first man ordered. "To keep anyone from following us, I need her to release you from the bond."

Rhianna growled. "I should blast you where you stand."

Bryn edged closer, ready to bring her elemental sword to life.

"Release him." The man put his hand on the back of Zane's neck. "Or I fill him with enough lightning to fry him from the inside out."

"How do I know you won't kill him, anyway?" Rhianna asked.

"He has what he wanted," Zane spoke to Rhianna. "Please release me."

Rhianna frowned. "I release you."

A shadow passed over Zane and then he looked at the dragon threatening to electrocute him. "It is done. And you can go to hell." He twisted and swung his sword upward in an arc, slicing into the man's stomach and up through his rib cage.

Stunned, the man growled and blasted Zane with enough electricity to make his body spasm before he dropped to the floor where he continued to twitch. The smell of burnt flesh filled the room.

"No." Rhianna screamed and scrambled to the floor, reaching for Zane.

Jaxon blasted frozen flames, creating a protective barrier between Rhianna and the enemy. Valmont charged, sliding over the table with his sword extended. Bryn lunged forward, turning her elemental sword on as she went. Her fire and ice blade penetrated the man's chest just as Valmont's blade slashed into his carotid artery, sending a shower of blood spurting across the room painting the wall where the secret door had now closed.

"Rhianna," Jaxon yelled.

Bryn performed the releasing motion to turn off her sword. Valmont tugged but his blade must have been stuck in the man's spine. He put his boot on the man's stomach, shoving him off of his sword and sending him crashing back into a bookshelf.

"Rhianna?" Bryn placed her hand on the ice barrier melting it with her flames. She sank to the floor where Rhianna cradled Zane's head on her lap.

Jaxon had his arms around his girlfriend's shoulders as he felt for a pulse on Zane's neck. "I'm sorry. He's gone."

"Why did Zane do that?" Rhianna sobbed. "I released him."

"Maybe," Valmont said, "Zane didn't believe the man would actually let us all go."

There was a loud pounding in Bryn's head.

"Do you hear that?" Valmont asked.

Okay, maybe the noise isn't in my head. It was coming from the entrance to the room. It sounded like someone was pounding the wall with a battering ram. All she could see was a dead knight. Tears welled up in her eyes.

"We need to open the door," Jaxon said, "without whoever is outside accidentally killing us."

"A phone would be handy right now," Bryn said.

Valmont walked back to the dead man's body and searched his pockets, retrieving a cell phone.

"Give me that," Jaxon said.

Valmont tossed the phone to Bryn who handed it to Jaxon. He dialed and spoke to his father. The battering on the door stopped.

"It's safe to open now." Jaxon looked at Bryn. "Do you mind?"

"I've got it." Valmont went to the door and pushed it open. Ferrin, Bryn's grandfather, and a half a dozen other people poured into the room.

"The traitor is over there." Valmont pointed to the back corner.

Everyone started asking questions.

"We need a moment of silence," Jaxon shouted loud enough to be heard above the din.

Amazingly, everyone quieted down. Ferrin and her grandfather approached. Ferrin squatted down and touched Jaxon's shoulder. "Who was he?"

"His name was Zane," Jaxon said, "and he came here to protect Rhianna's life."

"He was my knight." Rhianna sounded sad and lost.

Ferrin appeared confused, but he didn't make a rude comment like Bryn expected him to.

"I'm sorry for your loss," Bryn's grandfather said, "but, we need to know what occurred here, and we need to know if anyone is still in danger."

Bryn's head snapped up. "The dance. The man who escaped said they would attack the dance if their people didn't see them leaving when they were supposed to."

Ferrin grabbed his phone and started giving orders.

"Bryn, who escaped where?" her grandfather asked.

"A Blue-Black hybrid made Rhianna's knight open a secret door only Blue knights can access. He went through there." She pointed at the wall splattered with blood. "And the door shut behind him."

"Can you open it?" her grandfather asked.

"We can try." Valmont placed his sword on the wall. Bryn sliced her finger on the blade not feeling a thing. A faint outline of a door glimmered and then disappeared.

"At least we know where it is." Her grandfather frowned. "Maybe we can find a volunteer to open it for us."

"I'll do it," Rhianna said.

Jaxon opened his mouth to speak and Rhianna cut him off. "I don't want his death to be in vain."

"Whoever left by that door is probably long gone," her grandfather said. "Tonight we'll concentrate on keeping the other students safe. Tomorrow or the day after, Rhianna, we may ask for your help."

"Can we go back to the dance to check on our friends?" Bryn asked.

"Ferrin will have deployed our guards. I'd like you to come with me and give a more detailed description of the events." Her grandfather glanced down at Zane and then back up at Valmont. "Can you help us make the necessary arrangements?"

Valmont nodded.

• • •

Bryn followed her grandfather up to his office on the top floor of the library. Valmont sat beside her, quietly holding her hand. She could feel rage coming off of his body. Any answers he gave were brief. What was he feeling? Guilt? Anger? Fear?

She filled her grandfather in on the tragic events of the evening.

"We need to find someone to open that door," Valmont said. "That man could still be in there."

"The vaults were here long before the library, which currently sits on top of them. There is a series of tunnels connecting them to each other and to access points on and probably off campus. I'm sure he's made his way back to his friends by now."

Speaking of friends. "Since I'm not hearing any loud explosions, can I assume the dance was not attacked?"

"We found traces of a few small groups of the enemy across campus, but they appear to be gone now."

"Except for the traitors living among us," Valmont said. "Someone at the dance must have watched and waited for Rhianna to go someplace by herself so they could kidnap her."

"That is a disturbing thought." Her grandfather steepled

his fingers under his chin. "Do you think they targeted her in particular, or do you think they would have kidnapped any Blue they had access to?"

Bryn rubbed her temples trying to make her brain process all this bizarre information. "They must have known we were close to Rhianna and that we'd understand why they wanted someone from Dragon's Bluff. They mentioned Zane by name."

"I mean no disrespect toward the young man in question, but do you think he could have been a willing participant in tonight's treachery?"

"At first, that thought went through my head, too." And it made her feel like crap. "But he didn't seem to know about the blood magic. And he'd never met Rhianna."

"Valmont, how well did you know him?" her grandfather asked.

"Not at all. He started working at Fonzoli's after I moved here. My father told me good things about him over the phone. He's a new hire."

"So you didn't know him." Her grandfather mused. "It wouldn't do to start asking questions right after his death. In a few days, maybe you could ask your parents how his family is doing."

"I hate doubting him," Valmont said. "I'd rather do it now, so I know the truth."

Her grandfather pointed toward a phone on a side table. "As you wish."

Valmont dialed, and Bryn listened to his end of the conversation. When he got off the phone, he was shaking. "My father was surprised I'd heard of Zane's death so quickly since they only found his body half an hour ago."

"What?" That didn't make any sense.

"Zane was scheduled to work tonight. He loaded up the catering truck at the restaurant and left on schedule.

Somewhere between Dragon's Bluff and the school, someone must have hijacked the truck. They found the real Zane dead in a ditch with a bullet in the back of his head."

Bryn's brain spun in circles trying to put the information together. "So that wasn't Zane who became Rhianna's knight and gave up his life for her?"

"No." Valmont paced the office. "Who kills a man so he can impersonate him and then gets himself killed? Who does that?"

"Someone who is insane or desperate," her grandfather stated in a cold tone.

"Will there be an autopsy to identify the body?" Bryn asked. "Because how can we be sure he wasn't a dragon? He said he became Rhianna's knight, but we don't know if that's true."

"If he wasn't a knight, I don't think the blood magic would have worked," Valmont said.

"Right." She hadn't thought about that.

"We won't solve any more mysteries tonight." Her grandfather stood. "Before you return to your dorm, I do have one bit of good news. The Directorate agreed to appoint you and Jaxon as Student Directorate Council."

"What does that mean?" Bryn asked.

"Students can come to you with concerns. If their concerns are valid, you can contact me or Ferrin to discuss the issue. That way the students have a more direct line of communication to the Directorate which should help eliminate some of the unrest on campus."

"Sounds like a good idea."

He escorted them to the door of his office. "Both of you performed admirably this evening under difficult circumstances. Bryn, I know your grandmother would prefer it if you weren't in the thick of battle, if at all possible." He sounded like he was sort of making a joke.

"I try to stay out of the chaos, but weird stuff seems to happen around me."

"I am aware of that." Her grandfather put his arm around her shoulders and squeezed like he was giving her a sideways hug. She smiled up at him. He grinned and then pulled her into a real hug. She couldn't believe it. She hugged him back and then stepped away.

"Don't tell anyone I did that," her grandfather joked. "It would ruin my image."

"Your secret is safe with me."

Bryn and Valmont headed down the stairs and walked across campus holding hands. Guards lined the sidewalks checking out everyone who passed, which was kind of nice.

When she reached her room, she called Clint and Ivy to check on them. Her friends were worried about her, but they were fine. Exhaustion hit her like a tidal wave.

"Go change into your pajamas," Valmont said. "We're camping out on the couch."

Dressed in yoga pants and a T-shirt, she joined Valmont on the couch. In the back of her head, she thought about suggesting they sleep in her bed. It would be more comfortable, and they'd slept there before when she'd been sick, so it wasn't a big deal. But tonight after everything they'd gone through, it might be easier to stick with something close to normal. Not that her life was ever normal. Despite all the tragedy tonight, the one good thing to come of this mess was she'd become closer to her grandfather.

She seemed to be on a more even keel with Jaxon. That was good. And what had happened with Ferrin tonight? He'd actually acted respectful toward Rhianna and the dead guy who wasn't really Zane but had still been Rhianna's knight. She had never imagined Ferrin capable of such kindness. Maybe the expectation of a new baby had softened him up, after all.

The last sound she heard before falling asleep was Valmont talking in his sleep, something about pizza and lasagna. Maybe he was dreaming about working as a waiter. Would he be happy to return to his real job? Seeing Rhianna crying over a knight had taken Bryn's breath away. If she ever had to stand over Valmont's body like that… She shuddered… It was too horrifying to imagine. She'd do whatever it took to keep him safe. Even if it meant letting him go.

Wait. Where had that thought come from?

This whole night was messing with her head. She wondered how Rhianna was coping. Of course Rhianna was traumatized, but at least she'd released Zane before he'd died. Not that she would've gotten sick and turned to stone over a knight she'd known less than an hour. Right?

. . .

Jaxon showed up at Bryn's door way too early the next morning. She opened the door, bedhead and all, because she worried something might have happened with Rhianna. "What's wrong?"

"We need to talk." He studied her attire of yoga pants and Munch's "The Scream" shirt and shook his head, but he held a carryout box and a tray with three cups of coffee.

"Come in."

Valmont sat up on the couch, bleary-eyed and confused. He pointed at Jaxon. "Why?"

Bryn shrugged and snagged two cups of coffee, downing half of one and passing the other to Valmont. "He had food, so I let him in."

Jaxon sat at the library table. "I'm here because I don't know what to do about Rhianna. My father told me about the real Zane being murdered. How do I tell Rhianna she's grieving an impostor?"

Bryn opened the carryout box and chose a cranberry orange muffin. "Give me a minute." She ate half the muffin and finished off her coffee. "Okay, my brain is now engaged, but I don't have an answer for you."

"Do you remember what impostor-Zane said to Rhianna last night?" Valmont said.

"He apologized for what happened to her," Jaxon said. "Knowing what we know now, it makes more sense, but why did he try to kill the traitor he was working with?"

"The driver that attacked me earlier this year was actually my grandmother's driver. He'd worked for her for more than a dozen years. If someone had something powerful enough to blackmail him or threaten him with, I could see the same thing happening with not-Zane."

"For simplicity sake, let's call him Zane," Valmont said. "And say Zane was drafted into this situation against his will and he didn't want the traitors to get away with it. He could have attacked that guy because he didn't want him to succeed with whatever he was doing and he believed strongly enough that he gave his life to stop him."

"That paints him in a better light," Bryn said.

"Maybe he wasn't as evil as his counterparts, but he also wasn't the brave hero that Rhianna is mourning." Jaxon shoved his hand back through his hair. "How do I fix this?"

"You can't," Bryn said. "Even though Rhianna released him and he wasn't her knight any more, he did save her life, *and* he died right in front her."

"That is not the answer I came here for." Jaxon sipped his coffee.

"Maybe," Valmont said, "you should tell her the truth. It might help her recover a little bit faster."

"Maybe." Jaxon sighed. "Any other knightly logic you'd like to share?"

"Not really," Valmont said. "Bryn and I have been making

it up as we go along."

"Again," Jaxon said, "not helping."

Valmont shrugged and sipped his coffee.

Jaxon frowned like he was considering the situation. "There's something else. The fact that those hybrids were Black and Blue made me wonder about something. Remember Analise, who supposedly died in a car accident?"

"What's he talking about?" Valmont asked.

"Alec, the Black Radical Revisionist dragon who died at my grandparents' estate, had petitioned to marry his girlfriend Analise, but the marriage petition was denied so she took the only other option, which was a Directorate-sanctioned benefactor."

"How does that work?" Valmont asked.

Anger flared in Bryn's gut. "If a female is declared unfit to marry, for whatever reason, which the Directorate doesn't bother to explain, then an older married man will offer to keep her as his mistress after she graduates."

"And these men's wives are okay with this?"

"It's mostly Blues that engage in this behavior, since their marriages are based on money and political alliances."

"What does this have to do with Alec and Analise?"

"Jaxon and I looked into the whole benefactor situation and discovered all mistresses are required to undergo a procedure which keeps them from having kids."

"Are you serious?" Valmont stared wide-eyed.

"It gets worse," Bryn said. "Analise missed her follow-up appointment to make sure the sterilization worked, and not long after, she died in what we assumed was a Directorate-sanctioned car crash."

Valmont opened his mouth and pointed at Jaxon. No sound came out. He tried again. "I'll bypass the rant about how the Directorate is insane and go with the obvious reason you're bringing this up. You think Analise, or another dragon like her, could have faked her own death and given birth to a Blue-Black hybrid dragon."

Jaxon nodded. "In essence, maybe the Directorate isn't the only one responsible for car crashes and other mysterious deaths. Maybe women fake their deaths, with or without their benefactor's knowledge, and then they become a part of a secret community of hybrids."

"Who would have every reason to despise the Directorate," Valmont said.

"If someone denied my marriage, tried to sterilize me, and then told me my only choice was to shack up with a guy old enough to be my father, I'd be pretty pissed off at the Directorate, too." Bryn waited for Jaxon to respond.

Jaxon spoke in a quiet voice. "If the Directorate explained why a couple was not allowed to marry, do you think that might make a difference?"

"It might," Bryn said. "But it would depend on their reasoning. If the DNA of the two dragons would combine to create a super-evil genius or someone driven insane by lust for gold, *that* would be understandable. If the Directorate denied marriage based on something ridiculous like one of the people developing a limp…" She didn't bother finishing her sentence.

Jaxon stared into his coffee cup. "I now see some of the Directorate's decisions are not…as logical as I would like them to be."

Wow. For Jaxon, that was a huge confession.

"Maybe, since you're slated to be on the Directorate," Bryn said, "you can help change the system."

"Maybe, I could." Jaxon stood. "I think I'll go tell Rhianna the truth, because not knowing won't help the situation."

Bryn let Jaxon out and locked the door behind him. She turned to find Valmont smiling at her. "What?"

"You are like a pebble tossed into a pond. Everything you

do and say creates ripples in dragon society." He raised his cup of coffee to her in a silent toast. "Did you ever think you'd get Jaxon to admit the Directorate is less than perfect?"

"No." She grabbed the box of muffins and carried them to the coffee table. "If only we could convince whoever is attacking the campus that violence isn't necessary for change, everyone's lives would be a lot safer."

Valmont picked up a muffin and peeled off the wrapper. "Agreed. Any ideas on how to do that?"

"It's not like we can send an invitation to the hybrids to attend a welcome Back to School Gala like we did with the injured students."

"No, but you could have an open forum where students could share concerns. You could even do it online and keep it anonymous. That way, if anyone, hybrids included, wanted to ask questions or voice opinions, they could do so without fear of retribution."

"That's a great idea." Bryn went to sip her coffee and discovered the cup was empty. She pouted at Valmont.

He laughed. "Do you want to get dressed and go eat in the dining hall?"

A sudden idea had her smiling. "I have a better plan. We're going to have breakfast at the swanky cafe downstairs. And I'm going to speak to every person we come across, even if they don't talk back."

"Just to be obnoxious?" Valmont asked.

"Partly, and partly to reinforce the idea that I'm not going away. I'm a member of the Blue Clan, whether they like it or not. And with Jaxon's help, maybe we can convince more students it's time to change the way things are done around here."

As Bryn changed clothes, she thought about everything that had happened since they'd come back to school after Christmas break. The Back to School Gala had been a success in more ways than one. A good portion of injured students had returned to school and most of them had been accepted by their Clans. The Blue Clan might still be a little rigid, but the Blue females were now talking to Rhianna, and according to Akbar's experiment, Clan boundaries were definitely softening. She wasn't sure what her grandfather would think of that, but she enjoyed his company now. Both of her grandparents seemed like people she could depend on. And oddly enough, she now felt like she could depend on Jaxon in a crisis. They might not have the warm fuzzies for each other, but she'd grown to understand and respect him, even if he tended to act like an ass-hat on a regular basis. Then there was Valmont—her rock in these turbulent times. Even if the magic of the bond made them both a little unstable sometimes, she knew he'd always be there for her, not out of obligation, but because he truly cared.

If the Radical hybrids would stop attacking campus, maybe the peaceful hybrids could come out in the open. The Directorate might come to understand not all hybrids were bad. And the good hybrids could help broker some sort of peace between the Directorate and the Radicals. While she was dreaming, she threw in a new law, which would allow Jaxon to marry Rhianna. Who knew, maybe if they all worked together, dragons could be allowed to marry whomever they wanted....even their knights.

"Bryn, are you ready?" Valmont called from the living room.

"In a minute." She ran a brush through her hair and smiled at her reflection. "Ready or not, here I come."

Acknowledgments

I'd like to say thank you to all the readers who left reviews and star-ratings on Amazon and Goodreads. Without you, there wouldn't be a third dragon book. I'd like to thank Erin Molta and Stacy Abrams for their editing expertise. I'd like to thank Entangled Publishing for believing in my dragons.

About the Author

Chris Cannon lives in Southern Illinois with her husband and her three dogs: Pete the shih-tzu who sleeps on her desk while she writes, Molly the ever-shedding yellow lab, and Tyson the sandwich-stealing German Shepherd Beagle. She believes coffee is the Elixir of Life. Most evenings after work, you can find her sucking down caffeine and writing fire-breathing paranormal adventures or romantic comedies. You can find her online at www.chriscannonauthor.com. Subscribe to her newsletter at http://www.chriscannonauthor.com/connect/

Discover the **Going Down in Flames** *series...*

Going Down in Flames

Finding out on your sixteenth birthday you're a shape-shifting dragon is tough to swallow. Being hauled off to an elite boarding school is enough to choke on. Bryn needs to figure out how to control her new dragon powers to make it through her first year. But focusing on staying alive is difficult when you're falling for someone you can't have. Zavien, a black dragon, is tired of rules, and meeting Bryn is a breath of fresh air. Old grudges, new crushes, and death threats abound, but together they may be able to change the rules.

Bridges Burned

Also by Chris Cannon

Blackmail Boyfriend

Haley Patterson, honor student, has had a crush on popular, golden boy Bryce Colton for ages. But then she hears a rumor—Bryce is telling everyone that he hooked up with *her*. With Haley's reputation taking a serious nose-dive, she gives Bryce a choice: be her boyfriend for a month, or face the angry, cage-fighting boyfriend of the girl he actually *did* hook up with. Now Bryce is being blackmailed by a girl who has two three-legged dogs and lives on the other side of town. Can something so fake turn into something real?

only I can save the human race from extinction, it's clear my freeze didn't avoid a dreadful fate. It only delayed the horror...

SALT
by Danielle Ellison

When Penelope was a child, a demon killed her parents—and stole her magic. She's still a witch...but she's been pretending to be something she's not. When she's finally given the chance to join an elite demon-hunting force, Penelope is determined squeeze through the tests, find the demon, and take back her magic. Then she meets Carter. He's cute and smart, and he knows her secret. But he also has one of his own...